THE
WOMAN
AT NUMBER 6

BOOKS BY MATTHEW FARRELL

The Perfect Mother

ADLER AND DWYER PREQUELS
What Have You Done
I Know Everything

ADLER AND DWYER SERIES
Don't Ever Forget
Tell Me The Truth

THE
WOMAN
AT NUMBER 6

MATTHEW FARRELL

bookouture

Published by Bookouture in 2023

An imprint of Storyfire Ltd.
Carmelite House
50 Victoria Embankment
London EC4Y 0DZ

www.bookouture.com

ISBN: 978-1-83790-375-7
eBook ISBN: 978-1-83790-374-0

For my family and friends,
Thank you for your unending support. It means the world.

PROLOGUE

She watched them from across the street, hidden in the shadows of a dark dirt road where the halo of streetlights didn't quite reach. They were sitting two tables in from the restaurant's bay window, across from one another, their bodies leaning forward, their faces only inches apart. The other diners around them were oblivious. Everyone at each table had their own worlds to live in, just as they were living in theirs. Their smiles were both authentic and obnoxious. He said something to make her laugh and she almost spilled the glass of wine that was in front of her as she threw herself back in hysterics. Her laughter made him laugh which made her laugh harder and so it went. Such was the way new love unfurled itself.

Only that love wasn't hers to have. The young woman—the girl—was stealing it.

And stealing would not be tolerated.

She stood against the oversized elm tree, hands clenched into fists, staring at the couple having such a profound and lovely date. They were so natural together, their conversation coming easy. They were clearly relaxed in each other's company, like they were meant to be. But again, they weren't meant to be. Ever. He was hers. End of story.

A wind blew down the dirt road, kicking up dust and stinging her eyes. She coughed and ducked out of the way, stumbling back toward her car, which was waiting at the end of the block. She'd seen enough. She glanced over her shoulder one last time and watched as he took a piece of chocolate cake and fed her. He. *Fed.* Her. The young woman—the girl— slipped her plump lips around his fork and took the piece, her eyes never leaving his. The girl wore an expression so sultry and alluring that she thought they might have sex right there on the table in front of everyone else. His expression changed and he said something that made her nod with purpose. The playfulness was gone, replaced by lust now. She could see it as plain as she could see the waiter rushing to get him the check. Perhaps he could see it too. A new love can often be schizophrenic in its roller coaster of emotions. One minute you're having dinner, telling funny stories about work, then suddenly you find yourself playfully flirting, pushing the envelope to see how far your partner is willing to go with you, then something comes over you and all you know, all you can focus on, is the fact that you want him in you immediately so you can feel every morsel. That was new love. There was no rhythm or reason to it, just primal instinct.

That's what she missed the most.

She climbed into her car and watched as he paid and they got up from their seats. The young woman—the girl—looked happy, content, and in that moment, she sensed how easy it was for the girl. She had no idea what was coming. Poor thing.

A random thought popped into her head. The relationship between God and Man was such a lopsided one. God always knew Man's future. No matter what Man did, God knew how things would end. No matter how Man tried to change the outcome of things, God knew the inevitability of it all. Every road led to the same fate. And in the girl's case, her fate had been sealed the moment the little bell had jingled over the firm's front door and he'd walked into her life. Her road led to only one place. Her end. And *she* was going to make that happen.

She liked playing God.

DAY ONE

CHAPTER ONE

Tracy Cowan sat in her car in front of Dr. Devi's brownstone, staring at her knuckles as they turned from pink to white, her grip tightening around the steering wheel to keep her hands from shaking. She focused on the little cut that stretched across her second knuckle down toward her wrist. It looked raw and unsightly. She'd have to put some bacitracin on it when she got home. The cold weather kept the wound from healing and every time she tightened the skin, it would split and the process would begin all over again. A little bacitracin and a Band-Aid would do the trick. As soon as she got home.

Outside, Manhattan moved on with the afternoon, unaware of the woman who'd had a rebirth only hours before. The sound of car horns mixed with the growl of bus engines and the intermittent thunder of the 4 train somewhere below the street was supposed to be familiar, but today, Tracy found it distracting. Pedestrians filled the sidewalks as delivery people rode by on their bikes, hopping curbs and cutting off traffic, weaving in and out of lanes. No one seemed to notice her sitting pin-straight in her seat, staring at her hands, trying to calm herself as she came to the realization that the woman who'd woken up that morning was not the same woman who now idled in front of the brown-stone. She'd become someone else, a phoenix rising from the ashes of a life she now understood was not meant to be. And this new woman, in her new life, was ready to take her first step toward a journey that had no real plan or destination. It was frightening and exhilarating all at the same time. Her story was not over. This was simply a plot twist. Things were going to move in a different direction now. This was Act Two, Scene One. Go.

Manhattan had been where it all started. Funny that she would be validating its ending there as well. She'd been walking across 34th and 5th after lunch with an old college friend when she passed a disturbed homeless man who immediately turned to follow her, mumbling threats if she didn't hand over a few dollars. She'd kept walking and he kept following her, his threats getting louder and more violent. Other pedestrians—strangers—parted as she walked by with the man catching up to her, yelling for her to turn around. It wasn't until she almost reached the next block that a man she didn't know stepped between them and took her hand, gently guiding her into a pizza place, glaring at the homeless man who stopped for a brief moment before spinning back around and walking back toward 5th Avenue. She'd thanked him and he'd offered to buy her a slice. She didn't normally do spontaneous, but something told her to accept, so she did. That had been the first date she'd had with her husband. Now that marriage was over.

The phone in her pocketbook vibrated again, stealing her from her thoughts as she looked at her bag on the passenger's seat. The buzzing sound begged her to answer the call, prodding her to hit that green button and listen to the ramifications of her actions from earlier that morning. He had to have called ten times in the last hour. At first there'd been nothing. For most of the day there had been no effort to reach out and connect the dots she'd left scattered across their lives. But as the afternoon pushed its way toward dusk, the shock of what she'd told him over breakfast must've finally worn off and the calls had begun.

She'd been tempted to pick up the first two or three times, but as she reached for the phone, she kept asking herself what she might say. It was obvious how things would play out. He'd demand that she defend her decision and he'd be ready with a counterpoint to each point she'd make. He'd drag her into a discussion that would become a debate that would, undoubtedly, devolve into an argument where threats would be hurled without fear of repercussion. Knowing all that ahead of time, she simply never bothered to answer any of the calls. There was no point. There could never be any mutual understanding. Maybe one day, but not now. She'd turned the ringer off, set it to vibrate, and ignored the buzzing that emanated from her pocketbook as best she could. She'd said everything there was to say. The gauntlet had been laid. Now it was just a matter of letting it all play out. Things had already been set in motion. The first domino had already fallen.

Tracy grabbed her bag and opened the car door. As soon as she did, the muted sounds of the Upper East Side came alive and the familiar smell of roasted peanuts from the stand at the corner welcomed her back to the neighborhood. She shut the door and looked down at her reflection in the Kia's glass. Her blond hair hung in front of her face, covering the brown eyes he said he'd fallen in love with the moment he met her. She smiled at her reflection in the tiny SUV to see if there was any joy left, and thought she could see a hint of happiness somewhere in there. She'd have to dig it out if she was going to hit the reset button. Thirty-eight wasn't too old to start fresh. She could make a go of it. She had to. This was the only way.

Lights... camera... action.

Kingman, Poppy, and Quiet Boy were hanging out on the stoop in front of Dr. Devi's brownstone in the same three spots they were always in when she arrived. Kingman stood closest to the door while Poppy sat one step lower and Quiet Boy leaned on the railing at the bottom by the sidewalk. Tracy wasn't sure if all three boys were from the neighborhood or patients of Dr. Devi's, but she'd seen Quiet Boy slipping into Dr. Devi's office after her on more than one occasion, so she knew he was a patient. The other two, she had no idea.

"Hey, girl," Kingman said as soon as she turned to walk up the stairs. He was leaning against the outer frame of the door, a puffy ski jacket covering what she knew was a very muscular frame. He was clearly the leader of the three with his infectious smile and disarming charm. He tossed a tennis ball from one hand to the other as he watched her approach.

"Hi, boys," she replied. "How's everyone doing?"

"We're cool," Poppy said. He sucked on a vape stick and looked up at the sky as he exhaled. Unlike Kingman, Poppy was shorter and more round than fit. His winter coat looked snug on him, like he'd outgrown it two or three seasons before. He had no alluring smile or infectious vibe. But he was funny, and funny could always be attractive. "We was waitin' on you. We knew it was your day to come by. We had to make sure we were here."

"You guys were waiting on me? Why?"

"You know why. Don't play. Cause you're hot! You got that MILF magic and we need our fix. Just like we do every week."

Kingman playfully kicked Poppy, laughing. "Man, shut up! You crazy. She don't want to hear no nonsense from you."

"It ain't nonsense. Look at her. Hot magic, right there!"

Kingman's voice went down an octave. "Don't disrespect a princess like that," he crooned, winking at her just once.

Poppy shook his head, cackling. "You could never love her like I could! Never!"

The two boys laughed as Tracy smiled and shook her head. She got the same kind of cheesy pickup lines from them every week and every week they'd laugh at their own jokes, thinking they were cool and creative. When she'd first met them, she wasn't quite sure how to respond, but over time she realized they didn't mean any disrespect, so she got in on the act. These were boys who just weren't old enough to know how to talk to a lady yet. Give them all some time. They were charmers for sure.

She stopped in front of Quiet Boy and punched him in the side of the arm the way a big sister would to do her brother. "What's up?"

Quiet Boy was smaller and skinnier than the others, but when she hit his arm, he was solid. He always wore the same hoodie with the same wires from his earbuds snaking out from underneath. He looked young, but he was cute. His light brown eyes would be his calling card when he got a little older. He rubbed his arm and chuckled. "Damn, that hurt. You been working out?"

"Natural strength. I was born with it."

"You should sign up for MMA or something. Go professional. I'll be your manager."

"Then I guess I'll be the champion. Just lead the way!" She laughed and dug into her pocket. "I got a good one this week."

Quiet Boy rubbed his hands together. "Yeah, me too."

Tracy came away with a small flash drive. She held it up. "Prince."

Quiet Boy chuckled and waved a hand at her. "I know Prince! 'Purple Rain' and all that shit. That ain't new."

"Ah, but this isn't the popular stuff. This is his debut album from 1979. Self-titled. Just Prince. This was before he teamed up with the Revolution. Check it out. The vibe is old school disco with some dance in there. You'll like it. I promise."

Quiet Boy took the flash drive and held up one of his own. "Okay, mine is from Danger Mouse and Black Thought. The album is *Cheat Codes*. You got one of the most skilled producers in the biz teaming up with one of the most talented emcees of all time. No way you don't like this!"

Tracy snatched the drive out of his hand. "I can't wait. You've been on a roll lately."

"Man, you know she throws that out once she gets back in the car," Poppy barked through a laugh. "She don't like none of that shit!"

"I don't like all of it, but he's turned me on to some cool stuff," Tracy replied. "Just because you and I don't share music doesn't mean you have to be jealous about us."

Kingman hollered approval at her dig.

Poppy stopped laughing, but his smile remained. "Name me one emcee you got from Quiet Boy that you like."

"ShrapKnel. Curly Castro and PremRock are great together. I could go on if you want."

She climbed the remainder of the steps to the soundtrack of belly laughs from Quiet Boy and Kingman and the concession from Poppy that she'd shut him up. She'd been trading music with Quiet Boy ever since Dr. Devi was late to his office one day and she sat outside with him on the steps waiting. It had been just the two of them that afternoon, and the subject of music came up. She talked about bands like Fleetwood Mac and Green Day and the Backstreet Boys, and he talked about modern-day hip hop and rap. The next week she'd brought him a copy of *Rumours* and the week after, he'd brought her Meek Mill. It snowballed from there and quickly became their weekly traditional. She'd miss that. She'd miss him.

Tracy reached the top landing and traced her finger down the line of call buttons, ringing Dr. Devi. Kingman was suddenly behind her. His voice was low again. Serious.

"You different today," he said. "For real. I don't know what it is, but something's changed. You got this aura about you. It's powerful."

She could hear Poppy in the background.

"Man, what do you know about auras? Don't try and play like you some mystical pimp."

"I'm just saying something's changed. I can tell. I can sense it."

Tracy smiled although the boys couldn't see it.

"You're right," she said without turning around. "A lot's changed." She rang the office buzzer. "Today is my do-over. Today, everything starts new."

CHAPTER TWO

"You did it," Dr. Devi said. His voice still had a hint of the Indian accent he'd come to the country with when he was a child. "I can see it in your face. You actually did it."

Tracy fought the urge to grin like an idiot. She played it cool. "I did. I think I blindsided him though."

Dr. Devi's office was quite stereotypical: dark walls, bookshelves full of textbooks and periodicals, a large oak desk on the far end of the room, stacks of files piled on top. He even had the requisite two chairs that faced each other off to one side, just beyond the entranceway. Framed awards and certifications hung behind the desk. Plants lined the windowsill closest to the two chairs. It was a welcoming space, despite the clutter, and making it feel welcome was the whole idea. Tracy had felt that sense of ease the first time she'd stepped into the office a year earlier, and over the course of that time it had become a place of refuge. Dr. Devi himself had become a rock in her life, someone she knew she could tell any thought or secret or idea to without fear of ramification. And it wasn't because it was his job to listen without prejudice, but because he really did seem to care. He'd done nothing more than hear her and guide her, and that had been enough. She wished she could call him a friend, but knew that would be crossing some invisible line meant to separate the doctor and the patient. It was incredible to think an off-the-cuff referral from her primary doctor had led to this. Just as things looked bleak and she struggled through her frightening diagnosis, she was given a new life. A new beginning. Like it was meant to be. And Dr. Devi had been the angel she never knew she needed.

Dr. Devi himself was tall and slender. His well-manicured beard and mustache accentuated his almost perfectly chiseled cheeks and chin. His skin was dark, smooth. Jet-black hair was combed back and gelled into place. His hazel eyes held a kindness she'd never seen before. He'd been leaning against his desk when she walked in. A smile crept upon his lips as she shut the door behind her and sat in her usual seat. He knew before she even said anything. Maybe Kingman had been right. Maybe there was an aura about her.

"How do you feel?" Dr. Devi asked as he watched her sink into the overstuffed chair.

"I feel good." She paused, nodding to herself for confirmation, swallowing the smile. "And also scared. And anxious. And nervous."

"That's all normal."

"But I have to admit, I also feel so free. Like a weight has been lifted. Just saying the words out loud to him was like I was liberating myself. I'm happy. Or at least I think I can be."

Dr. Devi pushed himself off the desk and made his way toward her. He floated more than he walked, quiet and effortless. He slid down into his usual seat across from her and leaned forward, his eyes never leaving hers.

"You've taken an incredible step. You did the hard work and you really dug into your emotions."

"All thanks to you. You helped me realize the life I thought I wanted was, in fact, the very thing making me unhappy. You helped me see that my cancer diagnosis was the wakeup call I needed to show myself that there was only one chance at one life."

"Yes. You found your inner strength and your self-worth, and *you* made the decision to change things. I'm so proud of you."

A tear slipped down Tracy's cheek and she brushed it away.

"It wasn't all bad all the time," she said quietly. "I loved Malcolm. I still do. We had a good life together. It just wasn't my life anymore. It wasn't me. I realized that I thought I needed a protector, but what I really need is a chance to let go and be free so I can experience what makes me, me."

"You've been through a lot. The cancer was a turning point for you."

The phone buzzed in her pocketbook, and Tracy reached down to grab it.

"Sorry. I forgot to turn this off before I came in."

"Has he been calling?"

"Incessantly."

"That's to be expected. What has he said?"

"I don't know. I haven't answered."

Dr. Devi fell back in his seat. "Tracy, you have to answer. As difficult and uncomfortable as it may be, you have to allow Malcolm to express what he's feeling too."

"I know."

"You blindsided him this morning. You said it yourself. He didn't seem to know what you were feeling, so all of this is a complete shock to him. You delivered news you've had the luxury of having been able to come to terms with over the course of an entire year. He heard about this a few hours ago over eggs and coffee. It makes sense he'd be calling. I'd think it strange if he wasn't."

Tracy put up her hands. "You're right. I guess I didn't consider that."

"It's okay," Dr. Devi replied. "Just understand that he has to go through the stages to accept this, and right now he needs communication from you; he needs to talk and yell and cry and beg for you to reconsider and scream and everything in between. That is something you'll have to endure to a certain extent. I'm not saying you should allow yourself to be bullied or verbally abused, and God forbid he lays a hand on you. I'm just saying he needs to hear you and understand where you're coming from with this, and at the same time, he needs to be heard. Otherwise, he'll never have the closure he needs, and he'll never get over losing you like this."

Tracy turned the phone off and slipped it back into her bag. "You're absolutely right. I think I just wanted to meet with you first. Regain my center before I talk to him."

"That's fine."

"I'm heading home after this. I'll text him when I get in the car and tell him I'm coming. We can talk in person. He deserves that."

Dr. Devi took his pad and pen from a small table next to his chair. "Have you said anything to Finn?"

"No. He was already on the bus when I told Malcolm. I didn't want him home in case things turned into an argument."

"But he'll be home tonight when you get back?"

"Actually, I had my sister pick him up for a sleepover. It'll just be me and Malcolm."

"That's a good plan."

Tracy paused, knowing this would be just as hard to say as what she'd told her husband earlier that morning. She felt her stomach clench as she cleared her throat and wiped another tear with the back of her hand. There was a brief moment when she thought about keeping her mouth shut, but she knew she couldn't do that. Doing the hard things was what made her journey so fulfilling. He taught her that.

"There's something else," she began. "I... I'm not coming back. This is going to be our last session."

Dr. Devi stopped writing and looked at her. He cocked his head to one side. "May I ask why?"

"I'm heading north. As soon as I can. Vermont or Maine or something. I have a meeting scheduled with my lawyer tomorrow and my plan is to pack as much as I can for me and Finn tonight while I'm at the house and stay with my sister until my lawyer says it's okay to make the move. I need to get out of this area. If I'm really going to start fresh, I need to reinvent myself in a place that's still close enough for Finn to see his father, but far enough away that nothing reminds me of this life I'm leaving. I'm starting my own adventure now, and unfortunately, you're part of the life I have to let go of."

"It sounds like you've been pondering this for a while."

A small smile. "I think I've been planning this ever since I first walked in here. I just didn't know it until you helped me."

"I see."

There was something in Dr. Devi's expression that made Tracy a little uneasy. She thought she caught an angry tone in his voice and sensed he might be a little angry despite what he told her. Nothing over the top. Just enough of an edge to his voice to notice. The mood in the room changed. The office, a space that had been an oasis for the past year, suddenly seemed small and claustrophobic. She felt the walls closing in on her, reaching for her to keep her from leaving.

"Are you mad? I realize this is just as much a shock to you as it was to Malcolm earlier. I'm sorry for that, but I really do have to make a fresh start."

Dr. Devi put on a smile of his own. "I'm not mad. To be honest, though, I don't think this is the time to stop your therapy. We've gotten you to a place where you were finally able to make the kind of change you wanted to make. Now we have to take the next step. The next few months will be crucial."

"Maybe you can recommend someone up north?" Tracy suggested, trying to ignore the sensation of being suffocated. "I'm not saying I'm cured or anything even close to that, and you're right about the next few months being crucial. I'd like to stay in therapy. Maybe you can put me in touch with a colleague once I'm settled?"

"I'd be happy to recommend someone."

Dr. Devi dropped his pad on his lap and, for a moment, stared out the window where the plants were lined on the sill.

"And I can call you between now and when I get to wherever I'm going," Tracy continued. "We could have virtual sessions or phone sessions until I get settled with someone else."

Dr. Devi turned away from the window and reached over, gently taking her hand in his, holding it, his thumb rubbing hers. He'd never done that before.

"You can call me whenever you'd like," he said. "Day or night."

"Thank you."

"As your doctor I'm not supposed to say this, but I'm going to miss you, Tracy. I really am. You're an amazing woman. It's important for you to always remember that. What you've done over this past year is truly inspirational."

"Thank you. For everything. I'm going to miss you too."

Tracy looked down at his hand holding hers, waiting for him to release his grip, but he wouldn't let go. The room was quiet as she closed her eyes and tried to imagine what her future would hold. All of this change had to be worth it. It had to be. It might be a bit painful at first, but in the long run everything would pay off. She couldn't see any other way. She had to leave him, but first she had to show him that she knew about everything.

Nothing else would work if she didn't.

CHAPTER THREE

"Hi, you've reached Tracy's cell. I can't answer right now so—"

Malcolm Cowan disconnected the call and tossed his phone on his desk, slamming his fists down on the arms of his chair as he cried out in frustration, his voice echoing off the walls of the small trailer that looked out onto the job site. The rickety file cabinet that stood by the door swayed back and forth. Papers and invoices on his makeshift desk swept into the air and rocked gently back down to the floor. Beyond the tiny windows on the far end of the trailer he could see backhoes digging into the earth for a foundation that would eventually hold a six-story apartment complex in Hastings, on the banks of the Hudson River. This had been the fourth straight job his construction firm had been awarded and his reputation for a solid build with little-to-no cost overruns was spreading throughout the industry. Four jobs that spanned the last two years and things were finally happening. The company was taking off. His net worth was getting bigger. And the end game of selling off the company to a larger conglomerate in another five years was looking more promising than ever. Things were on the upside. After so much blood, sweat, tears, and hope, the worm was turning. Until Tracy had dropped her bomb that morning. Now everything was a mess.

She'd said it so matter-of-factly, sliding into the stool across the kitchen island from where he stood eating a bowl of cereal. *We need to talk.* He never thought those four words would be the precursor to something so life-changing. He thought they'd been happy. He thought the leanest and meanest parts of their marriage were over and there was smooth sailing up ahead for both of them. He figured she wanted to know where he'd been so late and why he'd slept on the couch when he got home. He had no idea she was planning to *leave.* Sure, she'd been a little distant and depressed since the cancer scare, but that was normal. They hadn't been sure she'd survive. It had been scary for both of them. He'd let her have her space, but never in a million years did he think things were so bad that she needed to actually give up her life with him. He couldn't figure out where that was coming from. She couldn't know, could she? No way. He'd been so careful.

"I've done a lot of soul-searching in the last year. I really dug deep and tried to get to the core of how I was feeling. At first, I thought it was some post-cancer depression thing, but it's so much more than that. Malcolm, I'm not the woman I was when you married me eight years ago. That woman was just coming out of a seriously failed relationship and before that, a relationship that literally almost cost me my life. I was a mess. I didn't know how to love or be loved, and you were a different kind of man. You were ten years older and in control of things. I was in awe of your drive and determination and fell in love with your ability and your promise to keep me safe. I thought we were a team and I thought that was all I ever wanted."

As she spoke, he could hear the neighbor's kids laughing and hollering to each other as they made their way out of the house and into the minivan that was parked in their driveway.

They sounded so happy and carefree, while the mood in his kitchen kept getting heavier and more ominous.

"I realized that I don't think I was ever really in love with you. I was in love with the fact that you could take care of me and protect me, but that's not real love. I can see now that the emotional investment I need to give you isn't there. It never was. I tried to deny what I was feeling and push through it, thinking maybe it was just a phase that I'd overcome, but when my diagnosis came and I started examining myself on a deeper level after I got better, I understood that we only have one life, one chance to make the most out of our time here. You don't deserve a wife who doesn't love you and I don't deserve a life where I feel trapped again. I can't do this anymore. As much as I appreciate what you've built for us, it's not for me."

At that point he'd stopped eating and was just staring at her, wondering what in God's name she was talking about. And before he could reply, she'd blurted the next two sentences that would change his world.

"I'm leaving, Malcolm. I want a divorce."

She'd hopped off the stool and walked out of the kitchen like she'd just reminded him to pick up the dry cleaning on the way home from work. There were no tears or yelling or fumbling over her words. She was emotionless, cold, determined. Before he could even react, she was gone. He wasn't sure how much time passed, but he stood against the island, bowl of cereal in hand, for what seemed like forever. The sound of the neighbor's car pulling out of their driveway had snapped him back to reality and he'd dropped the bowl in the sink, got dressed, and made his way out to the site, his wife's words echoing in his head the entire morning.

Eight years of marriage. Eight years of protecting his family, having their son, providing for them so Tracy didn't have to work and could stay home with Finn, taking jobs he knew were too small to grow the business, but doing it for the quick cash so they could get through the winter, the days taking care of her after her chemo treatments. The sacrifices he'd made were immeasurable. And for what? So the woman he loved and gave everything to for a decade could bounce down the stairs one morning and tell him she's leaving? No way. And what about Finn? Did she think she was going to take his son away from him without him putting up a fight? She couldn't be that stupid. Finn was his life. That boy wasn't going anywhere.

Malcolm snatched his phone from his desk and dialed again.

"Hi, you've reached Tracy's cell. I can't—"

He ended the call and pulled up his texts, accessing a different number. He paused, his finger hovering over the keypad as memories drifted in and out of his mind. There had been better times once. They'd loved each other unconditionally. And Finn. That boy had been the best thing that ever happened to either one of them. He still loved her. There was no denying that. How could she leave what they'd built? How could she leave him all alone?

He began typing.

IT'S ME

It took a few minutes before he saw the responding text bubbles appear.

                              YOU GIVE ANY THOUGHT TO WHAT WE
                                                    TALKED
                                                    ABOUT?

I DID

                                                    AND?

He sighed, thinking everything through one final time before he slowly typed the words he knew could change everything.

DO IT

She wasn't taking his son.
No way.

CHAPTER FOUR

It was dark by the time Tracy stepped outside. The rush out of the city was still about an hour away, but the streets were already much more deserted than when she first arrived. The sidewalks only held a handful of people. The rumble of the 4 train was always a constant, but sounded louder now that the neighborhood was quiet. Even the boys on the stoop were gone. She wished she could've said goodbye to them one last time and thought briefly about waiting for Quiet Boy to end his session with Dr. Devi. They had that sibling connection she couldn't deny and felt like she owed it to him to tell him she wasn't coming back and that their year-long game of introducing each other to music they loved would end with Prince and Danger Mouse and Black Thought. He'd become a familiar face over her year of being treated at the brownstone. But no, staying would be weird and she didn't like goodbyes. Besides, he hadn't been in the waiting room when she was done, so she wasn't even sure if he had an appointment after her. Dr. Devi would tell him eventually, and he would tell the others. It was time to go.

Tracy shivered as she climbed into her car and started the engine. The temperature had dropped by at least ten degrees since the sun set. She sat for a moment and took her phone out of her bag, powering it back up and watching as the screen came to life. The series of buzzes shook her. The texts and calls and voicemails were too many to count as they loaded into the phone, notification after notification, alerting her each time Malcolm had reached out. She could see the texts popping up on the screen, one after the other.

WHERE ARE YOU?

CALL ME

PICK UP YOUR PHONE!

YOU CAN'T IGNORE ME!

I'M GOING TO FIND YOU

PLEASE DON'T DO THIS TO US

I LOVE YOU

PICK UP THE PHONE!!!!!!!!!

YOU BETTER ANSWER YOUR PHONE NOW!

WHERE ARE YOU??????

WHERE IS MY SON!!!!!

CALL ME BACK!!!!!!

Tracy could feel the pit of her stomach drop as she thumbed through the texts that got angrier and more volatile. She'd expected a visceral reaction from Malcolm, but actually seeing the threats and the rage and the random confession of love on the screen scared her. She knew how easily he could lose control, if even for a second. She thought about heading straight to her sister's house instead of going home, but quickly dismissed the idea. Going home and facing Malcolm was part of the process. It had to be done. The hard stuff, right? She'd just have to be careful.

Her call log showed twenty-seven missed calls and her voicemail was waiting with seven messages. She deleted them all without listening and texted Malcolm instead.

FINN IS FINE. HE'S WITH MISSY. I'M ON MY WAY HOME TO TALK AND I DIDN'T WANT HIM THERE. I'M SORRY I DIDN'T ANSWER YOUR CALLS OR TEXTS. THIS IS HARD FOR ME TOO AND I JUST NEEDED THE DAY TO THINK. I'M COMING HOME NOW. ABOUT AN HOUR AWAY.

She placed the phone in a cup holder and pulled out of her parking spot. Tiny droplets of rain dotted the windshield and she wondered if the rain might turn to snow as she made her way north. It had been a relatively mild winter, but March was always so unpredictable. She hoped she could get to the house before the roads became too slick.

The phone began to ring as she pulled across the Third Avenue Bridge and onto the Deegan Expressway. She wasn't going to let it roll to voicemail this time. Dr. Devi was right. Malcolm deserved communication.

"Hello?"

"My God, where have you been?"

Malcolm's voice was sharp and full of vitriol. He spoke

slowly, but there was an unmistakable edge that told her he was fighting hard not to lose it.

"I just had a session with Dr. Devi and now I'm heading home so we can talk."

"Is that quack bastard the one who told you to leave me? Is that asshole the one who put all this crap in your head?"

Tracy turned on the Kia's rear wiper and as she did, noticed a sedan behind her among a cluster of other cars. It caught her attention because it only had one headlight. She instantly flashed back to her childhood with her older sister, Missy, punching her in the arm and screaming "Padiddle!" She could almost feel her bicep ache.

"Are you even listening to me?"

Malcolm's voice brought her back to the present.

"Yes. I'm listening. But I don't want to talk about it over the phone when I'm driving. I'll see you in a little while. We'll talk then."

Malcolm was seething. "Do you really think I'm just going to let you get up and leave because you say you need to find yourself? Do you think I'm so weak that I'd sit back and let you turn our lives upside down and destroy my son's life? You're crazy, Tracy. Insane. You can't come out of nowhere with this and expect me to be okay with it. None of it even makes sense." His voice softened. "Everything we've been through. You and me. We're a team. We love each other. You can't throw that away."

The car with one headlight was two cars behind her as she sped past Yankee Stadium. She kept glancing back, watching it and thinking about the long trips to Lake George in summers so hot she thought she'd melt in the backseat.

"I love you too, but not the kind of love that can keep us together. And besides, this isn't about you."

"Of course it is! You're leaving me and you think you're taking my son with you. This *is* all about me!"

She turned off the Deegan and onto the Sprain Parkway, tracking the car with the one headlight as it followed behind. She couldn't help notice how it was weaving in and out of its lane as it remained behind a small delivery truck that was between them.

"Malcolm, please. Let me get back to the house and we can talk. But I'm telling you right now, if you're going to be raging and violent, I'm not coming. I can explain everything, and I realize what I said this morning wasn't enough. I know it seems like this is coming out of nowhere from your perspective. I get all that. You deserve to know everything and I'm willing to share it with you, but if you're just going to be screaming at me the whole time, I'll sleep at my sister's."

"I was never violent to you," Malcolm replied. "How could you even say something like that after what you've been through?"

"I know. I'm sorry. But you sound pretty unhinged right now."

"Because my life just got all fucked up!"

She could hear her husband breathing heavily on the other end of the phone, panting like an animal.

"I'm coming now. We can talk. I'll tell you everything."

"Yeah, I'll be waiting."

He disconnected the call before she could say anything more. The rain that had begun in the city must've already passed through the Hudson Valley, and although the roads were still wet, the sky was now full of stars rather than clouds. She looked behind her again and could see the sedan in the left lane, keeping pace, its single headlight watching her.

Padiddle!

She focused on the road, and thought about what the next few hours would be like. She needed to stay firm and strong if she was going to make things happen the way she needed them to. It was going to be a long night and it was important to get it all done correctly. Talk with Malcolm, pack a suitcase for her and Finn, and leave. The rest would take care of itself over time, and by then, she'd be getting ready to move north and start over. The only question that remained once everything was said and done was would Malcolm let her leave once she got to the house?

She honestly wasn't sure.

CHAPTER FIVE

Missy Rollins placed the plate of chicken nuggets in front of her adorable nephew as he sat and watched the cartoon she'd set up for him so she could start dinner. He was absolutely gorgeous. Blond hair that hung over his tiny ears, cut in a bowl shape that allowed his bangs to stop just past his eyebrows. His blue eyes were almost translucent, which would make the ladies swoon one day. His soft, thin, lips were the lightest shade of pink. He was perfection, and she couldn't get enough of him. Such a shame his world was shifting right under his feet.

"Blow on those before you eat them," she said. "They're still hot."

"Thank you, Aunt Missy," Finn replied without taking his eyes off the screen.

"You're welcome, buddy. And after dinner we have to take a bath. Then I'll let you play on my iPad before bed."

Her cell phone started to ring. Missy made her way into the kitchen to retrieve it. The Caller ID told her it was her sister.

"Hey."

"Everything okay?" Tracy asked.

"I should be asking you that," Missy replied. "How'd it go? I called a few times, but you didn't answer. I didn't want to keep stalking you for gossip."

"Yeah, I wasn't really dealing with the phone today. I got your text that you picked up Finn, so I knew you had him."

"And you took care of everything?"

"Yeah. I told Malcolm this morning after Finn got on the bus. He didn't take it well. I think he was shocked at first. Then he got pissed. I'm heading home now to talk with him. Wish me luck."

"I'll do no such thing. You don't need luck. You need to come to your senses and realize you're making a mistake."

"You keep telling me that."

"Because someone has to." Missy spun around the slightly dilapidated kitchen that hadn't been renovated since the eighties. "You hit the lotto this time, Tracy. You have a decent guy who's a good provider and one hell of a businessman. He's not like the others."

"Except that he is."

"Look, there's no reason to mess this up. I don't want you to end up like me. Dead-end job, stuck in Mom and Dad's old place, no light at the end of my tunnel. You might want to just rethink this."

"Kind of too late now."

"Nothing's too late. Not yet. There's still a chance to undo what's been done. If you want that."

"Things are already in motion."

"I can help you make it right."

"No," Tracy replied. "It's done. You'll just have to trust me."

Missy made her way into the living room, listening as the worn floorboards gave under her feet. The water stain that ran down the wall from the leaking roof peeled the paint off in large flakes. The cracked window looking out onto the street hadn't been fixed in ten years. The same brown carpet that was installed when she and Tracy were kids was matted and stained and worn from decades of traffic. She looked at it all and knew everything would stay that way for the foreseeable future. A paycheck-to-paycheck life didn't afford such luxuries as fixing leaking roofs and broken windows.

"Has Malcom ever laid a hand on you?"

"No."

"Ever threaten you physically? Throw something at you? Hit Finn? Threaten to hit Finn?"

"Don't be ridiculous."

"Then how bad could things really be?"

A pause on the other end.

"It's bad enough that I want a fresh start." Tracy's voice was low.

Missy nodded. "I know. All I'm saying is take a moment and look around at the life you've built for yourself. You have security, money, a beautiful son, and the opportunity to give this kid brothers and sisters without having to worry about feeding and clothing them and sending them to good schools. You don't have to worry about anything. People would kill for that. Maybe you can move your line in the sand. Redefine your definition of bad."

Another pause. Missy watched Finn blowing on each nugget before shoving it into his mouth. He was such a good kid. He didn't deserve to have his life turned upside down.

"Can I speak to Finn?" Tracy asked. There was a cut to her voice now. She was annoyed.

"Sure. Text me later and let me know how things are going. I'll be up."

"Okay."

Missy crossed the room and held out the phone as she sat on the couch next to her nephew. "Mom wants to say hello."

Finn dropped the fork he was holding and grabbed the phone. "Hi, Mommy!"

Missy couldn't help but smile when she heard the joy in the

boy's voice. She wondered what that joy would turn into in the years to come. Would things work out? Would he be happy? Or would he look at the life his father had created and resent his mother for dragging him away from it? She knew Malcolm would be part of Finn's life, but not in the way any of them had imagined. Why was Tracy so willing to screw everything up?

Missy tilted her head back and let it rest on the back of the couch. Ever since Tracy's episode with Jake, she'd felt the need to protect her little sister. She'd always been there for her, and when she met Malcolm, she thought she could turn over those duties and get on with her own life. But now that was changing again. Tracy wanted to walk away from a life Missy would've given anything to have. She'd take the good with the bad and never look back. There wasn't even a question.

She'd do anything.

But not Tracy.

Tracy was different.

Tracy had lines, and when you crossed them there was hell to pay.

Always.

CHAPTER SIX

Tracy disconnected the call and fell back into her seat. Her heart ached hearing Finn's voice, so full of innocence and wonder. She'd done her best to sound cheerful when they spoke, but wasn't sure if she'd been able to pull it off. All she really wanted to do was drive straight to him, wrap her arms around his tiny little body, and never let go. In Finn's world, he was simply sleeping over his aunt's house for a fun night of games, TV, chicken nuggets, and bedtime stories. He had no idea his life was changing, and that the surroundings he'd grown up in and felt safe and familiar in were about to be replaced with a new life, somewhere different, somewhere alien. She hoped he'd understand as he got older and wondered how he'd be once everything was exposed and the dust settled. Kids were supposed to be resilient. He'd be fine. He had to be. She'd make sure of it.

The traffic on Route 9 was growing heavy as rush hour took hold. Tracy put on the radio to try and take her mind off things for a bit. She was tired. The adrenaline that had been carrying her throughout the day was waning and she fought to stay awake and alert as she drove. Her quiet reprieve wouldn't last long. She knew things would escalate as soon as she got home. Malcolm had had all day to think about what she'd said that morning, and from the sound of his voice and the tone of his texts, he'd been stewing in an anger that seemed to be growing. She'd try to reason with him, to make him see that she just wasn't happy and needed a fresh start, but she had little faith that he'd choose to see anything her way. At that point she'd be forced to tell him what she knew and that would be the end of it. She would take their son and move far away from the house and the life he'd built for them. And then he'd see the price he'd paid for the mistakes he'd made. She'd have a new life, but that was all down the line. She knew her husband wouldn't let them leave without a fight, and Malcolm had no problem getting his hands dirty to get what he wanted. She took her foot off the accelerator for a moment and let the car coast. For a second time since leaving Dr. Devi's, she thought that going home might've been a bad idea. Dr. Devi's voice echoed in her mind.

"You have to allow Malcolm to express what he's feeling too. You blindsided him this morning."

She put her foot back on the accelerator. Better to just get it over with.

Tracy flicked on her turn signal and looked into her rearview mirror as she eased her car over to the right lane. As she did, she caught a glimpse of the car with one headlight about three vehicles back, in the left lane.

Padiddle!

She felt her body tense as she looked on. The car with one headlight moved to match her lane change, sliding into the right lane, keeping pace. Her breath caught in her throat and the tiredness she was feeling immediately vanished. Who was that? There was no way that same car could've been following her all the way from the city by chance. Not from Dr. Devi's office. She'd taken, like, four or five different roads. What were the odds that car would still be behind her?

Tracy sped up and watched as the car with one headlight did the same. She took her foot off the accelerator and slowed until other cars around her began flashing their high beams and passing in frustration. The car with one headlight remained behind her, always two to three vehicles away, gaining speed when she did. Slowing when she slowed.

Padiddle!

With more traffic crowding around her, Tracy sped up and passed an oversized pickup truck on the left. When she was by the truck, she quickly merged into the left lane just in time to match the pace of a school bus in the right lane. Together, they had the entire road blocked. She checked her rearview mirror and could see the car with one headlight trying to maneuver its way up, but she and the bus were slowing all of the traffic just enough so everyone was bunched up and no one could make an offensive move.

The exit sign for *Montrose/Buchanan* appeared around a bend in the road. Half a mile until the turnoff. She sat up in her seat and waited, checking to make sure she was still parallel with the bus even as the other cars behind her were starting to tailgate while others flashed their high beams again, trying to get her to move over.

He's sent someone to keep tabs on me, she thought. *They've been following me all day and I never noticed. I only noticed tonight because of the one headlight. Otherwise, I'd have no idea. They were waiting when I got out of Dr. Devi's office. Can't be a coincidence. That son of a bitch had them follow me to make sure I went home.*

She reached for her phone in the cupholder and dialed Malcolm.

"Hello."

"If you're going to have me followed, you might want to make sure your guy has a car that doesn't stick out like a sore thumb," she barked, hearing her voice shake as she spoke. "I'm not a child. I said I was coming home and I am. I don't need a chaperone."

"Once again, I have no clue what you're talking about," Malcolm replied.

"Don't lie to me. They've been following me since Dr. Devi's. I don't need a goddamned tail."

The exit was just up ahead. Less than one hundred yards.

"Can I remind you that I'm the one who's been calling you all day trying to figure out where you were?" Malcolm shouted. "Why would I keep calling if I had someone tailing you? Make sense, Tracy."

Tracy pressed down on the accelerator and inched up ahead of the school bus. She was almost there.

"Someone's following me. I can see them. If it's not you, then who is it?"

"Why would someone be following you?"

"Because my husband is a control freak and needs to know where I am and has an army of workers who would be willing to do him a favor for a few extra bucks?"

Malcolm laughed on the other end of the phone. "I told you I didn't have anyone follow you. There's probably no one following you and this is all in your head. It's rush hour, for God's sake. People commute in and out of the city. You're fine."

"I don't feel fine."

"Okay then, where are you?"

"Route 6. Almost at Montrose."

"If it makes you feel better, get off the exit and drive to the trooper station on Post Road. If someone really is following you, they won't follow you there."

"Yeah, I'm way ahead of you."

Tracy slammed down on the accelerator and shot past the bus. As soon as she was clear, she tugged the car into the right lane just as the exit ramp was upon her. She flew down the ramp and watched behind her to see if the car with one headlight would follow. She stopped at the red light on the bottom of the ramp and turned around in her seat, staring, waiting.

Nothing.

"What's going on?" Malcom asked.

A few other cars made their way down the exit ramp toward her, but all of them had full sets of headlights. There was no sign of the car that had been following her. Tracy turned back around and pulled onto Post Road.

"I'm good. Maybe they weren't following me. I don't know. Maybe they're just going home like you said. My nerves are a little frayed today."

"Join the club."

"I'll take Post Road until I can get back on Route 9 at Welcher. Be home soon."

She could hear him breathing, but Malcolm didn't say anything more. She disconnected the call and drove down the familiar road that brought her through the northernmost point of Croton-on-Hudson until she crossed into the village of Buchanan. Malcolm was from the neighboring town of Verplanck. He'd grown up in a two-bedroom trailer, raised by a single mom who worked three jobs, and had an older sister who'd died in a car accident when she was in high school. They'd married at a church in the center of town and had their reception under a pavilion at George's Island, a small state park in town that was hidden deep inside the streets of suburbia and sat on the banks of the Hudson River.

She knew this area. She'd driven those roads countless times when they were dating and earlier in their marriage when they would visit his mother before she died. How could it possibly be that she was driving on these roads the same day she was leaving this part of her life behind? What were the odds? Perhaps it was a sign.

Without really thinking about it, Tracy found herself passing the VA hospital and turning down Dutch Street toward the park, the memories of her wedding day drifting through her mind as she went.

It had been a good day. The weather had been sunny with no humidity. The breeze off the river had been perfect. Tracy was in a beautiful white dress her mother found and Malcolm had been in his best, and only, suit. Friends and relatives filled the pavilion and danced until the band stopped playing at midnight. She'd honestly thought that day had been the beginning of forever for her. She never thought her life would take such a turn.

The road narrowed and grew dark. Tracy put her high beams on to make sure she could see where she was going. The mesh gate was open and she noticed the sign welcoming her to George's Island had been updated since the last time she'd been there. As soon as she entered the park, civilization slipped away and she was surrounded by woods on all sides and the Hudson River in front. She knew there were houses and streets and a neighborhood beyond the thick set of trees, but in the darkness, she couldn't see any of that. The loneliness made her feel at ease.

The parking lot was empty. Tracy drove her car down past the abandoned playground and empty grill pits to the edge of the water, next to the boat ramp. She could see lights dotting the mountains of Rockland County across the river but the way the Hudson bent, she was too far inland to see the Bronx or Manhattan. She shut off her lights and let the car idle, watching the current being swept south, whitecaps glowing in the moonlight. A gust of wind rocked her car and she could see a set of clouds making their way from west to east. She really had to get to the house before the weather turned again and the roads got too slick.

She leaned forward and stared at the dock rocking up and down in the current. She and Malcolm had taken their favorite wedding picture there. He stood behind her and she was leaning into him, his arms wrapped around the top of her chest, hugging her. The dock had been rocking that day too, but she never thought she'd lose her balance and fall in. She knew he was there and would protect her. Now all of it was gone. Just like that.

The tears came suddenly, unexpected. Tracy fell back in her seat just in time to see movement in her rearview mirror. The blurred image sharpened as she wiped her eyes and, again, her breath caught in her throat. She didn't know how he'd found her, but she was suddenly aware of how alone and vulnerable she was in the empty parking lot. Just two cars with no one else around.

Just her and the car with one headlight.

Padiddle!

CHAPTER SEVEN

Tracy spun around in her seat to get a better look. The car had come all the way down the winding road and snuck into the lot without her noticing. It crept behind her and stopped about two spaces away.

Blind hands reached for her phone as her eyes remained fixed on the car. She tried to make out the identity of the driver, but could only see a faint silhouette. Who was in there?

She looked down at the phone and unlocked it with her thumbprint, immediately hitting the red emergency button.

"911. What's your emergency?"

As if sensing what Tracy had done, the car's high beams suddenly came to life and the horn blared.

"I need help!"

"Okay, what's your name?"

"Tracy Cowan!"

The horn stopped. Silence again.

"What's the problem, Tracy?"

With the interior of her Kia still bathed in light from the other car's high beams, Tracy sat frozen as the car lunged once, then suddenly sped toward her, slamming into the back of the Kia, pushing it forward, tires squealing, engine roaring.

Tracy screamed and turned back around in her seat, watching as she inched past the concrete divider, onto the thin patch of grass, and closer to the river.

"Help me!"

"Tracy, what's happening?" the 911 operator asked. "Talk to me."

The car kept pushing her, its heavy frame and powerful torque no match for the tiny Kia. She was almost past the grass now. He was pushing her into the river.

"What are you doing? Stop! Please!"

"Tracy, what's going on? I need you to tell me what's happening."

The car stopped for a moment, but before Tracy could catch her breath, it blared its horn again and began pushing once more, knocking the Kia sideways. The phone fell from her grasp and onto the passenger's side floor. The left front tire fell into the water.

"Please! What are you doing? Stop!"

She pounded her horn to try and get someone's attention. She knew people lived beyond the woods at the top of the hill. She had to get someone's attention.

"Stop!"

The roaring engine died and the car backed up. Tracy fumbled for the handle and opened the door just as the car sped forward again, engine growling, this time hitting the Kia square in the back and sending the entire front end into the river. As soon as the current got hold of the small SUV, it began pulling her out further.

"Oh my God!"

Tracy pushed her door all the way open and fell out onto the grass as the Kia got knocked from behind one final time and the entire vehicle went into the river, quickly slipping into the strong current toward Manhattan, the bottom half sinking, as the wind whipped up.

The car with one headlight backed away at an angle, moving slowly as if knowing it had cornered her. The hunter had its prey. It washed Tracy in the strength of its high beams, watching as she scrambled to her feet and ran as fast as she could toward the tree line beyond the parking lot.

The world around her dimmed. The lights went out. She heard a car door open and close, followed by the slapping of footsteps on the gravel. The driver was chasing her. She had to get to the small patch of woods and hide. The darkness would be her camouflage.

Tracy crashed through the first line of bushes and trees and as soon as she did, all of the detail she'd been able to see only moments earlier was gone. The world around her had turned black. There were no details to anything. Just shapes and shades of darkness. She glanced behind her to try and see who was coming, but she was already too far into the woods to see back out onto the parking lot. She had to keep moving.

The footsteps pursuing her crossed into the woods. Tracy tip-toed the best she could, grimacing every time she stepped on dead leaves or snapped a branch. The air around her was cold and she shivered from both the dropping temperature and the adrenaline that coursed through her body. She held her trembling hands out in front of her, feeling as she went, trying to determine which way to go to get to the houses on the other side of the woods. She bit the inside of her cheek to keep from sobbing too loudly. Tears streamed down her face, blurring her vision. If she could get to the houses, she could scream for help and get someone to call the police. If not, she didn't know what she was going to do.

The person chasing her had no concern for staying quiet.

Twigs snapped and leaves crunched and still the footsteps marched through the woods with purpose, closing in on her as she tried to run without making any noise.

Who was this person? Why were they chasing her? What did they want? The questions flooded her mind as she tried desperately not to succumb to panic. She could feel her heart pounding in her chest and whimpered as quietly as she could, suppressing the need to cry out in panic.

It's Malcolm. Has to be.

There was a light in the distance and Tracy could see the woods beginning to thin. A clearing. The houses. She'd made it. She stopped to get her bearings, but there was no time to properly assess anything. She could hear the footsteps behind her getting nearer. She ran as fast as she could toward the light and the clearing. Low brush and thorn bushes tugged at her clothes, ripping the fabric and scratching her skin. She ignored it all and focused on the light and the clearing. If she could just get to the houses, she could get help.

It's him. He did this. He's angry.

She burst through the last line of trees and stumbled out into what she thought would be a line of small fences that marked the yards of several houses in this part of the neighborhood. Instead, she slipped on loose gravel and fell onto her back as she heard the sound of water lapping the shoreline. The light she'd been focused on was a set of barge lights from the Cuomo Bridge that stretched across the Hudson. She'd made a half-circle in the woods and had come back out on the riverside. The houses were in the opposite direction. She'd gone the wrong way.

"Help me!" she screamed as loud as she could, no longer caring about being quiet as panic took over. "Somebody help!"

The footsteps crunched on the loose gravel and stopped. Tracy spun around and tried to scramble to her feet, but all she could see were two legs running toward her, jeans and a pair of work boots. Before she could register anything else, she felt a flash of pain on the side of her head and then there was nothing but blackness and the ever-distant sound of the tide slapping the edge of the concrete boat slip.

CHAPTER EIGHT

Around the same time Tracy was running through the woods, searching desperately for an escape, Detective Dennis Taft was studying Kat Masterson's body from across the living room of her apartment, trying his best to keep his emotions locked down. He had to remain professional, but it was a hard sight to see. She was sitting on the floor, her back leaning against the bottom of her couch, her legs spread out under the coffee table, her head hanging straight down so he couldn't see her face. Her white silk robe was untied and open. She was naked underneath. The dog chain that had been used to kill her still hung around her neck. There was blood on the couch behind her, spatter on the upper half and a pool on the cushions. The rest of the apartment seemed clean and untouched. Outside the two large windows in the living room, Norwalk, Connecticut moved on as life always did. They'd been on scene for almost two hours.

He stood in his spot between the living room and the kitchen, perfectly still as he studied every inch of his surroundings, writing notes in his pad without looking down at the paper. The hand that held the pad also clasped a rusted old locket on a chain. His thumb rubbed the locket as he wrote, leaning the pad against his gut that stretched his dress shirt. How many times had he done this over his twenty-plus years as a detective? How many crime scenes had he come to in his over thirty years on the force? But this one hit home. The senseless violence. The heartlessness. It was too much.

The forensics techs worked around him, taking pictures, collecting samples, pulling prints, and processing the body as best they could before they'd ship it to the medical examiner for further analysis. A handful of uniformed police milled about, but mostly just stayed out of the way. There was an officer stationed at the door and on the porch of the three-family walkup. No one got in without proof of them living there, and before they were allowed up, they were asked to give a statement and timeline. So far, no one had seen or heard a thing, and judging from the neatness of the apartment and lack of any apparent struggle, no one would.

He'd gotten the call just after he'd finished dinner. Kat's employer had called 911 and requested a wellness check. Apparently, she hadn't been to work that day and no one could get in touch with her. Her cell phone went unanswered and there was no phone in the apartment. The officer stationed outside the door had been the first to respond. He'd got the landlord to let him in and found her just as she was now. The officer called headquarters and they called Taft. That's how these things went.

Lena Blau approached from the back bedroom and Detective Taft stopped writing. Lena was the lead investigator and had been with the Norwalk Police Department for almost ten years. She was an excellent cop. Her team was one of the best in the state.

Lena was short, maybe five feet, with cropped black hair

that was pinned back with a matching set of barrettes. Her blue eyes seemed to glow in the spotlights that had been set up in each corner of the room. He knew she was in her early forties, but she still looked like a kid fresh out of college.

"Hey, Dennis," Lena said as she sidled up next to him. She rubbed his arm. "You good?"

Taft pulled away. "I'm good. Just checking off the boxes. Making sure everything's done right. Any idea on time of death?"

"The ME will tell us more, but I'd say she's been dead for most of the day. About twelve hours, maybe? Could be longer. Body decomposition is already showing signs and her blood's pooled, so that tells me she's been sitting like that for a little while."

Taft nodded, clearing his throat. "So, the perp comes in last night. Yeah, that makes sense based on what she's wearing and the fact that no one's been able to get in touch with her all day today."

"The ME will take a rectal temp and do the math to pinpoint a time."

"Anything else I should know about?"

Lena looked at him. "You really want to do this?" she asked. "You don't have to be here. You have a retirement to get started on."

"This is exactly where I should be."

"We can handle it. We'll do it right. I swear."

"Consider this my last case." He looked at her and tried to keep it together. He could feel himself blushing. "Please."

Lena nodded. "Okay." She turned her attention back to the victim. "Preliminarily, it looks like she was strangled with that canine choke collar. We can see clear ligature marks on her throat and the chain was left there. The blood on the couch came from a blow to the back of the head. There's a paper-

weight on the floor behind the couch with blood and hair on it.
I'm assuming that's what was used. The rest of the place looks
pretty clean. We're processing everything and taking samples
for testing, but nothing jumps out at me. I'd say the scene was
tight. Right there in the living room. She gets hit, strangled, the
end."

Detective Taft scratched the white stubble on his chin as he
flipped the pages of his notepad with his thumb. "Kat's lived
here for two years. Works as an attorney in town. Nobody heard
anything last night or today. Doesn't sound like they would have
if it went down like you said. Blow to the back of the head,
choke her out, leave. Nothing stolen. Money and credit cards
are still in her purse. Jewelry's still in the bedroom."

"No signs of forced entry either. Door and windows are all
as they should be."

"Any cameras?"

"None. We'll check with the neighbors to see if they have
anything that looks out onto the street, but this place has nothing. Apparently, the landlord kept things pretty bare bones.
Rent was affordable, but none of the tenants get any extras."

Taft spun around, his eyes still searching for clues. "You
said her law firm called it in, right?"

"Yeah. Requested a wellness check."

"You notify them of what we found?"

"No specifics, but we let them know she won't be in for
work tomorrow. I'll follow up with them. Right now, we're going
to do the transport to the morgue. You need anything before we
wrap up?"

"Nah. Do your thing. I'm going to take one more cruise
around and then wrap it myself."

"There's an empty picture frame on her vanity in the
bedroom. Not sure if it's empty on purpose or not, but check it
out."

"Will do."

He watched Lena gather her team and give her final
instructions, and as the crime scene techs spread out to begin
the process of removing Kat's body, he walked along the edge of
the apartment, scanning for anything he might've missed.

The apartment was fairly small. One bathroom, one
bedroom, a living room, and an eat-in kitchen. The house itself
was built in the late 1800s and didn't have any of the amenities
a more modern multi-family home might have. There were radi-
ators in each room instead of gas heat. Window units instead of
central air. Closet doors against warped frames that didn't shut
all the way. A floor that sloped from north to west. But there
was also a charm he could see. Moldings you simply couldn't
find anymore. Antique wall sconces and a stained-glass chande-
lier in the living room. Crystal door handles. An original bear-
claw tub in the bathroom. He took it all in as he strolled from
room to room, wondering who it was Kat knew to so innocently
let them in the night before, only to be murdered in cold blood.

He could hear the body bag being unfolded in the other
room and his stomach clenched. He circled the bedroom, examining the blankets and sheets that were messy and unmade. A
small pile of clothes was stacked in the far corner. A tiny vanity
full of hair and makeup products stood next to the lone window.
Darkness outside as well as in.

Detective Taft leaned closer toward the vanity and looked
at the 5x7 picture frame Lena had mentioned. The frame was
bedazzled in fake diamonds and black gems. He picked it up to
get a closer look. It was hard to tell if a picture had been in
there. If there had been one in there, and it was removed, that
might help him identify the killer.

"We're all set," Lena called from the living room.

"Okay, thanks," Detective Taft replied. "I'll call you later."

He listened as the team carried the body into the hallway
and he made his way to the window that looked out onto

Bayberry Lane. Pulsating red lights filled the night sky. It was too cold for neighbors to be gathering to rubberneck, but he knew they were watching from their own windows. He'd seen it too many times over the years. They couldn't help themselves. Death had a way of making life more interesting.

CHAPTER NINE

Water. Distant. Waves, crashing onto the beach, loud and strong. Relentless. One after the other. Crash. Crash. Crash. Seagulls squawking. The wind pounding, but she can't feel it. Just the noise. The moan of wood giving way. The thump of a gust against an unsuspecting windowpane. Such violence. Anger.

The water has turned to ice. Smooth and clear. She's skating on it, listening to the steel blades cutting through the untouched surface, scratching as she turns, listening to the deafening silence of winter around her. The snow on the ground has muffled everything. No birds singing or people walking. No traffic or dogs or kids crying or the squeaking of rusted swings. It's just her, skating, circling, smooth and easy. The cloudless sky above her is blue, but there's no sun. The woods that surround the pond are caked in a thick white blanket. There's no ground to be seen. Only the rolling hills of white. So beautiful.

The wind is picking up, slamming against the wood and window, its urgency more apparent. It's trying to get in. To get to her.

There's something in the middle of the pond. It's hard to tell what it is from where she is, so she skates closer, trying to make out the small pile of shavings. She's close enough now to see that it's a hole in the center of the pond. Someone had dug it to go ice fishing, but no one else is around.

The waves are crashing against the shore more forcefully now, exploding when they hit the sand. They come, one after the other, punching the sand, climbing closer toward her.

She turns away from the hole, and as she does, she notices someone standing on the ice on the far end of the pond. She squints to try and see who it is, but the person's too far away.

"You thought you could run?"

His voice freezes her in place. She can see him clearer now, as if he's somehow gotten closer, but remains at the edge of the lake. It's Jake. He's smiling and holding his shotgun.

"You can't escape. I won't let you."

Jake fires a shot into the ice and she sees a large crack in the pristine surface. It approaches quickly and forms under her feet, then turns off in multiple directions, forming more cracks that grow from those. Something thumps and vibrates from below. She loses her balance for a moment, then regains herself and tries to skate back to the opposite end of the lake's edge where Malcolm is waiting, dressed in the same suit he wore at their wedding, his hands outstretched to try and reach her. Jake is laughing. His laughter echoes in the otherwise silent woods.

The seagulls are screaming now. Panicked. Crying. They sound desperate. They're in trouble.

The edge of the lake is so far. It seems the faster she skates, the further away Malcolm becomes. Jake's laughter pairs with the sound of the ice tearing and cracking. She has to get to land before the ice gives way.

The gusts are forcing their way inside. The tide is making its way toward her. The seagulls are crying for help. So much carnage. Her world is falling apart.

The ice cracks and becomes tiny cubes under her feet. She glances toward the safety of her husband and can see the hotel room they shared on their wedding night behind him. Even the rose petals he laid across the bed and the candles he lit while she was getting changed in the bathroom. It looks so romantic, but it's too late. She's under the freezing water before she can even take a second to hold her breath. It's so cold it shocks her body into paralysis. The weight of her skates and winter clothes pull her to the bottom. Her surroundings become darker and darker as the depths of the lake encroach on everything else. She's drowning. She'll be dead soon. There's no happy ending here.

Jake's voice. Somewhere on the surface.

"I'm here. I'm always here."

She tries to plead for help but the lake becomes a hurricane and the hurricane becomes a tornado. She's standing in the middle of a dirt road, watching a mammoth funnel cloud approaching. She knows she should run, but can't. She's too scared. She can see pieces of houses and cars and farm equipment and animals and people being sucked up into the funnel, and she waits for her turn.

"I'm here."

And then there's the warmth of the blackness again, soothing in its nothingness, calming in its void. She allows the blackness to engulf her and there's no more angry wind or relentless waves crashing. No more dying seagulls calling for help or icy water filling her lungs. No more Jake and his gun and his laughter. Just the caress of the blackness and all the serenity that comes with it.

And the voice, a different voice, somewhere out in the beyond.

"I'm here. You're safe."

DAY TWO

CHAPTER TEN

Snow flurries fell around the crime scene, contrasting the dark gray sky and almost black water. It was morning, but there was no sign of the sun that should've been at her back by now. The wind coming off the river was fierce, biting at her cheeks and nose. Everything in the parking lot was covered in a thin blanket of white making the task of finding evidence all the more challenging.

Detective Kelly Evans of the Westchester County Police Department stood on the banks of the Hudson, staring at the back end of a Kia SUV that stuck out of the water about fifty yards from the boat ramp she was next to. The current kept pushing at the car and in the quiet of the snowfall, she could hear the metal moaning as it tried to break free from the cluster of rocks it was caught up against. From where she stood, she could see the left front tire had been pinned between three boulders. The vehicle wasn't going anywhere, regardless of how hard the river wanted to dislodge it.

The lower half of George's Island was awash in police activity. The New York State Troopers had been stationed at the entrance to the park since that was their jurisdiction, but the park itself belonged to the county, so her team had gone in just after receiving the call from 911 dispatch. A dive team had been in the river for the last few hours looking for the driver and retrieving what they could from inside the SUV. She watched the small red flag bobbing on a Styrofoam float in the waves the wind kicked up.

She was alone where she stood, having just arrived on scene. It was her first case as the lead detective, the first time she'd come up on the rotation where a superior didn't have to shadow her. She'd heard the mumbling when the call came in. Some of the senior detectives didn't think she was ready to lead just yet and another argued that this kind of case, where foul play could be disguised as an accident, shouldn't be her first, but the chief refused to hear any of it and waved them all away. She was next up and the case was hers. Among the others now around her on scene, she was the superior, six months removed from uniform duty, just about five years with the department. She'd risen in the ranks quickly and that made some of the veteran officers a little uneasy, but she was a good cop and she knew it, and she knew they knew it. Having ambition wasn't a bad thing. Working to see that ambition through would only make the victory sweeter. Everyone else could fuck off if they didn't like it.

Kelly tucked the black hair peeking out of her knit hat behind her ears and took a step closer toward the water. Despite her ambition and confidence, there were definitely nerves. She could feel the butterflies fluttering in her stomach. She wondered if she should be doing more at that moment, jumping in and helping or directing action in some way. Instead, she kept spinning around in place, taking in the scene, trying to figure out what might've happened.

Sergeant Leeds, the uniformed supervisor on scene, and her old mentor when she'd come in as a rookie cop, broke away from a small group of officers who were huddled by the playground.

He made his way over and she watched him as he approached, his tall and meaty frame lumbering toward her with a kind of heavy grace large men often carried. Dirty-blond hair that turned white at the tips protruded from his ski cap, a matching dirty-blond-white mustache thick on his upper lip. His eyes were as dark as the sky and his face held the years on it for everyone to see. He'd been through a lot in his life, both professionally and personally. She didn't know any of the details, but one look at the man would tell you he had stories. Plenty of stories.

Leeds was one of the men in the department who didn't care about politics and didn't talk about who got what position within the chain of command. He'd been promoted to sergeant fifteen years earlier and that's exactly how high he'd wanted to climb the ladder. He was in his sweet spot and couldn't care less about who gave him the orders and who he gave the orders to. He'd been genuinely happy for her when she got promoted to detective. He was a rare breed and she considered him an ally.

"Morning, Detective," Leeds said as he sidled up next to her by the water's edge. "You ready for this?"

"Yeah, I think so."

"You know they wanted to skip over you and give this to Callahan?"

The butterflies churned her stomach again. "I heard something like that."

Leeds nodded, looking out at the water. "Good then. No surprises. You know where you stand. Time to throw you out of the nest. See how well you fly."

Kelly smiled. "I'm not going to hit the ground, don't worry."

"Have you been briefed?"

"I was just told that a couple of fishermen found the car half-submerged this morning and called it in. You guys matched the registration with the driver who called in to 911 last night."

"That's about the gist of it. We had a unit come down and

check things out after the fishermen called it in. Ran the plate
that he could see sticking out of the water. Car belongs to a
Tracy Cowan. Turns out last night at 5:17, a Tracy Cowan
called 911 to ask for help, but wouldn't give any other info. She
kept screaming and the dispatcher said she heard a lot of background noise, but the dispatcher never got her location and they
couldn't ping her cell phone properly. Call got cut off before
they could get any other information."

"So, this is no accident."

"Wouldn't appear so, hence the apprehension of giving this
to you as your first case." He pointed toward the SUV. "You can
see that the rear end is dented pretty severely. Dive team was
able to take pictures of the side that's underwater. Same kind of
damage. Dented from what looks like multiple impacts."

"Multiple impacts coincide with the chaos from the 911
call. Tells me this was intentional."

"Paint residue from the other car shows it was dark blue.
Maybe black, but we can get the forensics team to confirm as
long as we keep the rear end out of the water."

"Okay. We're looking for a dark blue, or maybe black, car
with a busted-up front end. Shouldn't be too hard. There's only
like, what, a million black and blue cars on the roads around
here?" Kelly turned and walked toward the boat ramp. She
gestured toward the red flag bobbing in the water. "Still no
body?"

"Not yet. We've alerted the police in the river towns south
of here as well as the NYPD. If the driver got dislodged from
her car, that current could sweep her right down to lower
Manhattan. Coast Guard is aware too. They're letting the
marine traffic on the river know to keep an eye out."

"What else have they been able to recover?"

Sergeant Leeds pointed to a small pile of items that sat on
the rocks near the riverbank. "We got Tracy Cowan's phone,
pocketbook, and keys that were still in the ignition. Her wallet

was in her pocketbook full of credit cards and some cash. Doesn't look like a robbery."

"Maybe started out that way and things went sideways? Or a road rage incident?"

"Sure. Could be."

Kelly stood over the items that were already in evidence bags. Aside from the things Leeds had just told her about, she could see a book, a handful of magazines, a bag full of clothes, and a box of tissues.

"We got any cameras in the park?" she asked.

"Not down here," Leeds replied. "They only have a camera at the ticket booth up by the entrance. We're pulling the feed now to see if we can catch anything."

"We do door-to-doors yet?"

"Just the houses that hug the woods here. No one saw anything and most of the people that live in those houses weren't home from work yet. One lady heard a car horn blaring, but nothing more than that. She looked out her window to see where the noise was coming from, but she can't see all the way down here. Her view is obstructed by trees."

Kelly walked back to the center of the parking lot with Sergeant Leeds in tow. She looked around again, trying to take it all in. The boat ramp was in the middle of nowhere. Woods on two sides, the river and a playground on the others. No cameras. No one to come help. Tracy Cowan really would've been alone out there, and now she was gone. But why was she down there in the first place?

"I want the park closed until we can get this snow to melt and see if we're missing anything. It's off-season so it shouldn't be a big deal. And I want a unit down here twenty-four-seven. No one disturbs the scene until the snow melts. Temps are rising in the next few days and the sun is supposed to be out. I want to make sure we're seeing everything there is to see."

"Roger that."

"Do we have an address for Tracy Cowan?"

"We do. She lives in Putnam Valley."

"Okay." Kelly took a deep breath to settle herself. The flurries blew against her face and she turned away from them. "Let's see what else the dive team comes up with and then we'll go make a visit. You're coming with me."

Sergeant Leeds nodded. "You got it."

She leaned in. "How am I doing so far?"

Leeds chuckled. "You're doing great."

"Better than Callahan?"

"You're a natural."

CHAPTER ELEVEN

The Cowan house was a good size. Although it was only built two decades earlier, years of neglect had begun to age it prematurely. The asphalt shingles on the roof were peeling up in some spots and the edge facing the yard and woods in the back had pocks of algae growing on it. The decorative pillars on either side of the stairs that led to the front door had undoubtedly looked stately back in the day, but now appeared fragile, the white paint chipped, the seams on both the top and bottom foundation pieces cracking away. Inside, the foyer had ceramic tile that led to a beige carpet in the formal living room and scratched oak floors in the dining and family rooms. The kitchen, where Kelly sat at an island facing Malcolm Cowan, who leaned against the stove, still had the dark wood cabinets of yesteryear and that same dated tile that welcomed her in the foyer. But the place was large and open and would've been a jewel when it was first built. Now, it looked outmatched by some of the upgrades she'd seen from the neighbors on her way into the complex. She wondered if a guy like Malcolm, being in construction, noticed or even cared. Like the shoemaker with no shoes.

She and Leeds had made their way over after the dive team surfaced without recovering any additional evidence. Malcolm had thrown the door open and ushered them inside before they even got a chance to knock. He looked disheveled, his face white, his eyes red. Without a word, he marched them down a hallway adorned with framed photos of a happy and vibrant family, which was in such contrast to the current mood. They walked into the kitchen and she sat at the island while Leeds leaned against the doorway that connected the kitchen and the family room. Malcolm took his position at the stove, folded his arms across his chest, and braced himself for the news.

"I called the police last night when Tracy didn't show up," he said, his voice cracking just a bit. He kept tugging at the fabric under his armpits. "I knew something was wrong. I *knew* it. She told me someone was following her and I brushed it off. Told her she was imagining things. But she was adamant about it, so I said to drive to the trooper barracks by the Buchanan train station. After an hour went by, I started calling her and she wasn't picking up. Another hour passed and I called her sister, thinking maybe she went there. Nothing. So, I called the police. They didn't do anything. Told me to wait by my phone. What kind of advice is that? I knew she was in trouble."

"We know you called," Kelly replied. "I got a transcript of your conversation with the 911 operator from their center. It was cross-referenced with the call your wife made through the name match, but Tracy hadn't been able to tell the dispatcher where she was."

"Couldn't you have, like, pinged her phone or something?"

"Hard to do in real time. The 911 operator who took her call tried to get a read on the cell signal. Unfortunately, there weren't any towers in the area to ping a good signal from. I'm sorry."

"You're sorry. That's good to know. But where's my wife?"

"We're working on it."

Malcolm looked at her, his eyes burning a hole through her, then going soft. "That's not good enough. Find her."

Kelly took out her notepad and placed it on the counter. "We have all of the departments that have jurisdictions along the river keeping an eye out. And our dive team is going to study the currents from last night to see how strong they were and in which exact direction they were going. They'll get back out there as soon as they redirect their search perimeter."

"Are you saying her body is out there somewhere floating around? You're saying she's dead?"

"I'm saying we're covering all of our bases."

Malcolm threw up his hands, his tone growing agitated. "Are you even going to try and look for her? She could still be alive."

"I know that. And we're not jumping to any conclusions. We're just trying to gather all the facts at this point."

Malcolm barked a cry, then wiped his eyes with the back of his hand. "Yeah, okay. Gather your facts then. Ask your questions."

Kelly exhaled slowly and opened her notepad. The mood in the kitchen was very unstable. One false move could send the man over the edge.

"Where were you last night between the hours of 5 p.m. and midnight?"

"I was on a job site in Hastings until about four o'clock. I own a construction company. After that, I came home and I've been here ever since."

"You never left the house last night."

"No. After I got home, I stayed in."

Kelly made some notes. "You mentioned you thought Tracy might've gone to her sister's house. What's her name, and where does she live?"

"Her sister is Missy Rollins. She lives in Dutchess. I can get you the address."

"And why do you think she'd go all the way up there instead of coming home last night?"

Malcolm hesitated and looked back and forth between the detective and the sergeant, a thin smile creeping upon his face.

"It's funny," he snickered. "I watch all the shows like *Dateline* and 20/20 and *True Crime* and all that stuff, and I always wonder how husbands and wives get themselves mixed up as prime suspects. I always wonder why they just don't tell all the truth at the start so they can be cleared. Now I get it. I understand how someone could fall into becoming a prime suspect. I'm going to tell you the truth and then I'm going to become yours."

Leeds pushed himself off the doorway. "What do you want to tell us?"

Malcolm sighed and shook his head, his gaze falling onto the floor. "Tracy told me she was leaving me yesterday morning. Stood right where you're sitting, Detective Evans. And I stood right where I am now. She told me she'd changed and after a lot of reflection, or whatever, she was leaving me. Getting a divorce. Throwing away an eight-year marriage just like that. Then she walked out the door. She had her sister pick my son up from school so Missy could stay with him, and Tracy was planning to come home and talk to me to better explain the goddamned bomb she'd dropped on our lives. When she didn't show up here, I thought maybe she decided to go straight up to Dutchess. Thought maybe she lost her nerve. And that's the truth. My wife went missing on the day she told me she was leaving me. I assume that makes me your prime suspect, right?"

Leeds nodded. "Right."

"Let's keep going," Kelly said. She didn't want to lose the momentum of the conversation. "You said Tracy called you and told you someone was following her."

"Yeah. She thought I had someone tailing her to keep tabs on her, but I didn't. I don't have the kind of manpower to take someone off the site so they can play PI all day. I tried to convince her it wasn't me and told her to drive to the trooper barracks. She said was going to do that, but then she said the car wasn't behind her anymore so she was going to take Post Road through Croton and Buchanan and get back on Route 9 at Welcher Avenue in Peekskill. That's the last I heard from her." He pushed himself off the counter and began pacing. "I told the 911 lady all that. She should've put cops out in those towns to look for her. And if she called 911 herself, they should've known where to look."

"Your call came in over an hour after hers," Kelly explained. "When they were cross-referenced, units were dispatched. That's protocol."

Malcolm was silent. Still pacing.

"Did your wife describe the vehicle she thought was following her?"

"No."

"Think for a second. Take your time. Did she say anything that might help us identify who was following her?"

Malcom was silent. He stopped pacing and closed his eyes tight. "Wait, she did say something." He opened his eyes back up and looked at her. "She said the car that was following her stuck out like a sore thumb, but she didn't say anything more specific."

"Do you know where she was coming from? Or where she was all day while you were at the job site?"

"She was coming home from her therapist's office. Dr. Devi. I don't know his first name. He has an office on the Upper East Side. I can get you an address."

"That would be great." More notes. "How long has she been seeing Dr. Devi?"

"A little over a year, I think."

"Do you know what prompted her to seek therapy?"

Malcolm nodded and began fidgeting, interlocking his

fingers and then unlocking them and then repeating the action. "She was a cancer survivor and it got pretty scary for a minute. She was having trouble coping with almost dying so she decided to talk to someone about it."

Kelly finished writing in her notepad, then got up from the stool and folded it closed. "We're going to need access to Tracy's cell phone records. Yours too. For all we know, she's still using the account and has a new phone."

"What're you saying? Why would she be doing that?"

"We need to come at this from all angles. It's true, something bad might've actually happened to your wife, but this could also be some elaborate way of trying to *convince* you something bad happened when, in reality, she could've just run away."

"Tracy wouldn't do that," Malcolm replied instantly. "She wouldn't leave my son. Something bad did happen, and I need you to look into me and clear me as quickly as possible so you can focus on whoever it was who did whatever they did. I need you to find my wife. You can have all the cell records you need. Anything you want. I've got nothing to hide. Just find her."

"I appreciate that." Kelly paused for a moment, then decided to push. She was curious to see his reaction. "Would you like to hand over your phone now?"

Malcolm stopped fidgeting with his hands and shook his head. "I would, but I need it for my work. I got sub-contractors calling me all day long. I have to make other arrangements if you're going to take my phone."

Push a little more. "I can stay and go through it. This way if you get a call, you'll be here. You can have it back when I'm done."

"I'd rather not."

"Okay." Kelly placed her notepad in her bag. "We'll get a warrant for both phones. Do it by the book. In the meantime, we're going to need you to come with us to the station so we can take a DNA swab, fingerprints, and a gun residue swipe to check all that off the protocol list."

"By the book."

"Exactly."

"Because I'm the prime suspect."

"Nobody's anything yet. This is just the beginning of our investigation. But if you want me to clear you as soon as possible, this is a good first step."

The three of them made their way down the hall, Leeds in front, Kelly and Malcolm falling in behind.

"In your experience, do things like this usually turn out for the worse?" Malcolm asked. His eyes glassed over with tears again. "Are you going to find my wife?"

Kelly looked straight ahead, focused on the front door. "In my experience, I find it better to stay hopeful. Facts will lead us to where we need to go. Keep the faith and let us do what we have to do."

"But you are going to find her alive... right?"

Kelly didn't reply.

CHAPTER TWELVE

Malcolm shut the front door and fell against it. He glanced out the side window and watched until the detective and the sergeant pulled away. When they were gone, he made his way into the family room and dialed Tracy's phone.

"Hi, you've reached Tracy's cell. I—"

He disconnected and looked up at the ceiling. They'd had him at the station for three hours. He was exhausted, his mind a jumbled mess. They'd taken his DNA and wiped his hands for gun residue and taken his picture and fingerprints and asked him the same questions in a thousand different ways, obviously trying to trip him up. After the second hour, it was hard to remember what his last set of answers were, but he guessed they'd been good enough to pass as the truth, because he only knew what he knew, despite them trying to catch him in a lie. They finally let him go and drove him home without another word.

The house was quiet. He didn't like that. It was unnerving, unsettling. He needed action, something to take his mind off things. This wasn't how anything was supposed to go. He wasn't going to let her leave. She wasn't supposed to have asked. He dialed the number he'd texted the night before.

"Hey."

"You took care of everything?"

"Just like you said."

"Good." He walked into the kitchen. The detective's perfume was still lingering in the air. "I need one more thing."

"What's that?"

"A lawyer. A good one. Tracy's missing and I'm the prime suspect. I know how these things work. I want someone on my side that can rattle a few cages if necessary."

"Not a problem. I know the right guy."

"Good. Get it done."

Malcom disconnected the call and hopped up on the same stool the detective had been sitting in earlier. He pulled up his text messages and scrolled to his exchange with Tracy the day before.

WHERE ARE YOU?

CALL ME

PICK UP YOUR PHONE!

YOU CAN'T IGNORE ME!

I'M GOING TO FIND YOU

PLEASE DON'T DO THIS TO US

I LOVE YOU

PICK UP THE PHONE!!!!!!!!!

YOU BETTER ANSWER YOUR PHONE NOW!

WHERE ARE YOU??????

WHERE IS MY SON!!!!!

CALL ME BACK!!!!!!

One by one, he began deleting the messages. It was better this way. Cleaner.

The less the police knew, the safer he was. At least for now.

CHAPTER THIRTEEN

It was a chilly night considering it was mid-August. Tracy and Jake had spent the late afternoon hiking up Anthony's Nose and sat in the perfect spot to watch the sun set over the mountains of the Hudson River. Jake was so good at romance. He understood the nuances of it, how something as simple as a rose on her windshield while she was at work could carry such meaning, or an unexpected card for no reason could make the very thought of the gesture the reason itself. He knew he didn't need to be over the top to profess his love and she understood how the little things often added up to something bigger than the big thing. They were a perfect match in that regard, and as they watched the sun set and the sky turn from blue to gold to black, she realized that night was one more of those little things that meant the world.

"You want to get back to the car?" she asked, rubbing her bare arms up and down. "I'm getting cold and we didn't bring a jacket or blanket or anything."

She turned and looked at Jake who was peering out over the river, his eyes glassing from the wind, his Adam's apple bobbing.

"Hello? Earth to Jake," she teased. "Can we go now? I'm cold."

THE WOMAN AT NUMBER 6   73

Jake finally turned and locked eyes with her. He didn't say anything, but there was something strange about him. He looked stern. Every muscle in his face was taut. His lips were curled in, his brow furrowed just a bit.

"What's wrong?" she asked.

Jake took a deep breath, but his expression remained. "Nothing, sorry," he replied, almost robotically. "We can go. I'm cold too."

Jake climbed to his feet and offered a hand. Tracy took it and he helped lift her up from her sitting position. As soon as she was standing, he fell to the ground.

"Before we go, I want to give you this."

Tracy looked down at Jake and time slowed. It took her a moment to understand that he hadn't fallen, but was actually down on one knee. He was holding something out in front of him. A ring. Her ring. Their ring.

"Tracy Rollins, will you marry me?"

Time sped back up again as Tracy reached for the ring, gently touching the diamond that sat atop a gold band. It was simple in its craftsmanship and exquisite in its simplicity. It was perfect.

Tears flooded Tracy's eyes. "Yes!"

Jake laughed as he stood, the pressure of the situation melting away, his face returning to normal again. As he slipped the ring on her finger, he whispered in her ear, his voice echoing in a chasm of nothingness as her world faded around her.

"You're mine forever now. And I'm yours. We'll always be together no matter what."

Blackness. The void. But she could sense something. A hand protruding from the darkness, reaching out to her. She didn't know how she knew it, but she could see it in her mind's eye, could feel its presence. She grabbed at it and it was there. She could feel its touch as she wrapped her fingers around it. Waves crashing. Louder now. And more sounds. Breathing. A digital beeping. A floorboard creaking over and over. But still the blackness. It was always there. It—

"Tracy. Can you hear me?"

She opened her mouth and this time she knew the words would come.

"Yes."

"Good."

Her voice echoed as if she were in a tunnel. It sounded different from what she was used to hearing. And the voice that spoke back to her... It was familiar. Soothing. She was calm when she heard it.

"I... can't see anything," she mumbled. Her words poured out of her mouth with no cadence. They seemed to come all at once. "All I see is darkness."

"You have bandages over your eyes," the soothing voice explained. "You were hit in the head repeatedly and there was some damage to your face. You'll be okay, but for now you need to keep your eyes covered. It's for the best."

She nodded, only half understanding what she was being told, but somehow she knew the voice was telling her the truth.

"What happened to me?" She tried to move, but her legs and arms refused to budge. She could feel a dull pain on one side of her body, but didn't know her left from right in that moment.

"I came just in time. If I hadn't come when I did, I don't know what would've happened. I suppose he would've killed you."

The dull pain began to run up her side and into her neck, spreading to her chin and jaw. She was aware of the pain, but somehow detached from it.

"He was beating you. I yelled and I guess I scared him

because I started running toward you. I wasn't even thinking. I was just running, trying to save you. That's all I wanted to do. I needed to get to you and make him stop."

Tracy's mind swirled. She had questions she wanted to ask, but her brain and her mouth were not working in conjunction with each other. Scenes from what the voice spoke of flashed through her memory, but all of it was distilled and blurry. She couldn't see any definitive detail. Everything was out of focus.

"When he saw me coming, he ran into the woods and I was able to get you out of there. I put you in my car and drove you here where you're safe. He doesn't know this place. No one can get you here."

She focused on her hands, trying to block out the pain that was becoming more prominent, inching its way up through her skull and behind her eyes, which remained shut. Just a finger. If she could move a finger then she'd know she could move another, and if she could move another she could move her hand. Then her wrist and arm. And then she'd know she wasn't paralyzed. But first, just a finger to start.

"I made sure no one followed us. I wanted to get your phone and your purse, but your car was already in the water and the current was taking it away. I figured your safety was more important than a phone you could replace or some money you might've had."

Her pinky moved. She wanted to smile, but the pain was clawing its way to the forefront, pushing out the blurred images of her memory and stealing any joy she might've been feeling. She was hardly listening to the voice anymore. The pain and her determination to move a finger had garnered all of her concentration.

"I had a doctor come in and check on you while you were asleep. He's a friend of mine and understood the sensitivity to the situation. He had some sleeping pills and some hydrocodone left over from an old basketball injury, so he gave you that to help with the pain and the stress of what you went through. The doctor won't tell anyone you're here. He's the one who bandaged your head and cleaned the cuts on your arms and shoulders. He said you probably have a massive concussion, but he doesn't think there's anything more dangerous than that, or that you need to go to the hospital. He'll be back in a few days to check on you. For now, he just wants you to rest."

The pain was intense now, covering her head, neck, and shoulders, shooting down both arms. She moaned as she struggled to get her index finger to twitch.

"You need to relax," the voice said, closer now. She could feel his breath on her face. "Shhhhh."

"It hurts," Tracy mumbled, her mouth full of marbles.

"I know."

"Make it stop."

"Okay."

Movement. The floorboard creaked again and she could hear footsteps cross the room and return. A picture of a man in a hood popped into her mind, standing in front of bright lights.

"The man," she said. "The man at the park."

"He's gone," the voice replied. "He's not coming back. And no one knows you're here. I promise you, you're safe."

A hand gently took her chin and a finger poked into the side of her cheek. She was helpless to pull away or react, and it was over before she could try and figure out how to make her body recoil. The bitter taste of the pill filled the inside of her mouth as it dissolved and slid down her throat when she swallowed.

"That should help with the pain," the voice explained. "Just give it a few minutes and you'll start to feel better."

Tracy took a deep breath and focused on the words.

"Who was the man?" she asked. A fog was growing thick around her.

"You don't have to worry about that."

"Tell me."

"I need you to rest."

It hurt to talk. "Please. Tell me."

"It was your husband," the voice said. "It was Malcolm. He was there at the river. He was trying to kill you."

CHAPTER FOURTEEN

As soon as she saw the door pull away from its frame, Missy burst through carrying Finn who was half-asleep from the car ride. She glared at Malcolm as she passed him and walked into the family room where she laid the boy on the couch and stomped back into the hall to face her brother-in-law.

"Where is she, you son-of-a-bitch?" she spat through clenched teeth. She wanted so desperately to scream and punch him in his smug face, but she didn't want to scare Finn. The boy was already going through enough. "Where's Tracy?"

Malcolm, looking pale and disheveled, put his hands up in surrender. "I don't know."

"Bullshit! She asks for a divorce and then goes missing? I know you did something to her. I know! And to think I defended you and told her to reconsider. But maybe she was right. Maybe she was right to want to get away from you."

"I swear, I have no idea what happened. I thought she went to your place. I called the police to let them know she never came home, and they didn't seem too concerned. Next thing I know, they're at my house telling me they found her car in the

Hudson at George's Island and there's a goddamned dive team searching for her body."

"What was she doing at George's Island?"

"I don't know," Malcolm scoffed. "It's where we had our wedding reception. Maybe she was passing it and decided to pull in and reminisce."

Missy looked him up and down. She was scared not knowing where her sister was, but at the same time, she was terrified about the plans that had already been laid. She needed Tracy there to help steer things. She'd be lost without her.

"You know I'll go to the ends of the earth for my little sister," Missy seethed. "After what she's been through, I'm the only one left to look out for her. You better be telling me the truth."

"I am!"

She couldn't deny that Malcolm sounded sincere, but everything was so up in the air at the moment. He told her about the car that was following Tracy and how she thought he'd been the one to send it.

"Okay then, if it wasn't you, who was following her?"

"I don't know. She thought it was a false alarm last time I talked to her. She turned off the Buchanan exit and the car didn't follow."

Missy shuffled into the formal living room. She glanced at the framed pictures on the wall, all scenes of happier times in the Cowan house. Finn's first birthday party. The day Malcolm bought the construction company. All three of them laughing and smiling as they rode in the back of Malcolm's new dump truck. Such great memories. Now everything was different. Darker. Chaotic. She used to look at the worn carpet and think about all the nights they'd sit together and watch movies. She saw the small hole in the wall at the base by the patio doors and could remember the New Year's Eve Malcolm had fallen down drunk and put a boot through the drywall. Those had been good times. Now the rug looked old and menacing, the hole gaping and unsightly.

"She told you yesterday morning that she wanted a divorce, and on that same day she goes missing and her car ends up in the river? That sounds fishy."

"No shit," Malcolm replied. He followed her into the room. "You don't think I realize how that makes me look? The police already had me down at the station answering questions and taking prints and DNA."

"Where were you last night?"

"Here. Waiting for Tracy to come home so we could talk. The police can ping my phone if they want. They'll see I was here."

"You could've been somewhere else while your phone was still here. I've seen the same shows you have. I'm the one who got you guys into true crime."

Malcolm leaned on the back of the couch. He looked exhausted. "Do you really think I'm capable of doing anything bad to Tracy?" he asked, his voice softening. "I love her. All I've ever done since we met is try and give her the world. I'm scared that something happened to her and I need to find her."

Missy sat down on the loveseat opposite Malcolm. "You say you love her, but she wouldn't be leaving you if there wasn't a reason."

Malcolm walked around the couch and plopped down. "Yeah, well if you know the reason, I'm all ears because she caught me completely off guard yesterday morning. Tells me she's leaving me out of the blue. Asks for a divorce. No opportunity for us to talk anything out. No chance to work on whatever was making her feel like she was. Just walks into the kitchen, drops the bomb, and walks out. I can't imagine my life without her and I would never hurt her on purpose, so if you know why she's leaving me, please tell me."

Missy studied her brother-in-law, asking herself over and over if he was capable of harming her little sister. She didn't see it as blatantly as you'd see it on some, but that didn't mean it wasn't there.

"I told her leaving you was a mistake," she said quietly. "I thought it was out of the blue too, and with Finn involved, I thought the least she could do was couples' counseling or something like that."

"But why was she leaving me?"

"I don't know."

"That's a lie. She tells you everything."

Missy shrugged. "I'm serious. She wouldn't tell me. But her mind was made up. She was leaving and no one was going to stop her. She was planning to head north to Vermont or Maine or something. As far as she was concerned, she'd already left."

Malcolm thought for a moment. "So maybe the cops were right. Maybe that's where she went. She just left and went north."

"She wouldn't leave Finn."

"Maybe she thought the boy should be raised by his father."

"So, she dumps her car in the river?"

"To throw us off."

"You're grasping, Malcolm. Something happened to her."

"Okay. What, then?"

"You tell me."

Malcolm leapt off the couch. "I swear to God, I didn't have anything to do with this!" he cried. "One second my life is normal and the next, my wife is leaving me, and the second after that, my wife is *missing* and everyone's going to think I did it. I don't know what happened!"

His voice exploded in the room. Missy recoiled, frightened by the sudden outburst.

"Daddy, what's wrong?"

Finn stood in the hallway looking in at them. His eyes were

half-shut and his hair was askew, some of it sweat-plastered to his face.

Malcolm quickly walked over and bent down to face his son, the anger and stress vanishing instantly. "Nothing, buddy. Everything's fine. I'm sorry I woke you."

"Is Mommy here?"

"Not yet. Soon."

He pulled his boy into an embrace and Missy watched the two of them in silence. As quickly as Malcolm's rage came, it was gone, replaced by a gentler, kinder person. Was that the act of a good father or a psychopath?

"We're going to find her," Missy said. She wasn't sure if she was talking to Malcolm or Finn or simply trying to reassure herself. "We're going to find her and she'll be okay and this will all just be a misunderstanding or something. You'll see." Tears came unexpectedly, rushing over her.

"Aunt Missy's right," she heard Malcolm say. "Mommy will be home soon and she'll have a crazy story to tell us."

"Okay, Daddy."

Missy got up from the couch. "And until she does, I'm staying."

Malcolm looked at her. "What?"

"You need help with Finn and the house and we need to work together to coordinate with the police and figure all this out. I'll stay and help and we'll work together. I'm staying."

"You don't need to do that."

"I do." She made her way over to Malcolm and Finn and stood over them both. "You know how I am when it comes to Tracy. She needs me and I'm not going anywhere until we find her." She leaned in closer, next to Malcolm's ear, lowering her voice so Finn couldn't hear. "And if it turns out you did have anything to do with this, I'll nail you to the wall and make you bleed. Slow and painful. Got it?"

Malcolm nodded, his eyes tearing. There was nothing else to say. He got it. Every word.

She was staying. For Finn. For Tracy. And for the plan.

DAY THREE

CHAPTER FIFTEEN

It was a new day, and at that point, a little over twenty-four hours since her team had found Tracy Cowan's SUV submerged in the Hudson River. The dive team had concluded their analysis of the currents and had been back in the water numerous times, and in numerous points along the shoreline, but there was still no sign of Tracy herself. It wasn't clear if this was a missing person's case or a homicide investigation, so Kelly treated it as both. She'd received two calls from the captain since she'd processed Malcolm Cowan, inquiring about her progress. Both times she went over where she was with everything and he seemed satisfied, but it was obvious he had a bench of more experienced men waiting to be called in to assist. He never reached out for updates so early in an investigation with any of the other guys. Just her. He was sending a message that was crystal clear. Find the woman. Figure out what happened. Now.

Kelly had gotten up early and made her way onto Manhattan before the bulk of the morning rush. Traffic was inevitable since she was, after all, heading into the city that never slept, but the starts and stops were sparse and she was able to make it to Dr. Devi's office with little fanfare. She'd left Leeds back in Westchester to manage the investigation locally and to oversee anything new that cropped up outside of her case. There was no need for him to accompany her into the city, and she knew the chief didn't like stretching the over-time budget, so she let him rotate back onto his normal shift and would reconnect with him later on should anything come up.

She sat across from Dr. Devi in one of two wingback chairs that faced each other, adjacent to his desk, near a window that looked out onto the street below. The psychiatrist looked to be in his late forties. Handsome. Kind with somewhat alluring eyes. She imagined his patients found it easy unloading their problems onto him. He had the kind of face that exuded kind-ness and placidity. His expressions and mannerisms seemed to invite disclosure.

"I'll keep this brief," Kelly began as she placed her notepad onto her lap. "I know you have a schedule to keep." She was still getting used to the idea of interviewing people, and it all seemed somewhat unnatural. She didn't have the smooth delivery or the authoritative yet caring cadence the other senior detectives had. They told her it would come with time and experience. Right then, it felt forced.

Dr. Devi smiled and waved a hand. "When you phoned yesterday and told me you were coming, I made arrangements. We have all the time you need. There's no pressure to rush. I want to help in any way I can. Tracy is a lovely woman."

"Can you tell me how long Tracy's been a patient?"

"Thirteen months."

"And what was the reason she initially came to see you?"

Dr. Devi paused. "You understand I can't divulge specifics about my patients. I must respect the privacy of our sessions. That being said, I know it's important for you to learn what you can in order to find her, so I'll do my best. Tracy first came to see me after she survived a medical episode. She was dealing with emotions around death and legacy."

"Her cancer."

"If you say so."

"Mr. Cowan told me when we spoke."

Dr. Devi said nothing.

"During her time with you, did she talk about her marriage?"

"Yes."

"Did she say if it was happy or not?"

Again, Dr. Devi smiled.

Kelly nodded. "Okay, let me rephrase. In speaking with Mr. Cowan, he told me that the morning Tracy went missing, she'd told him she was leaving him and wanted a divorce. Did you know that was going to happen?"

"Generally speaking, I knew," Dr. Devi replied. "But I didn't know she was planning on having that conversation with her husband on that particular day. She told me after the fact when she came in for her appointment."

"Were you surprised?"

"Not particularly. As I said, I knew it was going to happen at some point."

Kelly thought for a moment, creating her questions in her head before asking them, trying to find the right rhythm. There was something off that she couldn't place. The doctor seemed eager to help, but he was lacking concern for Tracy's well-being, or so it seemed. He was cold but friendly at the same time. It was strange.

"Based on the progression of her sessions with you over the course of thirteen months, were you surprised she wanted to leave her husband?"

"No. Often during ongoing therapy sessions, the patient realizes that what they thought they needed treatment for was just a symptom of the problem or an excuse to get themselves in front of someone like me. As they work through it, they start to buy into the healing and I help them understand what the root cause of their issue is. The more they learn, the more I help them unearth the true cause of their pain."

"And in Tracy's case, it was her marriage."

"Not her marriage specifically. It was about her relationships."

Kelly scribbled in her notepad.

"Did she tell you anything about Malcolm being violent? Did she ever tell you he hit her or scared her or intimidated her? Did you get the impression that Tracy's husband was a bad guy? Someone to be feared?"

Dr. Devi shook his head. "Our sessions and her marriage had nothing to do with violence. Without saying too much, it was about the need for rebirth. There were things that happened in her past that triggered her in certain ways. Made her seek safety over love. She'd come to see that in our sessions and understood that she could no longer put herself in those situations. Her marriage was one thing when she thought it was something else, so after some time, she decided that she wanted to start over."

Kelly put her pen down and sat back in her seat, staring at the doctor who appeared so calm and kind on the outside, yet perhaps *too* calm and *too* kind. He had every answer for her without pause. He was ready to alleviate any concern that she had and there wasn't a single speck of nervousness or uneasiness about speaking with a police detective. She studied his hands and found them still. She glanced at his lips and they remained stretched in a kind of half-smile to disarm her. There was no slight tremble or bouncing of the knee or tapping of his foot. Completely in control and detached. His years practicing had taught him how to hide certain mannerisms. He'd become a master at it. She decided to push a bit more.

"You realize you were the last person to see her the night she went missing."

"That's correct."

"Are you nervous about that?"

Dr. Devi laughed quietly. "I guess me being a suspect makes sense. That's fine. I understand. But I had nothing to do with it. You'll realize that soon enough."

Kelly picked her pen back up and made a few notes in her pad. Dr. Devi remained poised and in control. She couldn't shake him. Perhaps he had no reason to be shaken.

"Other than the fact that she was going home to talk about ending her marriage with her husband, did anything seem off?"

"No," Dr. Devi replied. He crossed his legs and leaned back on his chair at an angle, almost staring at her from the side. "Going home to talk about ending her marriage was bad enough. There was no need for anything further to be off."

"Was Tracy happy the day she saw you? Was she relieved that she finally said something to Malcolm? Was she nervous about what he might do?"

"She was nervous, but not in the malicious sense that you're suggesting. That morning had been a culmination of years of suppressed emotion, and thirteen months of us digging up that admission from the place where she kept it buried. Her nervousness came from the fact that she was facing her demon, acknowledging that she was doing something about it, and facing whatever might lie ahead."

"Facing Malcom."

"Yes."

Kelly dropped her hands onto her lap. "Let's get this out in the open," she said, not sure if her change in tactic would work. "Tracy Cowan is either missing or dead. If she didn't run away herself, then there's no *suggestion* of malice. Malice happened. I'm trying to find out what went down."

Dr. Devi looked at her, his kind eyes almost bending at the

edges as he rubbed his brow. His hand trembled ever so slightly. There it was.

"Look, I like Tracy very much," he said, his voice tightening just a bit. "She was kind and brave and always willing to put my suggestions into practice. She refused any kind of narcotic treatment, always wanting to try to really delve into her issues head-on. I admired that. She was a fighter and it took a strong will to get through to the root of her issue. I was proud that she was able to do that, but we must look at logic here. The day she asked her husband for a divorce, she goes missing. You find her car abandoned in the river. One must assume the husband is involved in some way."

Kelly folded her notepad closed and leaned forward in her seat. "That's the thing about being a detective," she said. "We're not allowed to assume. We have to present facts to get a conviction. That's the game."

"I understand."

She got up and stood over him, staring intently. "Did Tracy tell you she was going to George's Island on the way home that night?"

"No. I don't even know what George's Island is."

"She had her wedding reception there."

A shrug. "She just said she was going home to talk with Malcolm."

"And she never made it. She never had a chance to talk to her husband. Or to officially end things. Or to leave him."

"No," the doctor replied, his voice even. "She never had the chance to follow it all the way through. Seems like Malcolm is the beneficiary of that conclusion."

A tiny smile emerged at the edges of her mouth. "Thank you, doctor. I'm sure I'll see you again."

She left the office, trying to ascertain if Dr. Devi was a real suspect or just on her list because he was the last person to see Tracy the night she disappeared. She could tell she'd shaken him a bit at the end and couldn't help but notice how he steered his suppositions toward Malcolm, which was something he'd been so careful not to do at the beginning of their conversation. Maybe he was a real suspect.

Maybe.

CHAPTER SIXTEEN

Detective Taft sat in front of the Triaglia and Brown law firm and stared at himself in the rearview mirror. The same old man stared back. Same face. Gray. Wrinkled. Baggy cheeks and extra skin under the neck that hadn't been there in his younger days. His hair was thinning, and his day-old stubble seemed whiter than the day before. Was that even possible? He thought about his time when he was fresh out of the academy, as he often did as his days to retirement wound down. He'd had such vigor then. He was so amped to bring justice to the world and put the bad guys away. Over time, that enthusiasm became a thick layer of callous that built up with every murder and rape and beating and shooting and whatever else those scumbags came up with until the enthusiasm waned and the job became something automatic. It didn't take long before the callous ate away at love and relationships and family, until all that was left was the cases he got assigned. Whenever he thought about retirement, he thought about how much he'd miss being useful. A part of him didn't want to walk away from the chaos, but not because he thought he was doing good. It was because he didn't want to be an irrelevant civilian. He liked being a cop even though it dragged on him year after year. He liked that he mattered to the people he tried to protect. He never thought he'd end up alone though.

Taft opened the locket he was holding and stared at the tiny picture of his wife. He missed her so much. He couldn't believe she was gone. And his baby too. Life had a way of throwing devastating curveballs.

He folded the locket closed and stuffed it in his pocket as he climbed out of the car and made his way into the law firm, stopping just inside the entrance to take a look at his surroundings, a bell echoing in the otherwise quiet space. It appeared to be a small operation. The office was on the bottom floor of an apartment complex, next to a bank and an accountant on West Broad Street in Stamford. There was a young receptionist who greeted him when he walked in, and when he was taken in the back and placed in a conference room, he noticed only two other desks where he assumed the paralegals worked, and two offices on the far end of the space. Other than that, there was a wall of filing cabinets and a single bookshelf filled with black binders. The furniture seemed old. The aesthetics of the firm looked worn down.

John Triaglia was short and round, balding and fragile. His eyes were dark, and the thin wisps of hair on his otherwise bald head seemed to sway in a breeze he couldn't feel. Detective Taft rose from his seat when the old man walked in and they shook, Taft's hand swallowing the lawyer's.

"I appreciate you seeing me," Detective Taft began.

John shook his head and looked down at the table he sat at. "I can't believe what happened. We had a bad feeling when Kat didn't show for work without calling. Naturally, that feeling got much worse when no one could reach her. Such a tragedy. There's just no safe place anymore."

Taft took his phone out of his pocket, placed it in front of him, and hit the record button. "Kat was a corporate attorney, right?"

John nodded. "That's right. Our firm specializes in real estate. She was one of our best closing attorneys and a dynamite corporate lawyer. She had very good relationships with a few area banks we do closings for, and between her networking, and us being around since the dinosaurs, we had a nice little business going. She was loyal, smart, always up on any changing laws or regulations, and she was poised to become a partner once I retired, which is going to be sooner rather than later. She'll be missed, I can tell you that."

"Do you know if she was seeing anyone? A boyfriend or a new fling she might've mentioned?"

"No. I don't know of anyone."

"Any idea if she was close with a client?"

John laughed. "She was close with all of our clients. They loved Kat. Loved working with her and our referral business has grown tenfold since she came on board. She knew her stuff and got deals to the closing table in a hurry. Once you do a few deals with some of these real estate investors, they become like family."

Detective Taft shifted in his seat. "I'm going to need to see a list of the clients she's worked with since coming on board. I'll get you a warrant so you don't have to justify handing over the list to any client should they find out."

"Sure, no problem."

"I spoke to Kat's mother in Arizona. She didn't really know of Kat's friends. Do you?"

"I'm sure Kat had lots of friends," John replied. "She was personable that way. But she wasn't much of a talker here at the office and she was very good at separating her work and her social life. I wish I could rattle off some names for you, but I just don't know."

Detective Taft pulled his phone back toward him. It was

clear he wasn't going to get anything of significance from the firm and her mother had been just as useless. No one knew of any lovers or boyfriends or friends. No one he'd talked to so far knew about her personal life or what she did in her spare time. He needed to track down someone who could point him in the right direction, and he figured he'd get something once her phone was unlocked. Until then, he was just following procedure and going where he could to try and get answers. The door-to-doors the uniformed officers conducted had come up empty. He hoped someone in the neighborhood might've had a camera that caught something. There was still a chance that Kat's murder was random, but the fact that her apartment showed no signs of a struggle or forced entry told him otherwise. And that empty picture frame. Someone of significance was in that frame.

Maybe it was Kat Masterson's killer.

CHAPTER SEVENTEEN

Tracy was halfway across the football field when Jake finally spotted her. He was walking in from the opposite endzone, a cluster of small sheds and garages behind him. His hands were in his pockets as he lumbered along, a female student beside him, walking slowly, head down, hands hanging in front of her.

"Hey!" she called with a smile and an exaggerated wave.

Jake stopped for a moment, craning his neck to get a better look at her. The girl beside him stopped too. When he finally recognized her, his shoulders slumped and he smiled, waving in return.

"What're you doing here?"

"I booked the DJ and I wanted to show you the tablecloth pattern I picked out. If you like it, I'll call the hall and let them know."

"If you picked it out, I'm sure I'll love it."

They met at Tracy's forty-yard line and kissed. The girl remained awkwardly beside them.

"Uh, sorry," Jake said, motioning toward the girl. "This is Angela. She was helping collect the kickball bases after gym."

Tracy extended her hand, letting her engagement right

dazzle in the sunlight. "Hi, Angela. I'm Tracy. Nice to meet you."

"Hi."

Angela shook briefly, then looked at Jake. She bit her bottom lip and swallowed once as he stared at her. There was a look in her eyes that Tracy couldn't place. Fear? Pressure?

"You can go," Jake said. "Late bus should be here any second."

Angela ran off without another word. Tracy watched her go.

"Not very talkative."

"She's a good kid. Just shy."

"She seemed scared or intimidated or something. Was the clean-up a punishment?"

Jake nodded. "Yeah, she's pissed at me. I made her stay after school to help clean up because she was mouthing off to another girl during class and things were getting ugly. Now she has to take the late bus, and the kids hate that."

Tracy watched Angela disappear around the corner. There was something scratching at the back of her mind that wanted to come through, but before she could grab a hold of it, Jake spun her around, kissed her more passionately now that they were alone, and asked to see the swatch of tablecloth fabric. By the time she was explaining the color and pattern combination she was eyeing, the thought was gone and life pressed on.

Tracy could hear herself screaming as she half-woke from the memories, the images still dancing in her mind.

"Jake!"

His face, so young and innocent, morphing into the monster that was hiding beneath the surface the entire time.

"Stop!"

His beautiful blue eyes turning black and vacant. His heart

hardening as the truth came out and he realized there was no reason to pretend anymore. The mask was unnecessary. He could show his true self.

"No!"

She reached out in front of her, trying to grasp something to stay steady. Her head swam in the blackness and she knew that her balance was off. Her movements felt exaggerated and weak. She was aware of what would happen after he walked away, leaving her on the couch. At the time she thought it was over. That they were over. But it was only the beginning of a nightmare she simply couldn't wake up from.

"Jake!"

A door opened and footsteps scurried toward her.

"I'm here," a voice said.

"Help me," she stammered as she felt herself waking into a deeper shade of darkness.

"Shhh. I'm here. I'm right here. No one can hurt you."

"I..."

She felt the sting of a needle in her arm and almost instantly, a euphoric aura of calm and wonder came over her. Her eyes grew heavy and she could feel herself giving way to the pull of a beautiful unconsciousness where people like Jake didn't exist. Colors danced in the darkness and she giggled to herself. Again, she heard the voice in the distance, beyond the colors and the wonder.

"No one can hurt you," it said. "I'm right here. I'll always be here. All you have to do is call me. I... I love you."

CHAPTER EIGHTEEN
THREE MONTHS EARLIER

When the bell above the door rang, it reminded Kat of the ice cream shop she and her little brother used to go to on Cape Cod when their Aunt Bimy would take them for a week each summer to Yarmouth. Those had always been the best times when they would have the most fun and never had to worry about anyone saying no. Their aunt loved to spoil them, and it didn't matter if it was whale-watching, beach buggies, crab cakes for breakfast, or pizza at midnight, Aunt Bimy couldn't refuse them. She used to say it wasn't in her DNA to deny her niece and nephew anything, and that particular ice cream shop overlooking Follins Pond had always been their favorite. Aunt Bimy had been dead for almost a decade, but every time she heard a bell on a door, she was instantly transported back to those summers when the sun was never too hot and the water was never too cold.

Kat watched the woman step into the small foyer and crane her neck to look around. Her eyes searched the place, looking for someone to connect with. The small desk in the middle of the floor where their receptionist was supposed to be was empty, and the place itself was so quiet she could hear muted conversations from inside the bank that the firm was next to. Kat made her way around her desk and walked toward the woman, her feet sinking into the sagging wooden floor. The woman followed the sound of the creaking floorboards and smiled when Kat came into view.

"Welcome to Triaglia and Brown," Kat said, smiling in return. "How can I help you?"

The woman waved her hand around. "Half day today?"

"Actually, yes. We rotate Friday afternoons since that's usually our catch-up day."

"I almost turned back around and left."

"Well, I'm glad you didn't. Come on back. We'll talk."

Kat led the way to her desk and sat down. She motioned for the woman to do the same.

"What can I help you with?"

The woman eased herself into her seat and pulled her chair closer. "I'll get right to it since it's catch-up day," she said. "Bottom line, I need lawyer."

"Okay. Can't say you've come to the right place just yet. What kind of lawyer are you looking for?"

"A corporate lawyer. Someone who knows the ins and outs of business transfers and share assumptions and has the kind of expertise that could help with business continuity in the event of an emergency. For, like, just-in-case purposes."

Kat's smile broadened. "If that's what you need, then I'd say you've come to the exact right spot."

"You can help me?"

"Business continuity is one of my specialties." She extended her hand. "My name's Kat Masterson. It's nice to meet you."

The woman smiled in return, but there was something off about it. Kat couldn't quite figure out why, but there was an undertone of tension that the woman was fighting so hard to keep at bay. She slipped her hand into Kat's and they shook, the woman smiling and leaning forward.

"Hello, Kat. I'm Missy. Missy Rollins. I'm so glad you can help."

DAY FOUR

CHAPTER NINETEEN

The ride from Stamford to Farmington took an hour and a half up the Merritt Parkway. The Office of the Chief Medical Examiner was housed in a brown, nondescript, stucco building with black tinted windows that was perched up on a hill. Detective Taft parked his sedan in one of the open visitors' spaces and walked inside, anxious to find out if anything was uncovered during Kat Masterson's autopsy, yet at the same time dreading seeing the girl lying on the table. He'd seen too many bodies over his years. It was time to walk away for good, to go down to Florida and live the rest of his days in the warm sun and gentle waves of the gulf. There was nothing keeping him up north anymore. Just this last case, then he'd leave forever.

The Connecticut Medical Examiner's autopsy room was a familiar space. Two examination tables, a stainless-steel table on wheels that held the instruments needed for an examination, a scale to measure organs and the brain, and a drain in the middle of the floor for a thorough cleaning after the body had been removed. The morgue itself was behind a swinging double door at the far end of the room. He could see the sign next to the ME's desk.

Todd Fischer was standing over Kat's body when Taft walked in. Todd was very tall and very thin. He'd played basketball for Sacred Heart University and still had that toned and athletic look about him. He was young, early thirties, thick dark hair that matched the dark stubble that ran from the tops of his cheeks and disappeared under his shirt collar. He had a file in one hand and was looking at Kat's neck, comparing something Taft couldn't see. Kat was face-up and naked. A Y-incision had been made just under her breasts, which was standard in an autopsy. She'd been sewn back up by the time he'd arrived. Her skin was a sickening blue he'd come to accept throughout his years in law enforcement. He stopped when he saw her body, choking back the bile that wanted to spew forth. It never got easy.

"Hey, Todd," Taft said as he approached the examination table.

Todd looked up from his file. "Dennis? I thought Lena was heading this one."

"She is. I thought I'd get a head start. She's busy with the scene still, so I figured I'd come collect the information and pass it along."

"Sounds like a plan."

"Tell me you found something, because we're on Day Four with no leads, no motive, and no suspects."

Todd stood straight and handed over the file. "By way of sequencing the events, I'd say she was hit on the back of the head first with the paperweight you guys found at the scene. Then she was strangled with the dog chain. The blow was pretty severe. Base of the skull. Caused a fracture. The person hitting her would've had to be strong to cause that kind of damage."

"So, she falls from the blow and the perp strangles her."

"That's what it looks like. Based on the damage to the skull and some trauma I saw when I took out the brain, there's a very

strong chance she was unconscious when she was being strangled. I found no fingernail marks on her neck, which is common
when a person is being strangled. Even if it's a suicidal hanging,
the body's reflex is to dig under whatever is choking them, and
we have none of that here."

"Can't struggle if you're knocked out."

"Exactly." He waited for Taft to open the file and pointed to
the middle of the first page. "Cause of death is definitely stran-
gulation." He turned the page to the photographs the techs had
taken at the scene. Taft could hardly look at them. "You can see
deep abrasions and contusions of the skin of the anterior neck as
well as the thick ligature mark from the chain that was used. I
found hemorrhages in the skin as well as conjunctiva of the
eyes, which is caused by asphyxiation, furthering the evidence
she was strangled. Finally, we have the fracture of the hyoid
bone."

"We didn't pull any prints off the dog chain. You get
anything from the body?"

"Not prints, but I was able to retrieve skin flakes from under
the victim's nails. We'll examine them and see if any belong to
someone besides the victim. Also got some DNA."

"DNA? Really?"

Todd took the file back and walked over to his desk. He
retrieved a clipboard and spun around.

"Based on our vaginal examination, we found evidence of
sexual intercourse that same night, and we were able to recover
a few specks of dried semen on the victim's leg. We'll use the
DNA from the semen to match the skin flakes that were found.
See if it's the same person."

"That's great," Taft replied. "Sound like that might get us
somewhere."

"Let's hope." Todd walked back across the room and
handed Taft the clipboard. "Your copy's on top."

Taft took the copy and folded it without reading it. "Our

victim had sex the same night she was killed. No one heard anything that would cause alarm, and there was no sign of forced entry into the apartment. Nothing was rummaged through and no money or jewelry was taken. There was no real sign of anything bad happening aside from the homicide itself. Confirms what we thought."

"The victim knew her killer."

"Yup, and now you're telling me she might've had sex with him before he killed her. He thought enough to clean off the dog chain, but had no idea he left semen on her leg. Big mistake."

Todd looked down at the woman on the table. "I say we make him pay for his mistake. Let's find out whose DNA that is and catch this son-of-a-bitch."

Taft nodded. "Best plan I've heard all day."

CHAPTER TWENTY

The door opened and Kelly pushed herself inside, stepping forward, holding up her shield. The woman who answered staggered back inside a step.

"Detective Evans, Westchester County Police. Is Mr. Cowan here?"

"No. Can I help you?"

Kelly put her shield away and handed the woman a sheet of paper. "I have a warrant to search the house. You may want to give him a call. Grab your jacket. We need you to step outside so my team can get started."

The woman skimmed the warrant, then snatched her coat from a rack just inside the front door, and allowed Kelly to guide her onto the small porch as the Westchester County forensics team exited from their vehicles and began carrying equipment inside. Kelly heard the woman call Malcolm and leave a message.

"You're Tracy's sister," Kelly said when the woman put her phone away. "Missy Rollins, right?"

The woman nodded. "That's right."

"I've been looking for you. Went to your apartment. Work. No one's seen or heard from you."

"My sister's missing. I came down here to help find her. Been here ever since."

"You never told your job?"

"They'll be there when I get back."

Missy was tall, skinny, but not in a healthy way. Skin and bones. She had a pretty face though. Nice blue eyes. Brown hair that was tied back in a braid. Kelly noticed that she had stumps for fingernails, no polish. Her hands looked dry and rough. The winter could do that.

"And no contact from Tracy?" Kelly asked, watching the team scurry around inside.

Missy stuffed both hands into the pockets of her coat. "Don't you think I would've called you if I heard from her?"

"I'd hope so."

"Yeah, well, I would've. And no, I haven't heard from my sister. We don't know where she is."

Kelly stepped aside as some of the techs hauled two large storage boxes from their van through the front door. "Okay, we can go back in now, but you need to stay in one room."

"In here."

Missy led the way into the family room. Kelly followed. She noticed the place looked a bit messier than when she'd first come to talk to Malcolm. Action figures were strewn across the floor. A jigsaw puzzle was open on the table, but only one corner had been done. The rest of the pieces were still in the box. A tiny basketball sat next to the television, the small hoop waiting at the far end of the room. The sectional had folded laundry on it. A book had been laid face-down on one of the armrests to prop it open.

"What about you?" Missy asked as she stopped and sat against the couch. "You must've found something if you have your forensics guys in here looking through the house. I'm a true-crime fan. I know they wouldn't be here if you didn't have something solid. Tell me."

"If you're a true-crime fan, then you know I can't do that."

"But you found something."

"We're still gathering the facts."

Missy looked her up and down. "Yeah, well, it's been three days. Once we get to seven, the odds of finding her are almost impossible. I need you guys to make this your focus. Please."

Kelly paused, weighing how much she might want to tell this woman and how much she wanted to keep confidential. She felt like she owed it to her to explain how hard they'd been working, but knew she couldn't disclose anything of real importance. Not until they had a clearer picture. She also wasn't sure if she could trust Missy or not. There was something about her that put her off, but Kelly couldn't place it. She was right though. Three days had come and gone and she really didn't have too much. The others at the station had gone out of their way to remind her of that. She decided to stay as vanilla as she could.

"You know we pulled her SUV from the river?"

"Yes."

"Her phone and purse were still in the vehicle. At this point we can't say if something malicious happened to her or if this is a case of her simply walking away from her life and starting fresh somewhere else as someone else."

"She wouldn't leave Finn."

"Yeah, that's what I keep hearing."

"And her plan was already to start fresh somewhere else. That's what she was on her way home to do that night. Talk with Malcolm. Pack up. Stay with me and then move north. She had her eye on New England. Vermont or Maine. That was already the plan. She wouldn't change it at the last minute and leave her son behind."

"Maybe it wasn't a last-minute decision," Kelly said.

"Maybe this was the plan all along, but she knew she couldn't tell anyone because the pressure not to leave her boy would've been too much."

Missy grunted through her nose and shook her head. "No chance. Not when it comes to Finn. She'd never leave him. Never."

There was a moment of quiet between them.

"We'll find her," Kelly said. "I'm sure of it."

"You better."

Shouts of instruction came from the other rooms. The techs were setting up and someone was taking pictures. The snapping of the camera echoed through the quiet.

"What did you think of Tracy's plan to leave her husband?" Kelly asked.

A shrug. "Honestly? I thought it was a stupid idea. Malcolm gave her a good life. His business is just starting to really get going. Tracy and me came from nothing, and she was just about at the point where she could start enjoying some of the finer things, but she was walking away instead. I thought she should stay and work it out. Told her as much. I mean, even if he was an asshole, just hang out for the money, you know?"

"Was he an asshole?"

"Not that I saw. But Tracy said she had her reasons for wanting to leave, so I had to support her."

"Did Tracy and Malcolm fight a lot?"

"Never. They were happy. At least I thought they were."

Kelly was jotting notes as they spoke. She stopped for a moment and looked at Missy. "Is Malcolm the kind of guy who could hurt someone?" she asked. "Physically, I mean."

Missy's eyes narrowed. "I don't know. Maybe."

"Do you think he had something to do with what happened to your sister?"

"Would seem logical, right? She disappears the day she tells him she wants out? He'd be my primary suspect for sure. On the other hand, I don't know if I can see it. He swore to me that he had nothing to do with it, and he seems convincing, but I also know he digs a lot of holes for a living and he pours a lot of concrete. He's a proud man. Wouldn't be too much of a stretch to think his pride made him do something rash, and my sister's buried under a building slab or underground somewhere, courtesy of a backhoe. I just need you to get your answers sooner than later, because if Tracy is alive, and I pray to God she is, time's gotta be running out. One way or the other."

Kelly put her pen down. "We'll get some dogs out to the sites he's been working at. Not sure they can detect a scent through concrete, but if your sister was on the grounds, they might pick up something."

"Sure. Whatever you have to do."

Kelly studied the woman who sat next to her, careful not to flinch as the forensics team worked around them. "How is your relationship with your sister?"

A smile appeared. "We're fine," she said. "We're best friends. I'm her protector. Two peas in a pod. We're the only family we have. And you already know I was home with my nephew the night she disappeared. I'm clean as a whistle, but by all means, feel free to send your team over and CSI my house too. I got nothing to hide. I know how the shows work."

"True crime."

"Right."

"I think just a DNA swab will do for now," Kelly said.

Missy nodded. "Whatever you need. I'm here to help. Just find my sister and bring her home."

CHAPTER TWENTY-ONE

Tracy dug her phone out of her bag and checked the Caller ID. It was her mother. She held up a finger to let her best friend—and maid of honor—Charlotte, know to pause the conversation for a moment. The rest of the dinnertime crowd was loud around them and she turned in her seat to try and hear better.

"Hey, Mom."

"Oh my God, Tracy. Are you okay?"

"Yeah. Me and Charlotte are at MJ's getting some wings and a drink."

There was a pause on the other end.

"Mom?"

"You're getting dinner?"

"Yeah. With Charlotte." She leaned down and cupped her hand over her other ear. "What's wrong? You don't sound right."

Her mother started crying. "Oh, Tracy. It's Jake."

Tracy's stomach tightened at the sound of her mother's distress spitting out her fiancé's name. "Mom, what happened to Jake?"

"Something terrible. Just... terrible."

Tracy knew she was awake, but had no idea if it was day or night, what date it was, or where she was. She somehow felt more lucid as she rolled from her side onto her back. The dizziness and floating sensation were both gone. She felt grounded. She could think. She could remember.

Her first memory was that car with one headlight. It had followed her from Manhattan all the way to Buchanan. She could recall the sound of the horn blaring. The gravel giving way under her tires. Her bumper being crushed on impact. The water from the river rushing in through the floor. She could almost feel it freezing her feet. The SUV starting to float and sink at the same time, the current pulling it out and under. She could remember running through the woods, thinking she was heading toward the houses that backed up against the park and discovering she'd ended up on the shore. The dark figure running at her. And the words she swore she'd heard while she danced between reality and dream.

"It was your husband. It was Malcolm. He was trying to kill you."

Her second memory was of Malcolm and that girl. She'd followed them and watched them and confirmed what she'd suspected. It had all been lies. His love. Their life together. All of it had been built for nothing. He'd found someone else. Everything she thought she knew was over.

Tracy sat up in bed and raised her hands to her face. She could feel a thick layer of gauze wrapped around her head, secured with layers of tape, wide enough to cover both eyes from the bridge of her nose to the middle of her forehead. Panic suddenly got a hold of her as tiny particles of color made their way into her blackness and a sense of claustrophobia set in. She pressed down on the gauze and immediately felt pain in both eyes. There was something the voice had told her about her injuries, but she couldn't quite remember what it was. A doctor had seen her? Had that been it?

I can't see!

A dark vertigo took hold, coupling with the claustrophobia. The dizziness returned and she could feel the room spinning and tightening even though she couldn't see anything. Her heart beat loudly in her chest, her breath shallow and short.

I can't see anything!

She pulled at the bandage that was around her eyes but it was wrapped too tight to get it past her nose. She clawed at it, but the layers of tape made it impossible to dig in to. Without knowing what she was really doing, but needing to do *something*, Tracy turned her body and swung her legs down off the bed until her feet touched the floor.

Help me! I need help!

The rug was soft on her bare feet. She pushed herself up from the mattress and stood, balancing in the darkness, fighting the vertigo, feeling the soreness course through her entire body, listening as the floorboards creaked under her shifting weight.

The room was silent. Outside, she could hear the wind pounding the walls and waves crashing on shore, but inside the room, there was no noise except for the floorboards. More quick and panicked breaths. Her heartbeat thumping in her ears. Tracy put her arms out in front of her and shuffled her left foot forward. She stopped, surprised at how weak she was, the pins and needles traveling from her feet to her hips. Her neck and shoulders hurt. Whiplash, maybe? She pulled the right foot to join the left, and repeated this movement until her hands bumped into a window and her foot kicked a wall.

Help me!

The glass on the window was smooth and cold. Tracy felt all around it, touching the moldings that separated the panes, feeling the sill and the small handle that lifted the bottom section upward. She moved to her left, sliding her hands against the wall as she went, still fighting the sensation that the room was spinning and shrinking at the same time. There was a second window about four feet from the first. She kept going and knocked into a rocking chair. As soon as she hit it, she heard the sound it made on the floor and somehow recognized it from when she was asleep. The voice had been sitting in it, watching over her and rocking in the chair as she slept. She could picture the silhouette of a person sitting completely still with only the chair itself rocking back and forth. She couldn't see a face but knew that it was staring at her, its eyes piercing her dreams, its grip on the armrests tightening.

Help me!

The wall fell into a corner, and as soon as Tracy continued left, she felt the frame of a door. She touched the wood molding, feeling the crevasses and the smooth rounded edges as she ran her hand up and down and eventually over to the door itself. Six panels. Wood. She found the knob and was about to turn it when she heard something that made her stop. She strained to listen past the sound of her heart beating and the waves and the wind outside. There was a noise. In the same room.

Breathing.

Someone was with her.

Watching.

"Hello?" she said, her voice weak and scratchy. "Is someone there?"

She stayed put, pressed against the door, too scared to move, not knowing where she was or who she was with, listening to the sound of the other person breathing, mixing with her own panicked breaths. The breathing was shallow, nervous. Short and fluttering. But it was there. Behind her. Not close enough that she could turn and touch the person. Just close enough to be heard under everything else.

"Who's there? Please. I can hear you."

The breathing stopped.

The floor creaked behind her.

The person was slowly inching toward her.

"Who is that? Tell me who's there!"

Closer.

Tracy could hear the terror creeping up in her voice. She turned so her back was against the door, facing the person coming toward her, her hands out in front of her, seeing nothing.

"Please," she said. "Who's there? Please answer me."

The creaking stopped.

"You shouldn't be out of bed."

She recognized the voice immediately, although it did nothing to quell her panic. She was confused, thrown off by the voice she'd spoken to so many times before. The kindness behind that hint of an Indian accent. She could picture his face, his disarming smile, his caring nature.

"Dr. Devi?"

"Sam. Call me Sam."

"I thought your name was Viraj."

"My friends call me Sam. It's more... American."

Tracy pushed further against the door, her hands still out in front of her, her world feeling as though it was tilting. "How are you here right now? Am I dreaming again? Why are you here?"

"You're not dreaming. You're safe."

"I can't see. These bandages."

She reached up and grabbed the gauze again, pulling at it to try and loosen it. His hands gently took hers and she yelped when she was touched.

"It's okay."

He redirected her hands to her side.

"You shouldn't pull at the wrapping," he said. "I don't want you to do more damage. You're still recovering. Your concussion was quite serious and both eyes were swollen shut. You may have an orbital fracture, but we're not sure yet. It'll be a few days before we can take the bandages off and have another look. For now, the doctor who came to examine you wants to keep everything in place. I told him we would."

"A doctor came to see me?"

"Twice. He said you're doing well. Just need to rest."

His hands moved from Tracy's and touched her left elbow and wrist, carefully pulling her from the door and guiding her back toward what she figured was the bed. She allowed herself to be shown the way, all the while trying to puzzle together where she was and why Dr. Devi was with her. There was something so utterly unnatural about being with him outside his office. Her shin bumped into the bedframe and she eased herself down to sit on the edge of the mattress.

"Where am I?" she asked. "What happened? I can't remember everything. Just bits and pieces."

"You're safe," Dr. Devi—Sam—said again. "I brought you to my summer home so you can recover from the attack. No one knows you're here and I want to keep it that way for now. Your husband is after you, and it's important he doesn't find you. Once you get better, we can call the police and we'll tell them everything."

Tracy nodded as she balled fistfuls of sheets into her hands. Malcolm. Malcolm had tried to kill her. She couldn't believe it.

"I don't feel so great." Her vertigo and claustrophobia were turning into anxiety and adrenaline. She felt on edge and took a few deep breaths to try and calm herself. "Tell me what happened."

Sam sat next to her. "You stopped by a park and drove down to the banks of the Hudson River. Why?"

The memory came back. "It was George's Island. That's where Malcolm and I had our wedding reception. I wasn't expecting to be anywhere near there but..." She turned toward his voice. "The car with one headlight. I remember that. It was following me."

"Yes, it was."

"That's how I ended up at the park. I had to get off the main highway and was on a back road near the park. I was driving and thinking about how my marriage was ending, and all of a sudden, it's right there. Like a sign from the universe or something. I just drove through the entrance on autopilot. I guess I wanted to remember the good times."

"Malcolm came for you," Sam said. "He was the one in the car with one headlight. He tried to push you into the river while you were still inside your car. You got out and ran into the woods. He found you and started beating you with a bat. He was trying to kill you, Tracy."

The images of that night flashed through her mind again. She began breathing heavy, almost hyperventilating, her world spinning in her darkness. She thought she might vomit and held her stomach. "My God," she choked. "Malcolm?"

"I chased him away and took you to my car and drove you here. I didn't know what Malcolm was planning next, and I didn't feel safe going to a local hospital or the police. It would've been too easy to turn this into a he-said, she-said thing, and I was afraid they'd let him take you home. If he took you, he'd finish what he started. There was no doubt in my mind. I couldn't have that, so I brought you here and you'll stay here until you're better, and then we'll go to the police. Together."

As Sam – it felt strange to use his first name – spoke, she asked herself if her husband was capable of hunting her down and killing her instead of allowing her to leave their marriage. She let go of the sheet and could feel her hands trembling.

Yes, he was. He most certainly was.

The irony was almost too much.

"But wait," she said suddenly. "Why were you there? How could you be there to save me? You were supposed to be in the city."

There was a prolonged silence filled by the wind hitting the side of the house and the waves crashing somewhere beyond the bedroom.

"I was also following you," Sam said. His voice was barely audible. "I know that sounds strange, but it's the truth. I was planning to follow you to your house and sit outside in case your talk with Malcolm escalated into something violent. I admit, that's not normal doctor–patient protocol, but I felt like in this case, I might need to help. If everything worked out, you never would've known I was outside, but I wanted to make sure I was around in case anything went wrong. I wanted to protect you." Another pause. "When you turned off the road, I followed. When you went into the park, I stayed in the upper lot above the one you were in, so I didn't see Malcolm drive down and hit your car. It was only after I heard a car horn honking and then I heard screaming that I came running down. I'm sorry for following you, and I acknowledge that it breaks the trust between us, but I care about you. I didn't want you to get hurt."

Tracy's head was still swirling from the information she was being confronted with. Something tickled the back of her mind, whispering warnings that she couldn't hear but knew were there. He'd been following her too. He cared about her. That didn't sit right.

"How long have I been here?" she asked.

"A few days."

"So, you've been, like, feeding me?"

"Yes."

"I don't remember that."

"Between the concussion and the drugs, that doesn't surprise me. Now that you're a bit more conscious and gaining a bit of strength, I'll help you into the bathroom later and you can take a bath. Clean yourself up. I didn't want to overstep. There's a bedpan on your nightstand. You can keep using that until you're more stable on your feet. You can't be up and around though. It's too dangerous."

A thought broke through the darkness and Tracy almost fell off the bed. "Finn!"

Sam stood up, holding her steady. "He's fine. He's still with your sister."

"I need to get to him. He can't be alone with Malcolm. It's too dangerous. We have to call the police now. I'll tell them everything. I have to keep Finn away from Malcolm!" Tracy tried to stand, but hands gently took her by the shoulders and guided her back down. "If he can try and kill me like that, there's no way he can be trusted with my son. Please! We have to call the police. We have to get Finn away from Malcolm!"

"You're not strong enough just yet."

"I need to get to my boy!"

The grip around her shoulders tightened, pushing and squeezing.

"This is not up for debate." Sam's voice was calm, but firm. "You need to rest."

"You're hurting me!"

The grip immediately vanished.

Silence between them.

"Okay," Sam said. His voice was back to normal now. Friendly. Unassuming. "How about this? I'll reach out to Missy myself and make sure she stays with Finn. We won't let Malcolm near her."

"I need to talk to him."

"You will. Soon."

Pills rattled in a bottle. Sam opened the top and dropped two into the palm of her hand.

"Take these. You've been too active. Your brain and your body need to relax."

"But I—"

"Do as I say and you'll recover quicker and we can get to the police. You have to take care of yourself before anything else can happen."

Tracy took the pills and chased them with water Sam gave her. When she was done, hands laid her down on the bed and covered her with a blanket. She tried to think of more questions and wanted to sit back up and discuss ways she could get to her son, but her head suddenly felt heavy and things that had been so important only moments earlier, faded into the background. Before the darkness turned deeper and the lucidness she'd felt earlier began slipping away, she had a different thought.

The plan.

Things had already been put in motion, but she was not there to guide them. What was going to happen if...

Then there was nothing. Not even the sound of the waves or the wind hitting the house outside. Not the whisper of warning or the uneasiness she knew she felt but wasn't yet ready to acknowledge. It... nothing.

DAY FIVE

CHAPTER TWENTY-TWO

Missy stared at the dark ceiling, her mind churning and jumping from one thing to the next. Things were already spinning out of control. All the meticulous planning and the lies and the fake smiles and now everything had changed. Tracy was gone, maybe dead. So where did that leave her? It looked as if she'd have to do this herself and try and find her sister at the same time. What was happening? Where was Tracy?

The detective's question kept slipping into her thoughts, repeating in Missy's mind, a loop that spun endlessly in the background of everything else. It started at dinner and remained in the wee hours of the night.

"Is Malcolm the kind of guy who could hurt someone?"

Everyone had a breaking point. Everyone had a switch that could flip. It was just a matter of being pushed to that point. Most weren't. Some were. But the general question Detective Evans was asking wasn't whether Malcolm could hurt someone. The real question was could Malcolm kill Tracy? Did he have it in him?

Missy pushed the covers off her body and sat up in the bed.

The guestroom was spacious but sparsely furnished. There was the bed, a nightstand, and a dresser. A small flatscreen sat atop the dresser and a few framed paintings from Bed Bath & Beyond hung on the walls. The clock on the nightstand read 3:17. The house was dark and quiet. Finn had gone to sleep at nine and she'd laid down at eleven. At the time, Malcolm was still awake in his office. She'd heard him come up to the second floor just before midnight. Since then, she'd been tossing and turning, listening to the detective ask her question over and over, knowing she could be sleeping in the room next to the man responsible for her sister's disappearance. But she wasn't scared. Not of Malcolm. She was focused.

"Is Malcolm the kind of guy who could hurt someone?"

The wall-to-wall carpet silenced her footsteps as Missy snatched her phone from next to the clock and crossed the bedroom, making her way out into the hall. She tip-toed down the corridor, past Finn's room, and stopped at the double doors to Tracy and Malcolm's en suite. She carefully placed her hand around the knob and held her breath as she turned it and cracked the door open ever so slightly.

With the help of a nightlight that was always on in the en suite bathroom, Missy could see Malcolm was lying faceup in his bed, shirtless, the covers pulled to his waist, leaving his toned chest exposed. One arm was across his face and the other at his side. A faint snore came rhythmically from the bed. He was in a deep sleep.

"Malcolm," Missy whispered. She waited for a response, but he didn't budge.

"Is Malcolm the kind of guy who could hurt someone?"

Missy quietly pulled the door closed again and released her hand from the knob. She turned and made her way downstairs, wincing whenever she caught a step that creaked under her weight. When she reached the main floor, she scurried through the foyer, across the kitchen, and into Malcolm's office. She stood in the doorway and turned on the flashlight from her phone, scanning the room before taking another step.

The office was small, holding only a desk, a file cabinet, a printer, and a bookcase. A laptop was on the desk along with rolled up drawings she knew were blueprints from the projects his company had been hired to work on. The bookcase held binders and books on engineering and construction. She had no idea what was in the file cabinet.

"Is Malcolm the kind of guy who could hurt someone?"

Let's find out.

Missy went to the desk first. She tapped on the laptop and was thankful it came to life without the need for a password. Malcolm wasn't very inclined when it came to changing technology, so it didn't surprise her that he felt no need for a password. It would've only been one more thing to forget or lose. Better to keep it simple.

She went to all the usual places. Word docs held job contracts and construction budgets, but nothing else. Excel spreadsheets were filled with Sources and Uses tables for fundings and job requisition checklists. His internet search history listed addresses and job sites and material research and pricings and websites for subcontractors, but nothing incriminating. Even the little bit of porn he seemed to dabble in was vanilla by today's standards. His laptop was all business. Nothing that would prove he had anything to do with Tracy's disappearance.

Missy tugged on the desk drawers. She found two keys in the top drawer, and all of the other drawers were unlocked but one. The unlocked drawers had books on construction, his bank ledger, and job contracts. One of the keys unlocked a drawer that contained a black handgun. She had no idea the make or model. It was heavy and large. She held it up to her nose and tried to determine if it had been recently fired. The gun smelled of oil and metal. She didn't know if that was normal or not.

The other key unlocked the file cabinet, but there was nothing in there that had anything to do with Tracy. Same with the binders in the bookcase. She sat back in his seat and scanned the room with her phone's flashlight one last time. There was nothing there. She was wasting her time. Missy got up from the chair, made sure to put everything away the exact way she'd found it, and walked back through the bottom floor, up the stairs, and stopped, again, at the double doors.

"Is Malcolm the kind of guy who could hurt someone?"

That question kept repeating in her head. She had to know. She had to learn the truth, and if Malcolm was involved, she had to get Finn as far away from him as possible. For Tracy.

Missy clasped her fingers around the door handle and, again, turned it. She opened the door further this time, slipping in and carefully making her way toward Malcolm's bed. She could see his phone sitting on his nightstand, the red power button on and ready, the screen dark. Malcolm's rhythmic snore was the soundtrack to her harrowing journey across the bedroom until she was standing over him, her breath held in her throat, staring to see if he was able to wake up while she reached for his phone.

Everything was so quiet. Even detaching the power cord from Malcolm's phone caused a clicking sound that might as well have been a freight train going by outside. She grimaced as she waited for Malcolm to stir, but he remained still, his one arm still over his face, the covers undisturbed by his waist.

She hit the power button as the phone came to life with a series of vibrations and chirps. Missy held her breath to see if the noise was enough to wake Malcolm and slowly exhaled when she saw that it wasn't. He remained asleep.

The phone was locked, asking for a FaceID or his passcode. Damn. She'd hoped he'd taken the passcode off as he'd done on his laptop. No such luck. Now what? She knew she only had a few attempts at a password before the phone would lock further, and there was no way she'd ever figure what the passcode might be besides trying *Tracy* or *Finn*, both of which she tried and failed. The FaceID was the only way.

Missy eased herself down beside Malcolm, and with her index finger and thumb, pinched his wrist and slid it away from his face. As soon as he began to wake and move, she ducked down so he wouldn't see her. The snore stopped, followed by a large exhale, and Missy waited, the room cast in a blanket of tension, until the faint snoring started anew.

Kneeling up, she placed the phone in front of his face, but it didn't unlock. She tried again, and still, nothing. She ducked back down and took her own phone out, Googling the procedure. Her heart stopped when she read that the FaceID could not be activated with a person's eyes closed. There was no other way to unlock the phone.

Missy stood back up and returned Malcolm's phone to the nightstand. She heard the detective's voice again.

"Is Malcolm the kind of guy who could hurt someone?"

Then she heard her own question, never spoken before until just then.

"Did Malcolm kill my sister?"

She took a quiet breath, grabbed the phone, and held it in front of Malcolm's face. She flipped on the light that was on the nightstand.

"Malcolm!" she whisper-called. "Malcolm, wake up! I hear something."

Malcolm stirred and opened his eyes, confused with where he was or who was calling him. Missy had the phone in front of him, and the flashing strobe light quickly scanned his face and unlocked the screen. As soon as it did, she shut off the light, spun around, flipped to the phone's settings, turning off the screen lock function to ensure it stayed open.

"Wha—" Malcolm muttered, still asleep and slowly climbing toward consciousness.

"Never mind," Missy whispered. "You're dreaming."

Malcom grunted something, then turned on his side, and quickly fell back to sleep. The faint snoring returned before she even made it to the bedroom door.

CHAPTER TWENTY-THREE

"Wake up, you son of a bitch."

Missy stood at the foot of Malcom's bed, watching as Malcolm stirred, turned over onto his back, then opened his eyes into slits. It took a moment for him to wake up enough to understand what was happening, but when she saw his eyes widen and his body instinctively push away from her, she knew he recognized the gun she was pointing at him and that he was fully awake now.

"Is Malcolm the kind of guy who could hurt someone?"

Apparently so.

"Missy, what are you doing?" Malcolm asked, his voice scratchy and dry. "What the hell?"

"You killed her," Missy spat, hardly comprehending the words she was forced to speak. "You killed Tracy."

"No, I didn't. Put the gun down."

"I read your texts. You killed her. Or you had someone do it. You couldn't handle the fact that she wanted to leave you. She was going to leave and she was going to take Finn with her and you couldn't let that happen so you got her killed. Maybe you didn't pull the trigger or plunge the knife into her or whatever happened, but you ordered it, and that means you killed her."

Tears streamed down Missy's face as she spoke. She knew she was supposed to stay quiet so as not to wake Finn, but she couldn't help the emotion that was pouring out of her. All of the love and the memories and the heartache she'd shared with her sister over the years came spilling forth. Behind that, she knew, was an anger she was afraid she wouldn't be able to control. Everyone had their breaking point. Missy wondered if this was hers.

"You took my phone?"

"I had to know the truth. And now I do."

"Put the gun down."

"Why was she leaving you?"

"I told you I don't know."

"You know!"

"I don't! I swear!" Malcolm pushed himself further against the headboard and sat up. He raised his hands in front of him. They trembled as he fumbled for his words. "Look, I don't know what you think you found, but I'm sure I can explain."

The gun was heavy and hard to hold with one hand. Missy fumbled with Malcolm's phone and flipped through the screens until she arrived at his texts.

"Neil says, 'You give any thought to what we talked about?' and you say, 'I did.' And Neil says, 'And?' and you say, "Do it.' You ordered her to be killed, you bastard."

Malcolm quickly shook his head. "Neil is Neil Scranton. He's my CPA. I called him the morning Tracy told me she wanted a divorce and I told him I wanted to remove Tracy from my business. I told him to take her off the bank accounts and to file the paperwork to remove her as a partial owner and beneficiary of anything that had to do with the business. That's what we were talking about. Jesus, Missy, if I was ordering Tracy to be killed, do you think I'd do it over text? And if I did, do you think I'd leave the text in my phone? Think about it."

Missy stared straight ahead, her mouth sliding open. The gun shook in her hand and she tossed Malcolm's phone onto the bed so she could hold it with both hands.

"Why was she leaving you?"

"I wish I could tell you."

"She was leaving you and you were going to take the business away from her?"

"How can I keep her on if she divorces me and moves away?" Malcolm asked, slowly lowering his hands. "I built that company. It's my legacy. She doesn't get any of it if she's not with me. That's the way it goes."

"You killed her."

"I didn't. I want her back. I wasn't the one trying to leave. I love her. You know that."

Missy dropped the gun and fell to her knees. A wave of confusion and anger and sadness and grief washed over her and she cried, loud and uninhibited, wailing into the otherwise quiet night. Despite what she'd just done, Malcolm climbed from his bed and knelt by her side, hugging her close to him. She could smell the perspiration on his skin as he whispered reassurances she couldn't really hear. Somewhere in the background, she knew Finn had woken up and come in. He was suddenly beside her too, hugging her with his tiny arms and little hands. The three of them were huddled on the bedroom floor in the middle of the night, exorcising all the fear and sadness that had been bottled up, worried about Tracy and what might've happened to her, all the while Missy asking the same question over and over, knowing she'd have to keep pushing forward with the plan herself and wondering if she had the strength to pull it off.

"Where is she? Where is she? Where is she?"

CHAPTER TWENTY-FOUR

Tracy pulled herself from a peaceful sleep as the remnants of her dream still lingered in her mind's eye. It had been a memory more than a dream. She and Malcolm had taken turns standing over Finn's crib the first night they'd brought him home. As she rocked in the chair in the corner, she watched her husband peering at the infant, an expression of focus and determination about him, even at three in the morning. He was a protector. It was in his blood. And in that moment, his sole reason for living was to watch over his son no matter how tired he might be. Tracy had closed her eyes that night feeling at ease, knowing Malcolm was there. For both of them.

Tracy's head ached and her eyes felt like they were full of glass shards. Her neck and shoulders were still tangles of knots. She tried to sit up, but immediately fell back against the pillows when a wave of nausea hit her. The blackness around her was thick and she still didn't know exactly where she was. As she woke up more and her mind came into focus, a single thought spun in her mind, whispering to her over and over. She needed to get back home. Things had been put into motion that she needed to guide. She couldn't trust that Missy could do it alone.

Her sister wasn't as invested in the outcome as she was. There wasn't enough at stake for Missy to give it the attention it deserved. Too much had been planned up to this point and she couldn't let it all fall apart. Not now. It was important for her to be there. So much could still go wrong.

"Try not to move too much." Sam's voice was right beside her. She jumped when she heard it. "You're still feeling the effects of the concussion. It's going to take some time."

The proximity of Sam's voice was a bit too close for her to feel comfortable. She wanted to push him away, but swallowed the instinct and tried to remain calm. She needed him. There was no question about that.

"My eyes hurt," Tracy said. She sounded as if she was another person listening from two rooms away. The echo in her mind was cavernous. "Can we take the bandage off to check them?"

"The doctor said to give it a few more days. The swelling needs to go down."

"But maybe we can wash them or put a cool cloth on them or something. They hurt so much."

"No." His breath was suddenly on the side of her face, whispering, tickling her cheek. "What you're feeling is normal. The pain will go away in a few days, we can take the bandage off then and check. In the meantime, I can give you something to help with them hurting. I don't want to see you in pain."

"No more pills. Please."

"They'll help."

"No. Thank you."

"Okay. Tell me if you change your mind."

Tracy felt Sam's hand take hers. It was cold to the touch, thin and small. He squeezed it.

"You're going to be okay," he said. "I'll make sure of it. I won't let anything happen to you. I promise. I care very deeply for you, Tracy. I'm going to protect you. Whatever it takes."

There was an unsettling uneasiness about the quiet that surrounded them. Tracy tried to act natural, but there was a sensation of dread in the back of her mind, scratching at her, warning her of something and urging her to get back home to see things through. She'd only known Dr. Devi for a little more than a year, and never imagined they'd grown close enough for him to be acting as her protector. He'd always kept a professional distance, doctor and patient. Perhaps her ending their professional relationship somehow gave him permission to become her friend? She took a breath and allowed her hand to remain in his.

"Can we call my sister? I want her to know where I am. I want to talk to my son. It's important they know I'm safe."

Sam let go of her hand and she listened as his footsteps retreated.

"We'll call them. Soon."

"I'd like to call them now."

"Soon."

The pain in Tracy's eyes was distracting her from everything else. She lifted her hands up to try and adjust the bandages on her face when she felt a tug on her left wrist and heard a chain clang against something metal at the side of her bed. With her right hand she traced her fingers to what felt like a smooth rope chain that looped snug around her wrist, fed back down to the mattress, and around the metal box spring.

This is not okay.

"What is this?" she asked. She wanted her voice to be calm and in control, but she could hear it cracking a bit as panic slipped in.

"I made it," Sam replied. His voice was even, matter-of-fact. "It was the best I could do for now. I don't have access to a hospital bed with safety rails, and I had to make sure you stayed in bed. When I came in the other day and you were up and around, I got nervous. Between you not being able to see and the concussion, being up and walking could be very dangerous. I wanted to make sure you stayed put while you're recovering."

"You chained me to the bed?"

"For your protection."

"Can you take it off? I don't like that. I'll stay in bed. Just take it off."

"It's only a precaution to keep you safe."

The mood in the room was turning darker. Tracy could feel the tension rising. Sam's voice was still even-keeled, but was also getting deeper, his words curt. She was scared.

This is not okay.

"Sam." Her voice was trembling now, on the verge of tears. "Take the chain off. I want it off."

Sam didn't respond.

"Sam!"

Nothing.

"Okay, look, I need to call my sister." Tracy was crying now, her voice barking through sobs she tried to control. "Right now. I want to call her, and then we can call the police. We can't wait any longer. It's important for everyone to know what happened with Malcolm, and I feel lucid enough to be able to talk to the police and to my sister. I think we need to involve the authorities at this point. Give me your phone."

Tracy tugged on the chain as she spoke, bending her wrist, turning her arm, fumbling with it between her fingers, testing its strength and trying to figure out how it was tied around her. She felt what appeared to be a tiny padlock, no bigger than her thumb. She took a breath to calm herself.

"I appreciate everything you've done for me and I can never thank you enough for saving me the other night, but I think it's time we alert the police about what Malcolm did and let the law take it from there. We can make sure he gets arrested and I'll be able to get to my son. It's time."

"You think it's time?" Sam finally said.

"I do."

"Interesting."

Sam's voice was cutting now. He was getting aggravated.

"What if he gets out on bail and comes home? Have you thought about that?"

"I'll get a restraining order."

"A restraining order would take too long. That's a stupid idea. What if he gets out and comes home and you can't see yet? How will you defend yourself and your child against Malcolm when you can't see?"

"I'll go to my sister's."

A chuckle. "You always have an answer."

A beat of silence between them.

"I saved your life."

"I know, and I'm grateful."

"Your husband was trying to beat you to death, and if I hadn't come when I did, you wouldn't be here."

Tracy started to cry again. She tugged harder on the chain, the fear taking over. "I know. And now we have to call for help."

"I am your help." Sam's voice was getting louder, his words coming faster. "I brought you to my house to give you the safety you need. You can't see. You have a bad concussion. You're still vulnerable. I brought you here to get you better."

"I appreciate that. All of it. I really do."

"But you want to leave."

"I just want to call the police and let them know what happened."

"So you can leave."

"So I can make sure Malcolm goes down for what he did and so I can see my son again. It must be frightening for him not knowing where I am. I have to let my family know I'm okay."

"All I've done for you, and you don't care."

"I do! I do care."

"The piss and the shit I clean out of your bedpan. The meds

I give you on a schedule that I have to keep. The food I prepare. The fact that I can't leave this place because you need to be taken care of all the time. You think you're the prisoner here? *I'm* the prisoner. *I'm* the one who can't leave."

Tracy felt like she was freefalling as the conversation spiraled out of control. Sam's footsteps slapped the floor, crossing to one end of the room, then back, then back again. He was pacing, getting angrier and more manic with every word, and there was nothing she could do except sit on the bed and hope he'd calm down. She'd triggered him and now had to wait for it to play out, for better or worse. She continued to play with the chain around her wrist, searching for a way to escape from it, but it was bound too tight.

"You'd be dead if it wasn't for me."

"I just want to call my family."

"I am your family!"

The room went quiet. The waves and the wind outside. The seagulls squawking. Nothing else.

Tracy could hear Sam breathing heavily. The footsteps stopped.

"Tell me about Jake."

The name came out of nowhere and felt like a punch to the gut. Tracy recoiled upon hearing it.

"Jake?" she asked through her tears.

"I heard you say his name a few times when you were sleeping. Who's Jake? You never mentioned him in any of our sessions."

"I... I don't like to talk about him."

"Why?" Footsteps coming closer. "Who is he?"

"An old boyfriend. A bad experience."

"Is he the reason you were leaving your husband?"

Tracy choked back her tears and shook her head. "No."

"Then why not bring him up during our sessions? If he's conscious enough in your mind that you call his name when you're sleeping, then he must be someone you think about often."

"I think about him every day."

"Then tell me who he is."

"No. I don't want to talk about him."

Another step closer.

"Were you cheating on your husband with him and using your supposed breakthrough with me as an excuse to leave Malcolm for him? Was I a prop in your game? Did you use me to get to the man you really wanted?"

Tracy remained silent, shaking her head as Sam hurled his accusations.

"Who is Jake?"

"Leave me alone."

"Tell me!"

"No!"

Something crashed next to her. Glass shattered on the ground. Tracy screamed and pulled away, cowering toward the opposite side of the bed, unable to go much further because of the chain wrapped around her wrist.

The room went silent again, then the footsteps retreated. She listened as the bedroom door opened, then slammed shut. She stayed where she was for what seemed like forever until she was convinced she was alone. She sat up in the bed and took a long, deep breath, trying to calm herself, knowing now what her subconscious had been screaming since the day she heard Dr. Devi's soothing voice in between consciousness and sleep.

Things were not as they seemed. Dr. Devi was not the man she thought he was.

Tracy was in danger.

DAY SIX

CHAPTER TWENTY-FIVE

Detective Taft decided to meet Jill Toomey down in the cafeteria of the office building she worked at on Summer Street. He was already sitting at a table for two when she arrived with a steaming cup of coffee in one hand and a stack of files in the other.

Jill was Kat Masterson's best friend. She was thirty years old, worked as a financial advisor with Merrill Lynch in Stamford, and graduated from UConn a year earlier than Kat. She was pretty, young and vibrant, had dark hair that was wrapped in a professional bun, olive skin, and dark eyes. Not too much makeup. Conservative suit. She looked like the real deal as far as he was concerned. A far cry from the funny and outrageous texts he'd found on Kat's phone. What he was seeing was, undoubtedly, Jill's professional persona.

Detective Taft stood when Jill approached the table. He extended his hand and waited for the young woman to put the coffee and files down before shaking.

"Thank you for meeting me," he said.

Jill dropped her stuff and hugged the man. He stumbled

back a few steps, caught off guard by the gesture. "I can't believe this happened," she said.

Taft did not reply.

Jill pulled away and sat down at the table. "Sorry. I didn't mean to get unprofessional. I just can't believe this happened. I don't know what to do or say. Please, make sure whoever did this stays behind bars for a very long time."

Taft sat in his chair and took out his phone, hit the record button, and placed it on the table.

"We're not resting until Kat's killer is brought to justice," he said. "I can promise you that. We're turning over every rock and investigating every lead. We're doing everything we can."

Jill's eyes glistened. "My heart's broken for real."

Taft waited for a moment. "Was Kat fighting with anyone? Someone at work giving her a hard time? Did she break off any relationships?"

"No. Everyone loved her."

"Was she seeing anyone?"

A nod. "It wasn't serious. Kind of like a friends with benefits thing."

"What was his name?"

"I don't know. None of us in our friend group did. We called him Big Daddy because he had money and when they got together, he would take her to fancy restaurants or Broadway shows or concerts that were hard to get tickets for. They'd spend a weekend here and there at posh bed and breakfasts. They had fun together, but she knew it wasn't anything serious."

"But you don't know his name?"

"Kat knew we'd disapprove so she never told us. Plus, she said it wasn't serious and she was just having fun. Calling him Big Daddy was a joke at first, but then it stuck." She leaned forward. "Do you think he had something to do with what happened?"

"Like I said, we're following through on every lead." Taft

shifted in his seat. "Why would Kat know you'd disapprove of who she as seeing?"

"Because he was married. And I think he was a client at her firm."

"Big Daddy was a client?"

Jill nodded. "It's just a theory, but the timing works out. She was working so hard with the way the real estate market was. I'm talking eighty-hour weeks, seven days a week, for a while. I invited her out to lunch, dinner, drinks, the club, and she kept refusing and telling me she had to work. There were a few nights she slept at the office before a handful of closings just because there was no time to go home. How are you going to work like that and still meet a guy and develop a relationship that turns into expensive weekend trips and exotic dinners? No one at her office is datable, so I figured it was a client. I asked her about it and she played coy, but she never denied it. That's as much as she'd give me. After a while I stopped asking. At the end of the day it was her business and not mine. Now I wonder if I should've kept pushing her to tell me who he was. If you think he had something to do with what happened, then I'm thinking maybe he wanted to get more serious and she didn't. Maybe after all the money he spent on her, he wanted to take things to the next level. And then he got pissed when she wouldn't give him what he wanted and..." She looked at him with desperation in her eyes. "You need to check and see who she was working with over the past few months."

Taft nodded, his mind working. "I asked her boss about Kat seeing any clients. He didn't suspect anything, but I know a warrant is being drawn up to get a list of the firm's customers."

"I'm sure he's going to be on there."

Jill started quietly crying at the table. Taft looked around and could see a couple of people sneaking glances, curious as to why the old man was making the young woman cry. He pushed a few napkins he'd gotten with his coffee across the table. Jill took one and dabbed her eyes. He pulled out a piece of paper from his jacket pocket, unfolded it, and slid it across the table.

"When we were in Kat's apartment, I noticed a picture frame on her vanity. Nothing in it. Struck me as odd. I saw a few pictures she'd taken on her phone and the same frame is in the background, and there's something in it. It's not a picture though. I was hoping you might know what it is. We haven't gotten access to her social media accounts yet, so if she posted about it, I wouldn't know."

Jill took the paper and looked at the black-and-white photo printed on it. She nodded immediately.

"She had a guitar pick in that frame. Belonged to Chris Martin. You know Coldplay?"

"Sure," he lied.

"Big Daddy surprised her one day with front row tickets at Madison Square Garden. She said it was one of the best nights of her life. Chris Martin tosses a pick into the crowd and she was right there to catch it. Took it home and put it in a frame the next day. You won't find any posts about it on her social media though. I don't think she wanted anyone else to know where she was or who she was with. She didn't even tell the others in our group. Just me."

"Any idea when this was?"

"Last winter. January maybe? I'm sure you can Google it."

Taft nodded again, smiled. "I'm sure I can."

"So, this confirms it," Jill said. "Big Daddy is your prime suspect. Why else would the killer remove the pick from the frame unless he was trying to take any items that linked him to her? That's the only logical explanation. Find Big Daddy and you'll find Kat's killer. I'm sure of it."

CHAPTER TWENTY-SIX

Missy sat on the floor, leaning against her bed. The room was dark. The edges of each window glowed from the sunlight outside, but inside there was just gray and black. Her thoughts tumbled upon one another, clarity turning to confusion. At first, she wasn't sure if Malcolm had anything to do with what happened to Tracy, but the more she thought about it, the more she realized it was simply too big of a coincidence for him not to. The day she asked for a divorce was the same day she goes missing? What are the odds? But she couldn't discount Malcolm's reactions to what was happening. He seemed so convincing that he had nothing to do with it, and he also seemed vested in finding her. The doubt began to creep in. Maybe he was as lost as she was. Maybe.

Neil Scranton was, indeed, a CPA from White Plains. Missy had looked it up on her phone after she returned to her bedroom. Too much information was coming at her at one time and it felt like nothing was connecting to what happened to her sister and where she might be. It had been almost a week since Tracy had vanished, which meant it had also been five days since the other investigation had most likely gotten started. She wondered how long it would take the police to put the pieces of that puzzle together and worried that she'd let something slip in Tracy's absence. She needed her sister back. She needed that steady hand in her life.

Missy got up from the floor and left the bedroom, bouncing down the stairs and hurrying into the kitchen to find Malcolm. As soon as she passed the refrigerator, she stopped. Malcolm was in the family room with Finn. She could hear the little boy's squeaky voice as he talked to his father. It was apparent he was crying. The tiny sniffles and crackling tone echoed through the otherwise quiet first floor.

"Are they going to find Mommy soon?"

"I hope so, bud."

"Can we help look for her?"

"The police just want us to stay put for now. If they need help, they'll ask us. They're doing everything they can. We need to try and be patient. I know it's hard, but that's what we have to do."

More tears.

"I saw on TV that we can ask people in the neighborhood to help look for Mommy and they can bring their dogs to help sniff for her and they can bring big sticks to walk in the woods with and a bunch of people can look at the same time and help the police. Can we do that too? Please?"

A deep, long, sigh.

"Maybe we can put something together soon. Right now, the police want us to stay out of their way so they can do what they have to do to find her."

"But if we can help the police, why would they say no?"

"Because they have their way of doing things and we can mess that up for them even when we're trying to help."

Finn began crying harder.

"I miss her."

A long pause before Malcolm's reply. His voice was beginning to crack as well.

"I miss her too, bud. I wish she was here with us right now. We'll find her. We have to."

Missy made her way into the family room and stood in the entrance, watching the father and his son having their moment. Finn was nestled in Malcom's embrace as he cried into his chest. Malcolm was running his hand through Finn's bushy hair, trying to soothe him as tears ran down his own cheeks. It was both endearing and heartbreaking to watch.

"I think Finn's right," Missy said, interrupting the scene. "I think we should make a call for some community volunteers and I think we should start looking for Tracy ourselves. It's been long enough. We can't sit around forever."

They both looked up at her, their eyes red and swollen, their tears shining in the overhead light.

"I've asked Detective Evans a few times if I could help and she keeps saying no," Malcolm said.

"That's because she's not done looking into you," Missy replied. "But I don't think we need to ask permission. It's my sister and your wife. This is our business. I say we don't ask anybody anything and we take matters into our own hands. I'll blast something out on my Facebook page and we'll hold a press conference. I'll set up a page dedicated to tips and posts about it, and once we get the public support, it'll be hard for the police to shut it down."

Malcolm thought for a moment. "Yeah, I guess that could work."

Finn looked back and forth between his father and his aunt. "We can help look for Mommy?"

"I think so, bud."

"Thank you!"

He hugged his father tight and his entire demeanor

changed. Hope could do that to a person. Hope could be a lifeline.

"Finn," Missy said as she walked over to the couch and sat on the edge of it. "Go get dressed and we'll figure out what we're going to do next. I have to talk to your father a sec."

"Okay."

The little boy scampered out of the family room and ran up to the second floor. She could hear the pitter-patter of his socked feet climbing the stairs with ferocity.

"I think a search might help," Malcolm said as he got up from the floor he was sitting on and wiped the tears from his eyes. He sat back down on the loveseat across from Missy. "What's up? You find any more evidence that I made my wife disappear?"

The jab stung. She couldn't deny that.

"I'm sorry I jumped to conclusions," Missy began. She folded her hands in front of her and squeezed them. "I want to say something like 'I know you loved her and could never hurt her' but she was leaving you for a reason. Maybe you *were* hurting her."

"I wasn't. I don't know why she was leaving me."

Missy stared at him, unblinking. He stared back.

"Malcolm. I know you're lying. Why was she leaving you?"

"I don't know."

"Who is she?"

"What?"

"Who is she?"

Malcom held her gaze for a few more seconds, then looked away, letting his chin fall against his chest. "It just happened and it was a mistake," he whispered. "I wasn't out there looking to have an affair. I was happy with my life. Tracy didn't do anything wrong. As far as I was concerned, our marriage was fine. There's no real explanation for it. I wish there was."

"Damn you."

"I'm sorry."

Missy wiped her eyes and took a breath. "She must've known. That's why she was leaving you. And after what she went through with Jake? How could you hurt her like that? She must've found out and you know there's no forgiveness when it comes to infidelity. Not with her. She's not going to let herself fall down that rabbit hole ever again. Jake messed her up forever."

"I wish I could take it all back. I love her and I want to find her."

"I'm thinking maybe your other woman had something to do with Tracy disappearing. Maybe Tracy was the one person holding up some kind of new life this woman had planned for the two of you. Gotta get rid of the last obstacle so you two can be together forever. Something like that."

Malcolm shook his head. "No way. What we had was fun and casual. It was nothing serious. Totally superficial. She wasn't looking for anything long term."

"Did she know you were married?"

"Yeah."

"Then she knew there was a wife to get rid of if she wanted you all to herself."

Malcolm was quiet, thinking.

"Who is she?"

"There's no way she had anything to do with Tracy disappearing. She's sweet and kind. She doesn't have a harmful bone in her body."

Missy slid to the edge of the couch and stared at him. She didn't like hearing him speak of his mistress that way. She spoke slowly, the tension in her voice cutting through the bird song outside the picture window.

"Who. Is. She?"

Malcolm looked down at the floor, then back up. He rubbed the stubble on his chin and shook his head again.

"Her name's Kat. Kat Masterson. She works at the law firm I have my business at. I'm telling you, she has nothing to do with this."

Missy let the name slip from her lips as she repeated the identity of Malcolm's secret lover.

"Kat Masterson. Got it."

DAY SEVEN

CHAPTER TWENTY-SEVEN

"I didn't do what they said!"

Jake's voice was pitching higher, his eyes bulging as he crossed the foyer into the living room where Tracy was curled up on the couch, crying. He stood over her, his chest rising and falling in great heaves of breaths. He was panicked and furious and terrified all at the same time. She could see the tips of his fingers were still dark with the ink the police used to fingerprint him at the station.

"They're lying! I didn't touch that girl!"

Tracy looked away, burying her head in the cushions, crying harder. She could feel him towering above her.

"Tracy, look at me. I didn't do any of it."

She refused to lift her head from the couch. She was scared and furious and so confused.

"I saw you with her!"

"She was a student helping me clean up as punishment. That's all you saw."

"I saw the look in her eyes. I should've known something was wrong."

"I didn't do anything!"

"You're saying this girl just suddenly decided to make up a lie and come forward?" she sobbed. "Why, Jake? Why would she lie like that?"

"To get back at me for punishing her? I don't know."

"She's not lying! I saw her face. This... this relationship. Us. Your life with me. That's the lie!"

Jake knelt down next to her and pulled her hands away from her chest, tightening his grip around them, leaning in and pulling her toward him. "I love you, Tracy. I need you by my side right now. I need you to show everyone that what this girl is saying about me doesn't mesh with the man I am to you. I need you to love me."

He lifted her face from the cushions and she looked him in the eyes, her tears coming so fast she could barely see.

"I love you," he said.

She shook her head. "The police showed me the video from the equipment shed. I believe Angela. I don't believe you. I don't even know who you are, and I don't love you. Not after this."

Time stopped between them. Jake just looked at her, transfixed, as if each letter of each word had to penetrate his psyche before he could understand the full breadth of what she said. After a few minutes passed, a tight little grin spread across his face and his gaze turned distant. He slowly nodded and let go of her hands.

"You believe this girl over me?"

"I want you to leave."

"You believe that lying whore over your fiancé? The man you've loved for all these years? The man who wants to spend the rest of his life with you? You're tossing that all away over this lying bitch?"

"I saw the video."

"More lies."

"Get out, Jake!"

Tracy turned back into the pillow and felt Jake climb to his feet. He stood over her again, breathing, panting.

"Last chance," he said. "Tell me you love me."

"Get out of this house!"

"Okay, then. If that's what you want. We'll end it. Right now."

———

There was no way to track time in the blackness, but it felt like it had been a while since Sam had been in her room. Tracy woke up when the pain in her eyes got too bad to sleep. She moved as best she could in the bed, stretching her arms and legs, flipping around within the confines the chain would allow. The sheets were starting to smell. Her skin was oily and her hair dirty. She needed a shower and a change of clothes. There was a general funk in the room that was getting worse.

The bedroom door opened and footsteps came in. Tracy tensed up and looked toward the door, although she could see nothing.

The footsteps stopped.

"Hello," Sam said.

Tracy was quiet.

"I'm sorry for losing my temper at you yesterday." His voice was back to normal, reserved, safe. "I've been under a lot of stress lately with what happened to you, and me bringing you here, and it just got away from me for a second. I'm sorry. That's not the person I am. I'll be better."

"Thank you," Tracy replied. She could tell he was sorry, but it was too late for such simple things. She seen a glimpse of the man he was behind his mask of stability and calm. She was scared. Of him. He was unstable and volatile. She knew she'd have to be careful.

"I contacted Missy. I told her you were safe, but left it there for now. She knows you're alive and that you're okay and that I'm nursing you back to health. I'm going to try and get Finn up here so you can see him."

Tracy couldn't believe what she was hearing.

"How did you get Missy's number?"

"She's listed as one of your emergency contacts in your file."

"Does she know Malcolm tried to kill me?"

"No. I just told her to keep Finn and not to let Malcolm near her. She was yelling at me, trying to get me to tell her where you are, but I told her I can't right now. She was very upset."

"Yeah, that sounds like Missy."

"I explained that I'd tell her more once I got what I need from you."

Again, the mood in the room suddenly changed.

"What do you need from me?" Tracy asked.

The footsteps came closer. The rocking chair creaked as Sam sat in it.

"Tell me about Jake. I need that, and then we'll see about getting Finn up here."

Tracy slumped against the headboard. All of a sudden, there was nothing but the memory of that day. The day that everything changed.

"I don't like to talk about Jake. I never told you about him."

"No, you didn't. Which brings me to a point about trust. All those sessions we had and those moments you shared with me. They were lies."

"I never lied."

"You did. Your omission was a lie. You told me you were leaving Malcolm because you needed to rediscover yourself and no longer needed the protection you thought he provided. It was my fault for allowing you to guide me with this self-diagnosis, but we'd made such progress, I thought you were telling me the truth."

"I was."

"Then why are you calling out Jake's name in your sleep? Who is he? Are you leaving Malcolm for him?"

"No."

"Then tell me about him."

Tracy was numb. In the darkness, she could see the scene play out before her as if she was watching a movie on a screen. The pain associated with the mere mention of his name was sharp and all-encompassing. She wanted to look away, but there was nowhere to turn. In her darkness there was no on and off switch. He was there and he wasn't leaving. Not unless she exorcized him.

"You can do this. I believe in you."

Sam's voice was soothing. It sounded like she remembered back in his office when he would help her talk through the things that were bothering her, and him getting her to open up always felt better in the end. She wanted that again. She wanted to purge the nightmare that was Jake Bollard by giving their story a voice. Just once. Maybe that's all it would take. She took a deep, uneven breath as the most horrific time in her life spilled out before her.

"Jake was the love of my life. He was everything I thought I wanted in a man. He was strong, confident, sure of himself, and funny. My God, he was so funny. He used to make me laugh until my stomach hurt. He was self-deprecating and always willing to admit when he was wrong. That takes a special kind of strength, you know? To be comfortable enough with yourself to admit when you made a mistake. I loved that about him."

"Did you fall for him right away?"

"Yes and no. I'd known him since he moved to our town in eighth grade, but we didn't really get to know one another until the summer going into sophomore year in high school. Then we started dating and we never looked back. I dated him all the way to graduation and I went away to college and he got a job with the district right out of high school. We were three hours away from each other, but we talked every night and he'd drive up to see me every other weekend. Time stood still when I was with him. We were perfect together."

"It sounds like you were happy."

"I was."

"And you trusted him."

"Implicitly."

"What changed?"

Tracy choked back her tears. "Everything. I was two years out of school when we got engaged. We were the happy ending that everyone in our town got a kick out of. High school sweethearts getting married. We were written up in the local paper and everything. Then one day I get a call from my mom. Jake got arrested. I couldn't understand why and my mom wasn't making any sense while she was crying through the phone. I got down to the police station to find out what was happening, and I waited for hours."

"That must've been a confusing time for you."

She could feel her tears dampening the bandages. Her stomach turned as she could see herself sitting across the sheriff's desk as he recited the crimes Jake was being charged with.

"He knew how to target her. He was a gym teacher at the high school, so he was always around, just on the periphery of things, hearing conversations and assessing the students while at the same time being the cool teacher with the easy class. He waited. He was patient as predators typically are. He only chose the one who he knew had too much to lose by saying something. Going after the popular cheerleader or student body president or the hot girl everyone knew would be too risky. If they talked, people would listen. They would believe them. Or at least be open to hearing what they had to say. He chose the voiceless. He chose the loser who had no friends and was in her third foster home. Angela Martinez. A girl like that knew how to keep her mouth shut. She knew if she did speak, no one would believe her and she'd be moved out of town and swept under the rug."

"What did he do?" Sam asked.

The room was quiet, but Tracy could still hear herself crying at the police station as she watched the love of her life being whisked away for processing.

"It started with dirty talk, then moved to touching, then escalated to rape. Went on for two years. And he was right. She didn't say a word. He said it was consensual, but Angela was underage. It was rape any way you looked at it. He got caught because he didn't know the school had installed security cameras in the back of the building by the supply shed because someone had been cutting the lock and stealing sports equipment. The custodian's supply room was right next to the equipment shed. They saw him escorting her inside. The rest snowballed from there."

"That must've been hard. Learning that the man you thought you knew was someone completely different."

"I was in complete shock. Then one day he shows up at my house, out on bail his parents posted. He told me all of it was a big misunderstanding, and that Angela was lying and that he didn't do any of the things he was being accused of. But he'd already told the police that the sex was consensual, so he was lying to me. I knew what he was. He tried to get me to understand, but how could I? He was a monster."

"What did you do?"

"I told him to get out. I screamed at him and told him to get away from me. He kept trying to reason with me, but after a while he knew he'd never get me to see his side of anything. He knew I didn't want to see his side of anything. So, he left. What I didn't realize was that he'd gone to his car, grabbed his shotgun he used for turkey hunting, and come back. He kicked down the door, took me hostage, and made me listen. Spent the next few hours explaining and apologizing and trying to get me to forgive him. All the while the police are surrounding the house. Things are escalating. I knew how it was going to end. He said he was going to kill us both so we could be together forever. I could've tried to talk him out of it, but the truth is, I wanted him to die, and a part of me wanted to die too. It would've been so much easier to just be another Jake Bollard victim instead of being the surviving fiancée who had a hard time convincing others that she never knew the secret life her lover led."

"But you did survive."

"I guess. I don't really think of it that way. He could've killed me. He just didn't."

"And you found Malcolm. Who you thought could offer a protection you felt you needed."

"Until I didn't anymore, I found out he was cheating on me, which is the one thing there's no coming back from. Not with me. That's why I had to end it."

"You never told me Malcolm was cheating."

"Well, there you go," Tracy sighed. She bit her bottom lip to keep from crying again. It still hurt to admit it. "I just did."

The rocking chair creaked again as Sam stood up. Tracy waited for him to say something, but all she heard were his footsteps pacing the floor in front of her bed and his light breathing.

"Are you mad?" she asked.

"No. I'm just taking in everything you told me. I understand better now why you felt the need to be so definitive when it came to Malcolm. You want to be loved and protected, but most of all, you want a true partner. Someone you can rely on. Someone who will always be there for you regardless of the circumstance. Someone you can trust."

"Yes."

The waves crashed in the background of their conversation.

"No more lies, Tracy. This can't work with lies or omissions.

The more I understand about you and your past, the more I can help. All I want to do is help."

"Okay."

He began to walk away.

"I want to see my son," Tracy said as the bedroom door opened.

"I'll see what I can do."

The door shut and Tracy was alone again. She closed her eyes and listened to Sam's last sentence replaying in her mind, trying to determine if he was being sincere or not, knowing how alone and vulnerable she was. She was scared, but knew she had to stay calm and play it as cool as she could. She wanted so desperately to see Finn. And she could only imagine what her sister was going through, as alone as she was, with the weight of everything on her shoulders, wondering where she was. Nothing worked without Tracy. She had to get home. She had to see her little boy.

She wondered if either of those things would ever actually happen.

CHAPTER TWENTY-EIGHT

Malcolm stood at the top of his driveway, hugging his son who held a blown-up picture of his mother, her face bright and smiling, his face pale with wide and frightened eyes. The small array of microphones that had been propped up in front of them looked like a giant flower blooming from thin stalks in the ground below. It had taken a few hours to put together the press conference, but a few strategic calls to people he knew in the local media helped. Missy had been instrumental with her social media contacts as well. The reporters who worked with the local Gannett papers and some on the community news team were able to reach out to surrounding affiliates and before he knew it, the three stations from the major networks in the city had pulled up in their news vans, ready to hear what he and Finn had to say. Now, the reporters were huddled beyond the microphones and floodlights, newspapers, internet, and television alike, waiting for him to begin. He could see most of them had their phones out, recording what he was about to say. A handful of cameras had been set up on tripods, ready to catch every moment. Behind the reporters, some of his neighbors had

emerged from their homes to watch. Of course they did. Someone's drama was always someone else's entertainment.

"Thank you for coming on short notice," he began. "I know
it's cold. I'll make this brief. My name is Malcolm Cowan. This
is my son, Finn. He's seven years old. We just wanted to bring
to the media's attention that my wife, Tracy Cowan, has been
missing for almost a week now." Finn held the picture of his
mother higher. "Tracy was driving home from the city when she
called me and told me she thought someone was following her.
The police found her SUV in the Hudson River at George's
Island in Buchanan, but there was no sign of my wife. Her
purse and cell phone were in the car. The back of her SUV was
smashed up like someone hit it, so we're figuring foul play. I'm
asking anyone who thinks they might have seen her or her SUV
in that area seven days ago to call the Westchester County
Police. Detective Kelly Evans is working the case."

"Where is Detective Evans now?" a reporter asked.

Malcolm shrugged. "Working the case, I hope."

The reporters moved in as a group, calling out their questions, one after the other.

"Are there any suspects?"

"Are you a suspect?"

"Do you know of anyone who might've wanted to hurt your
wife?"

"Has anyone considered she might've run away on her
own?"

"Why has it taken a week to bring this to the media's
attention?"

Malcolm instinctively placed a hand on Finn's tiny chest
and pushed the boy behind him. He held up his other hand to
stop the press from advancing.

"I'm not answering any questions at this time," Malcolm
shouted as he backed away from the microphones. "This press
conference was just to make everyone aware of the situation. If

anyone has information about where my wife might be, I'm begging you to please call the Westchester County Police. My son wants his mother home."

"What do you want to say to your wife if she's listening?" a voice asked from behind one of the spotlights.

Malcolm recognized the voice, but couldn't place it in the current setting. He looked into the cameras that were lined in the back. "Tracy, I love you and we're doing everything we can to find you. Finn loves you too. Please be strong."

The reporters kept coming, shouting their questions and moving past the set of microphones. Malcolm picked Finn up and was about to scurry toward the house when that same voice carried over the others with a question that froze him in his tracks.

"Mr. Cowan, is there any truth to the rumor that your wife asked for a divorce the morning she went missing?"

The other reporters stopped shouting and turned. Malcolm stood still, Finn pressed against his chest, as he watched Reagan Hart emerge from behind the lights like the star that she was. Reagan was in her late thirties, beautiful and sophisticated in every way. Her red lipstick against her bronzer was absolute perfection and her dark hair was a stylist's work of art. Even her navy-blue pantsuit was tailored to fit every curve. She was the anchor for the evening news that came on nationally after the local news was done. He couldn't believe she was standing in his driveway. None of it felt real.

"Reagan Hart?" he stammered. "What are you doing here?"

Reagan stepped closer, her underlings parting as she approached.

"Young pretty wife goes missing in suburbia," she replied. "I want to know why."

"Yeah, me too."

"In my experience, it's usually the spouse."

"Not this time."

"But your wife did ask you for a divorce the morning she went missing. Is that correct?"

Malcolm's heart started pounding. All of a sudden, the spotlights were hot against his face. He blinked against the brightness and could feel each and every reporter staring at him, waiting for him to answer, ready to convict him as soon as he told the truth.

"I can't comment on any of that," he said quietly.

"That's too bad," Reagan replied. "I didn't want to have to make you the prime suspect on my show. No choice now."

"I just want Tracy found."

"Then tell us where she is."

Malcolm felt Finn move under his arms and he was instantly present again. "Jesus Christ," he seethed. "My son is right here. I came to you all for help, not to be accused."

"Okay. Answer the question."

"Go to hell."

Malcolm turned away from the crowd just as the others began shouting new questions to him. He could hear accusations and innuendo mixed in with other things they wanted to know. He took Finn and walked quickly down the slate pathway, up the front steps, and into the house.

Missy was standing in the foyer, leaning on the banister, watching them.

"Jeez, that went a little sideways," she said.

Malcolm put Finn down and locked the deadbolt on the door. "Yeah, well, Reagan-friggin-Hart came out of nowhere and ambushed me."

"I saw that. Maybe we were stupid to think the press could help us."

"Maybe. I'm not answering any of their questions so they can spin this all around on me. We got the word out. Now they'll help spread that word when they report on it, and hopefully somebody saw something and can call the police about it."

Missy huffed a laugh as she peeked out a side window. "In the span of about two seconds, that press conference became all about you and what you did to Tracy. No one's going to care about finding her unless it puts you in their crosshairs. Buckle up because they're gonna spin this their way, and if you're not answering any questions, they'll keep spinning until the court of public opinion convicts you."

"I don't care. As long as we find Tracy. I'll sacrifice myself for her."

"I hope you mean that."

"I do."

Missy turned away from the window and looked Malcolm up and down slowly, taking him in. "Okay then," she finally said. "I got spaghetti boiling. Dinner's almost ready. Wash up. I'll meet you both in the kitchen."

Finn held up his picture. "What do I do with this?"

"Bring it with you," Missy replied. "We'll put it on Mommy's chair. She eats with us tonight. That's an order."

CHAPTER TWENTY-NINE

Kelly Evans sat at her desk scrolling through Tracy Cowan's Facebook page while the rest of the department operated around her. Uniformed officers made their way across the expansive floor, some heading out to patrol while others headed to desks of their own to make out reports or log their changeovers. A few of the other detectives worked silently across from her and still others barked into phones or called out commands to whoever might be listening. The unit was always noisy, but she'd found solace in the chaos. No need for noise-canceling headphones or a quiet place to hide out in. The bedlam was where she honed her skills as a police officer. She would carry that forward as a detective. Pandemonium was her security blanket.

Sergeant Leeds made his way over and leaned on the top of her workstation wall. "All the snow's melted at the park," he said. "We found some broken glass from the taillight and this." He placed an evidence bag down on her desk. Inside it was a small black box, no bigger than a book of matches.

Kelly picked up the bag, peering inside. "What is it?"

"A tracking device. One side is a magnet, so you stick it on the car you want to follow and the GPS signal tracks onto a phone. You can get them on Amazon and eBay and whatnot."

"Tracy *was* being followed. Just like she told her husband."

"Looks that way." Leeds took the bag back. "I'm sending it to tech to see if they can figure out what phone the data uploads to. We find the phone, we find the person who was at the park that night."

"And hopefully we find Tracy. I need a win here soon. The chief is getting restless."

Leeds pointed to a flatscreen television that was mounted in the center wall of the detective's wing. "Malcolm Cowan's press conference won't help. You see it?"

"Unfortunately, I did."

"Reagan Hart did a number on him."

"That's what he gets for going rogue."

"Any clue he was planning it?"

"None. And now all he's done is made himself the suspect and add a ton of busy work while we field phone calls about possible Tracy sightings. Plus, we're going to start getting pressure to arrest him, and we're not there yet. Maybe not ever. I would've talked him out of it if I'd known. Idiot."

Leeds nodded. "The house sweep came up empty too. Nothing out of the ordinary. No traces of blood. No traces of the Hudson River. A ton of prints and general findings you'd expect in a house with an active family, but it can all be discounted. Our last step is pulling footage from his Ring doorbell. Shot in the dark, but we'll see if anything unusual shows up."

"Damn. I was really hoping we'd get something solid."

"Have you had a chance to look at the surveillance camera footage from the security camera at the entrance to George's Island?"

"Also a dead end. It was too dark. They don't put the extra lights on in the off-season. Saves money against the budget. The camera catches Tracy's car coming in and another car about five minutes later, but you can't make out the model other than it's a sedan. Can't see a license plate. The only distinguishing feature was that one headlight wasn't working."

"Yeah, Malcolm Cowan mentioned Tracy said something about the car following her sticking out. Maybe that was it. The one headlight."

"Maybe."

Leeds handed over a file. "Not all is lost," he said. "I have a feeling this'll get us stepping in the right direction."

Kelly took the file and opened it. "What's this?"

"These are the texts and call records from Tracy Cowan's cell phone. No unusual calls from what I can tell, but you'll need to take a closer look. I just skimmed through. The texts are interesting though. Malcolm's texts are on top."

Kelly flipped to the page with Tracy's texts to and from Malcolm. Each one was printed out. She guided her finger down the page as she read.

WHERE ARE YOU?

CALL ME

PICK UP YOUR PHONE!

YOU CAN'T IGNORE ME!

I'M GOING TO FIND YOU

"Jesus," she muttered. "Seems a little unhinged."

"His wife just told him she was leaving him and then she split for the day. Truth be told, I'd be angry too, but this looks like it's enough to go ask him about it."

"Maybe."

"Turn to the next section. Those are Malcolm Cowan's texts from *his* phone. I highlighted what you need to see in blue."

Tracy flipped to the second set of texts. The exchange on top was between Malcolm and a contact named Neil.

IT'S ME

> *YOU GIVE ANY THOUGHT TO WHAT WE*
> *TALKED*
> *ABOUT?*

I DID

> *AND?*

DO IT

Tracy dropped the paper as if it might burn her. "Whoa."

"My thoughts exactly."

She looked up at the sergeant who was rocking back and forth on his heels, waiting for her next instruction. A little smirk was on his face. He knew they were getting somewhere. So did she.

"You think Malcolm would be smart enough to call the press conference and ask for tips on things like missing wives and broken cars in an effort to overwhelm the department and throw us off him?"

"I don't know," he said. "If he did, it backfired when Reagan Hart showed up."

"We need to play this cool. These texts aren't enough for an arrest warrant and even though they're enough for me to be able to bring him in for questioning, I don't want to let him know we're aware they exist. I'm going to go through the rest of the stuff and see if there's anything else. In the meantime, let's get a unit on him. I don't want him to get nervous and run while we're putting this all together."

"Consider it done. Eyes on him at all times. Ten-four."

THIRTY
TWO MONTHS EARLIER

Missy Rollins sat down across from Kat and gently placed her coffee on the table between them. "Sorry I'm late. Had a rough start this morning."

Kat brushed the thought away with a wave of her hand, but the truth of the matter was, Missy did not look like herself. Her hair was windblown and she was kind of panting like she'd been running. A thin layer of sweat made her skin glisten in the overhead lighting and her outfit looked a bit mismatched. This was not the woman who'd visited the firm a few weeks earlier. It looked as if Missy was, indeed, having one of those days.

"No worries. You're not that late. It's only been a few minutes. I'll survive."

Missy caught her breath and let out an exhale. "Were you able to get everything I need?"

"Yes." Kat pushed a file across the table. "Basically, we can draft you a Business Continuity Agreement as well as a Legal Transfer Certificate. I've put samples of both in the file for you to look at. The Continuity Agreement names a successor in the business should the principal become incapacitated or unable to perform the duties of running day-to-day operations. It allows a smooth transition to ensure the business keeps functioning in the event something happens to the principal."

"And the Legal Transfer?"

"That actually transfers ownership of the business. That's usually done in the event of death. Think of it as a will for the business, but death doesn't necessarily have to be the trigger. We cater the language to how you want it to work."

Missy opened the file and flipped through the pages, skimming the language. "Thanks. I'll take a closer look when I get back to the office."

"No problem," Kat replied. "Call me with any questions. After you let me know the structure you want to set up, I can have a draft out to you within a week."

Missy closed the file and took a sip of her coffee. She sat back in her seat and stared at Kat for a moment. Kat could feel the mood between them change just a bit.

"This is out of the blue," Missy began. "But any chance you were at the Coldplay concert the other night at Madison Square Garden? I was pretty sure it was you, in the front, almost center stage, but your back was to me and it was too packed for me to get to you to say hi."

Kat nodded and laughed, the tension in her shoulders immediately relaxing. "Yeah, that was me! You totally should have said hello. That was a great show."

"They're the best."

"I caught Chris Martin's pick."

"No way!"

"Threw it right to me."

"I'm jealous!" Missy laughed and leaned forward, lowering her voice. "And that guy you were with. Cute."

Kat smiled and shrugged. "Yeah, he's okay."

"He looked familiar. What's his name?"

Kat could feel herself blush as her stomach tightened. "I know this sounds strange, but I'd rather not say. I hope you don't think that's rude. It's just that everything's kind of new and he's older and I like to keep my personal life private. I've always been that way."

"Come on," Missy coaxed. "Attorney–client privilege. I won't say anything. I just thought I knew him and wanted to see if his name rang a bell."

Kat looked at her and shook her head. "I'd rather not say. Please."

"Okay." Missy finally said as she held up her hands. "I don't mean to pry and I certainly don't take offense. You do you. I can respect that. I just thought I knew him, is all. Anyway, good luck. He's a cutie."

"Thanks."

"I'll call you with the language I need in these documents."

"Sounds good."

Missy got up from her seat. "Things are going to happen sooner rather than later, so you'll be hearing from me."

Kat forced a smile. She wanted the woman out of her office. The talk about Malcolm was unsettling. She hated the fact that Missy had seen them. "I look forward to it."

Missy smiled in return. "I bet you do."

DAY EIGHT

CHAPTER THIRTY-ONE

"This goddamned phone won't stop ringing!"

Jake stalked his way over to the phone that was sitting on a table next to the television stand and tore the cord from the wall. The ringing instantly ceased, bringing the house quiet again.

Tracy was hyperventilating from crying. She remained on the floor near the couch, her knees tucked against her chest, her face resting on her hands as she heaved breath after breath, trying desperately to calm herself, to get her breathing under control. The sun was beginning to set and dusk was taking hold. The flash of emergency lights illuminated the otherwise darkening room, bringing a strobe effect of red and blue that danced on the walls and ceiling.

Jake positioned himself against the wall next to one of the living room windows so he could peek out and see what the police were doing. He had a look of determination about him as he gripped his shotgun against his body, his index finger lingering dangerously inside the trigger guard.

"I'm not going to jail," he said more to himself than to Tracy. "There's only one way the cops are carrying me out of here, and *that's in a body bag." He looked over at her. "Maybe they'll be carrying two."*

"Don't say that," Tracy sobbed. "You're going to get through this. I'm going to help you."

"There's no getting through anything. I'm not going to jail. I'm not going to let them make those lies into truths. I didn't rape that girl. I didn't do any of the shit they're accusing me of!"

"Then give yourself up and tell them that. Make them prove it at trial and if you're innocent, you'll go free."

Jake began to laugh. "Nah, that ain't how that works. Not for people like me."

Tracy lifted her head and sniffled. She stared at her fiancé, her eyes narrowing. "Then just kill yourself," she said. "Get it over with and pull the trigger. Why wait? Why make everyone sit around and try and negotiate with you? If your end game is to kill yourself, do it."

Jake turned away from the window and stared back at her. "I'm not deciding whether or not to kill myself," he growled. "And I'm not buying time or delaying my end. I'm deciding if I should take you with me. And I haven't made up my mind yet."

A clap woke Tracy from her sleeping memory. She was in the blackness again, but she could hear the world around her.

"I did it."

Sam sounded happy. Almost too happy. Perhaps a bit unhinged. Her stomach tightened when she heard him and she instinctively pulled on the chain.

"What did you do?"

Footsteps into the room.

"I found your story about Jake online. You *were* telling me the truth. I appreciate that, Tracy. Building trust is important."

Tracy didn't reply. She didn't like how jovial he sounded. It was a happy kind of madness and it scared her.

"You didn't tell me about Frank though."

The name exploded in her darkness and she recoiled, remaining silent.

"Two serious boyfriends and they both ended up dead?"

"Frank died in a car accident," she choked. "And he wasn't serious."

"It's no wonder you sought strength and safety with Malcolm. Your track record was a mess! What are the odds of two boyfriends dying within a few years? They must be astronomical!"

Sam didn't sound professional or empathetic. She'd never heard him like that in any of their sessions.

"Another important point in your life that you didn't tell me about. But that's okay, because I have a treat for you. Something to show you that I can be trusted and that I'm a friend. Maybe more than a friend."

Tracy knew she should reply, but had no idea what to say.

"Would you like to see your son?"

A pause, the mood in the room lifting a bit. Tracy waited for a moment, not quite sure she'd heard the words correctly, then shot up in her bed, dizziness overtaking her for a moment as white lights exploded in her blackness. "What did you say?"

"Finn is here. Would you like to see him?"

"Yes!"

Tracy couldn't help but let a little-girl giggle slip from her lips. Suddenly, the blindness and the chain around her wrist and the fear she felt being in a house she'd never been to with a man she didn't really know dissipated. These things were all insignificant nuisances now that she knew her son was there with her. Perhaps her situation wasn't as bad as she thought. Maybe Sam really did need her to get better before they could go to the police. Maybe he was acting in her best interest this entire time and she just wasn't prepared to trust anyone. But now her son was here and things seemed logical instead of frightening. Or perhaps the questions that should've been popping through her mind were muted by the excitement that took over.

Sam's footsteps exited the room and everything drew quiet. She could hear muted conversation, but couldn't tell exactly what was being said. The footsteps returned, and behind them, she could hear the skip-walk of a little boy's tiny feet scurrying across the floor.

"Go see your mom."

"Baby!"

Tracy sat all the way up in bed, arms outstretched, a smile beaming from ear to ear. The skip-walk grew louder and Finn fell into her chest. She hugged him tight, sobbing as joy filled her. She couldn't believe her boy was with her. Safe. Unharmed. Her hands began touching and feeling every bit of him. His frail little back. The vertebrae that stuck out of his skin. His thin wrists and small hands and skinny fingers and plump lips. His long neck. His...

Tracy stopped what she was doing and pushed the boy away from her. She pushed so hard she heard him fall from the bed and onto the floor. The smile that had been plastered on her face morphed into a scowl. The joy that had filled her heart turned cold. Terror engulfed her.

"What are you doing?" Sam asked. His footsteps crossed the room and she could hear the little boy whimpering.

"I'm sorry," Tracy choked. She put on a smile again, trying desperately to hide her fear. "He hit my face by accident and it was just a reflex from the pain. Come here, baby."

She felt the boy climb back up on the bed and she held him, rocking him against her chest as she kissed the top of his head. Her instincts told her to play along because if a man could do something like that, there was no way of knowing what else he might be capable of.

"Are you happy?" Sam asked.

"I am. Thank you."

Sam was standing over her. She kept the boy pressed up against her, running her hand down his back over and over, feeling his hair against her cheek.

"I can be the man you've been looking for," Sam said quietly. "I can give you stability and protection and something the others couldn't. I can also give you unconditional love. I can give you the relationship you've wanted since you were a girl in high school. The fairy tale. Happiness like you've never experienced before. I can give it to you, Tracy. You and Finn. We can be a family."

Tracy couldn't look at him. She buried her face in the boy's head, remaining quiet. There were no words to fill the silence between them. All she knew at that moment were two things. The first was that no matter how she looked at her situation, she knew she was trapped. In the bed. In the house. With Sam. Trapped. There was no way out. She could see that now. He would never let her leave. She was her prisoner and the weight of that fact finally sinking in crushed her.

The second thing she knew beyond a shadow of a doubt was that the boy she held against her chest was not her son. She had no idea who it was, but it wasn't Finn. A mother knows such things.

CHAPTER THIRTY-TWO

The air was frigid and froze Missy's body as she walked out of the police station and down the ramp toward the parking lot. The meeting with Detective Evans had been useless. A week had already passed and the only things that were clear was the fact that the detective had no new leads and no idea where Tracy was. All the corporate speak and false reassurances could only be tolerated for so long. She didn't give a rat's ass about an ongoing investigation. She wanted answers. It appeared she might have to go looking for them herself. As for the other thing, she had no idea where those cops were. Just as useless as the Westchester County PD. The entire game was waiting on the police to make their move. She wondered how long she'd have to continue to wait.

"Miss Rollins!"

Missy turned to find Reagan Hart winding her way through the cars in the lot, approaching quickly on heels that clicked the concrete. She was stunning, even with the cameras turned off. Perfect hair. Perfect makeup. A light blue overcoat that made the woman look like she was worth a million dollars. Missy stood frozen, half star-struck and half bewildered that such a celebrity would even know her name in the first place. She pushed her stringy hair out of her eyes and looked down at the cheap yoga pants, oversized sweatshirt, and faux leather jacket she was wearing. How embarrassing.

"Miss Rollins," Reagan repeated as she finally caught up with Missy and stood in front of her. "It's so nice to meet you. I'm Reagan Hart."

"Yeah, I know who you are," Missy replied, cursing herself for not coming up with a more dignified response. She backed up a step, not quite understanding why the reporter would be calling for her. "How do you know who I am?"

"I'm not just a news anchor. I'm an investigative journalist and your sister's disappearance is big news. It's my job to know all the players."

"Oh."

Reagan pointed toward the police station. "Anything I should be made aware of?"

"No. I was just meeting with Detective Evans to find out if there are any updates. There aren't."

"Must be frustrating."

"It is."

Reagan gently took Missy by the arm and guided her away from the building. "I was going to meet with Detective Evans myself, but maybe you can save me the trouble."

"Okay."

"Your sister is a recent cancer survivor. Breast that spread into the lymph nodes? Mastectomy?"

Missy stopped walking and looked at the woman. "How do you know that?"

A beautiful, disarming smile. "Like I said, I'm an investigative journalist. It's my job."

"But I mean, who told you? Isn't that, like, doctor–patient confidentiality?"

"I'm sorry, I can't reveal my source. I was just wondering

why her cancer diagnosis and subsequent victory over it hasn't been brought up in the investigation."

"Why would it?"

"Oh, honey," Reagan said, concern taking over her tone. "It's important. Going through something like that can change a person. Could be the reason why your sister decided to leave Malcolm. Sometimes people look into the jaws of death and it changes them forever. Underscores how you only live one life and it's better to be happy and live in the now than pretend you're happy just to get through the day. Maybe Tracy had that realization and decided to leave Malcolm and Malcolm wasn't having it. He snapped, and now she's gone."

Missy just stared at the woman, speechless. She wanted to tell her the real reason Tracy was leaving Malcolm, but stopped herself before she went down a road she had no business going down.

"Or maybe your sister decided to just up and leave. Start a new life. She ditches the car and all of her belongings in it and starts fresh."

"She would never leave her son." But even as Missy said this, a bit of doubt crept in. Was the plan maybe too much? Did Tracy freak out and leave? She wasn't sure anymore. That thought had crossed her mind in the early hours of the morning when she'd lain awake in the guest room, replaying what was and what could be. If Tracy had gotten cold feet and fled, there would be hell to pay.

A quick laugh. "Oh sweetie, you'd be surprised what people do after a near-death experience. Anyway, I was coming by to ask Detective Evans why she hadn't talked about that to the press."

"I don't think she knows about it."

"Then she's not much of an investigator. I mean, I found out about your sister's sickness in a single day. These guys have had a week. I hope they know what they're doing. For Tracy's sake."

Missy sighed as she balled her hands into fists in her pockets to keep them warm. "I'm not sure they do, and it's starting to piss me off."

"Good," Reagan said. She leaned in close and lowered her voice. "Anger produces results. Hang on to it. It'll be the fuel you need. Keep looking into your brother-in-law and I'll keep digging around to see what the police come up with. We'll report back to each other."

"I don't think Malcolm had anything to do with what happened."

"Do you really believe that?"

"Yeah. I... I think so."

Reagan Hart touched her chest and made a face like she was looking at a pathetic, sickly animal, like she felt sorry for Missy for believing in something so obviously flawed as Malcolm's innocence. She extended a gloved hand that matched the blue of her overcoat. Missy shook it, feeling shame for trying to find the best in people, contemplating what the woman said.

"Maybe Tracy had that realization and decided to leave Malcolm and Malcolm wasn't having it. He snapped, and now she's gone."

"Do we have a deal?"

Missy couldn't believe that she could be teaming up with a woman she'd watched on television for so many years. They'd be quite the duo and maybe just angry enough to get results the cops couldn't. Maybe this was her chance at finding her sister once and for all. And maybe Malcolm really did need a closer look. From the inside. At the very least, she could use Reagan in the other matter. A person like her could be quite beneficial.

"Deal."

A warm, beautiful smile. "Excellent."

CHAPTER THIRTY-THREE

Malcolm climbed out of his car when he saw Dr. Devi open the front door of his brownstone and usher a boy inside. He rushed past two other boys who were loitering on the stoop and hopped the steps two at a time, catching the door just in time to slip inside.

"Hey! Hold up!"

His voice reverberated off the antique tile wainscoting and fifteen-foot ceilings. The boy, hidden behind a large hood, was halfway up the meticulously carved staircase. Dr. Devi was still on the landing. The older man turned and looked him up and down, studying him, trying to make a connection.

"I'm Malcolm Cowan. Tracy's husband. We need to talk."

Dr. Devi exhaled and seemed to lose all of his stature and dimension. His youth and vigor were gone instantly, and he was suddenly hunched over a bit, his face forlorn, his eyes magnified behind his glasses, sad and wet from the rain outside. He spun around and motioned to the boy who remained halfway up the stairs.

"Go on up. I'll be there in a moment."

The boy nodded and thumped his way to the second floor,

his oversized hood swaying with each step. Malcolm watched him disappear, then turned his attention to the doctor who was walking toward him.

"I've come by the past two days," he said. His voice had a sharpness to it. He wasn't in a pleasant mood. "You haven't been here."

Dr. Devi nodded. "I didn't have office hours. I don't see patients every day."

"We need to talk."

"Yes, you mentioned that."

Malcolm waited for the doctor to ask him up, and when the silence got to be too long and awkward, the doctor pointed toward the ceiling.

"I'm sorry, but I have a patient waiting. We'll have to talk here."

"Have the police been by to see you?"

"They have. I think it was the day Tracy went missing. Maybe the day after."

"And what did you tell them?"

"I told them Tracy had come to see me for her regular appointment. Our session lasted for the normal allotted hour, and she left."

"What did you guys talk about?"

"You know I can't reveal that."

"Did she tell you about her asking for a divorce?"

Dr. Devi smiled as if he was talking to a deranged patient. "Mr. Cowan, as much as I'd like to help you in this awful circumstance, the doctor–patient relationship must remain confidential."

"But what if she told you something that could help us find her?"

"She didn't."

"How can you be sure?"

The smile disappeared. "I reviewed my notes and listened

to our session recording after the police left for that very reason. There's nothing that was said or discussed that would point us in any direction with regard to your wife's whereabouts. I'm sorry."

Malcolm studied the doctor. He looked like he was in good shape. Attractive. His charm was what surely suckered his patients into handing over their cash week after week to talk about their problems without ever finding resolution. Those charlatans were all the same. Always dangling the carrot. No cure yet, but keep writing those checks. We're getting somewhere, I promise.

"Did you tell my wife to leave me?"

The question hung in the air for a moment and Dr. Devi took a slight step backward.

"That's not how therapy works," he replied. "I don't offer advice. I merely guide my patients through whatever it is they want to talk about. Sometimes it's their problems. Sometimes it's things that are on the periphery of the problem, but I let them talk and find their way. If Tracy wanted to end your marriage, it was something she wanted for herself. I would never suggest such a thing. Ever."

Malcolm nodded and snickered. "When she first told me she wanted to see you, I thought it was because she was having trouble dealing with life after she got sick. I didn't think it would actually help, but I figured what the hell, you know? Go talk about what you went through and acknowledge your feelings or however else it works, and come back to me all fixed up. If I'd known you'd lead her toward ending our marriage and taking my son, I never would've agreed."

"I didn't make her decision."

"Yeah, but you didn't tell her to stay with her family and work it out either."

"Again, that's not how it works."

An overwhelming desire to punch the doctor in his smug

and educated face came over Malcom and he stuffed his hands in his pockets to keep himself from doing anything rash. He began pacing the tight hallway, back and forth.

"It's been eight days," he said. "Where the hell is she? The cops don't have a clue. The public thinks I had something to do with it and the press is making this story bigger every day. I've had to sneak out the back of my house for the past two days. I can't go to the job site anymore. They follow me and film me and shout questions and then they run their own version of what they think happened on the news later that night. It's sick. I don't know what to do. Where is she?"

Dr. Devi watched him pacing, following him with his eyes, standing completely still.

"They'll find her. I'm sure of it."

"Yeah? When?"

"When they're supposed to. And not a second sooner."

"What the hell is that supposed to mean?"

"Nothing. It's what I believe. Things happen when they're supposed to happen. That's all."

Malcolm fell against the wall and slid down to the floor. He cupped his hands over his face and choked down tears that wanted to burst forth.

"What if she's dead?" he asked.

Dr. Devi crossed the room, bent down next to Malcolm, and put a hand on his shoulder. "Then we'll deal with it. But until we have proof of such a fate, we remain optimistic. It's the only way."

Malcolm wanted to respond, but couldn't. Instead, he began to cry and listened to the sound of his sobbing echo through the corridors of the ancient first floor. Somewhere in the background, Dr. Devi was consoling him, but he didn't want to hear what he had to say. He just wanted his wife back.

CHAPTER THIRTY-FOUR

There was no wind this time. The waves seemed muted against the shore, gently rolling in with the tide, no fury or anger that had been there before. She could hear seagulls squawking in the distance and she imagined them circling over the water, then diving head-first for their prey. She had no idea what time of day it was, but she sensed it to be afternoon. She imagined the sun was hanging in a bright blue sky, the kind of sharp blue that only comes with the cold weather. No clouds. The sea, calm. It must be beautiful.

Tracy propped herself up on her elbows, then shifted herself into a seated position on the bed. She felt like she was going to vomit. Her head ached as if a migraine was coming on, and her eyes were millions of tiny needles stabbing her. She waited for the dizziness to subside, then took a few deep breaths to try and settle her stomach, but after the third breath, she vomited all over the comforter.

She heaved and spit, then reached up to her eyes that hurt so much. She touched the thick bandage and felt a bolt of pain shoot up through her face and down her back. She must've taken quite a blow. The bandage was tight and she followed it around to the back of her head where she felt a series of metal clips keeping it in place, the clips covered in layers of tape. She pulled at the bandage as hard as she could, then tried picking at the tape with her nails, but the chain on the side of the bed prevented her from being able to maneuver properly.

She wondered what was going on back home. Surely the police were investigating. Too much time had passed for them not to be. Had they found any clues that would lead them in the right direction? Was everything playing out? She feared things had already gone off the rails. Would they ever find her? Would they find him?

The hinges on the bedroom door creaked and Tracy immediately dropped her hands to her sides and froze. The house was unnervingly quiet. Just the gentle waves and the seagulls outside.

"Hello?" she said, her voice raspy and dry.

No reply.

"Is someone there?"

Nothing.

Tracy could sense a presence in the room. She could somehow feel a body standing in front of her, staring. She began to tremble.

"Please. Answer me. I know you're there. I can hear you. I got sick. I'm sorry."

Silence.

"Who's there?"

Her voice was becoming more panicked. She could taste the bile in her throat.

"Answer me!"

Feet shuffled in front of her. The hinges on the door whined again. Two small steps.

"Wait!" Tracy cried, her voice instantly calming. "Don't go. You're the boy Dr. Devi introduced me to. Am I right? Is that you?"

Silence.

Tracy pointed to her bandages and smiled, trying to disarm. "I can't see you because I got hurt. If I ask you a question, you'll have to answer with your words or else I won't know you're answering me. Can you do that?"

"Yes."

The voice was high-pitched and sweet. There was fear and trepidation in it, which made Tracy immediately want to protect him.

"What's your name, honey?"

"You pushed me before."

"I'm sorry about that. I didn't mean to. You surprised me, that's all. Please, tell me your name."

"Finn."

Just hearing her son's name sent a shiver across her body. She stopped herself from yelling and took a breath. "No, I mean your real name. What's your real name?"

"He told me it was Finn."

"I won't tattle that you told me your real name. I just want to know. It'll be our secret."

"Enzo."

Tracy's smile broadened as she raised her hand to wave. "Hi, Enzo. I'm Tracy. Thank you for telling me."

A few more footsteps came closer.

"The man told me my new name was Finn."

"I know. Do you know where the man is now?"

"No. He leaves sometimes. And when he leaves, he locks the big lock on the doors and I can't reach them. When he comes back, he checks to make sure I didn't leave my room, but this time he was gone for a while and I had to pee. I didn't want to pee in my room."

"Of course not," Tracy replied. She tried to keep her voice even so as not to scare the boy, but so many questions were running through her mind. "I wouldn't want to pee in my room either." She motioned around her with her hand. "Do you know where we are?"

"The lighthouse."

"We're in a lighthouse?"

"It's big."

She could feel her head clearing, but her body still felt heavy, her muscles sore. "Do you know the name of the town we're in? Or maybe the street?"

"No, I just know we're at the lighthouse by the beach."

She tried to figure out where that might be, but couldn't come up with anything. They could be anywhere.

"Is it cold outside?"

"Yes."

They were probably still in the northeast.

"Are there people on the beach?"

"I don't know."

"Where do you come from?"

"El Salvador."

"Where's your family?"

A pause. "The man said you could be my family. He said he could be my dad and you could be my mom and everyone would call me Finn."

Tracy's heart crumbled as she heard the boy talk.

"Has the man been nice to you?"

"Yes."

"Do you feel safe or are you scared?"

A few more steps closer. "I'm not scared."

"How did the man get you to come up to the lighthouse?"

"He came to the school I was at and brought me food and candy and comic books and then asked if I wanted to live with a real family and I said yes."

"Where's your El Salvador family?"

"I don't know."

Tracy tried to figure out a way to call for help. She was

trapped on the bed, but if she could get the boy to leave and find help, they could both be freed.

"Enzo, is there any door you can open that goes outside?"

"No. The lock is up high and I can't reach it. Not even with a chair."

"Can you open a window?"

"They all have metal over them."

Tracy paused. Metal over the windows? They must be hurricane shutters. That was the only thing she could think of.

"Does the house look clean or dirty?"

"Clean."

She sat straighter up in bed and pulled the chain tight so the boy could see it. "Do you think you can come over here and help me out of this?"

This time the footsteps retreated.

"I'm not supposed to be in here," the boy said. "I'm not even supposed to leave my room."

"I won't tell."

"But he'll know. If I help you, he'll see that you got out of the chain and he'll know I was here and I don't want to go back to the school. The man said that's where he'd take me if I didn't follow the rules. I don't want to go back there. I want to stay here."

"You will stay here. I promise. I just need you to come look at how I'm fastened to this and explain it to me. Can you do that?"

"No. I'll get in trouble."

"You won't. You'll be helping me, and that's a good thing. You want to help your mom, right?"

"The man said I wasn't supposed to leave my room when he's away, and I just had to pee. I wasn't supposed to come in here, but I wanted to see you."

"It's okay that you came in. I'm glad you did."

"I have to go."

"I won't say—"

"No! I'm not going back to the school! It's scary there."

The footsteps quickly faded and the bedroom door slammed shut. In the silence of the house, Tracy could hear the boy running back up the stairs to his room and it reminded her of how Finn used to run to the dinner table from his bedroom on the second floor. She lay back down and let the blackness wrap its claws around her as it pulled her deeper into the nothingness, her voice floating in her mind.

He's never going to let you leave.

You'll never see things through at home.

There's so much at stake.

You're destroying the plan. All that work.

How can you get out?

It's up to you to escape.

You'll have to do whatever's necessary. Nothing's off limits.

CHAPTER THIRTY-FIVE

Malcolm burst through the front door and quickly closed it behind him. He leaned against it, breathing heavy, his chest rising and falling under his parka.

"Anybody home?" he asked aloud. The house was quiet.

"In the kitchen," Missy replied.

Malcolm kicked off his shoes and made his way into the kitchen. He could feel his heart hammering in his temples and he concentrated to get his breathing under control. Finn was sitting at the table coloring and Missy was busy taking plates, glasses, mugs, and bowls out of the cabinets and lining them on the counter. Music played softly from Missy's phone. He hadn't heard it when he first came in.

"What happened to you?" Missy asked. She stopped what she was doing and looked him up and down. "You're all wet and haggard."

"It's sleeting again. I wish it would either rain or snow. This in-between stuff is too much. I had to park around the corner and come in through Philip's backyard into ours. I didn't want anyone from the press seeing me. I was able to get out earlier without them knowing. Wanted to keep it that way."

"I never would've thought our press conference would end up with you having to sneak in and out of your own house." Missy looked at Finn. "Honey, go get your father a towel. He's soaked."

"Okay!"

Finn hopped off the chair and ran upstairs to retrieve a towel. Malcolm sat down in one of the chairs and wiped his wet hair from his eyes.

"What're you doing?"

"I'm rearranging the kitchen so it matches my kitchen at home." Missy spun around and began opening the cabinet doors that were under the countertops. "If I'm going to be here helping you guys out, I can't keep wasting time hunting for things. I thought that if I put things here the way that are at my place, I can just grab whatever I need and keep going."

"I didn't know there was a specific pattern to go by."

"There isn't. And Tracy's placings were fine. They just weren't what I was used to and it was getting annoying. You see, I put the pots and pans with the baking sheets and Tupperware on the bottom. Flatware, glasses, and mugs go up top."

Malcolm grunted. "Now I'm going to be the one hunting for things that I need."

"Wrong. If it's up to me, you won't have to do anything. Just let me know what you want and I'll get it or make it or whatever. I don't mind. Seriously."

There was a brief silence before Malcolm reached across the table, grabbed a napkin, and wiped his face. "Last week, you barge in here accusing me of hurting Tracy. Few days after that, you wake me up by pointing my gun at me, again, convinced I did something to Tracy. Now you're rearranging cabinets and offering to be my short-order cook. What gives?"

Missy placed the glasses on a shelf. "Where were you today?" she asked, ignoring the question.

"I went to see Tracy's shrink. Dr. Devi."

"Why?"

"I wanted to know what happened that day she saw him. I wanted to hear it directly from him. I was hoping he'd mention something that would point us in the right direction."

Missy closed the cabinet and leaned against the stove. "Funny, I did something similar. I went to see Detective Evans to ask her why there hasn't been any leads or updates after eight days. She had no answers."

"Neither did the shrink."

"But when I was walking to my car, Reagan Hart approached me. Knew exactly who I was."

"What'd she want?"

"She made me an offer. She said she'd give me tips and leads that she finds along the way, that maybe the police don't want to share, in exchange for me doing the same. Mostly about you."

"Great."

"It got me thinking." Missy crossed the room and stood in front of Malcolm. "If you really did have something to do with this, why would you be acting exactly like I'm acting? Why would you be driving around looking for answers from people because the police aren't finding her fast enough? Why are you bothering to go on TV and have a press conference and put yourself out there so the world can judge you if you weren't as desperate to find Tracy as I am?"

"I could be playing the role of distraught husband. It's been done before."

"Not like this. Not with it being so authentic. You care."

"Yeah, I care. A lot. I'm her husband. Even if I was in the process of screwing it all up, I still love her." Malcolm fell back in his chair and looked at Missy. "Maybe I deserved it."

Missy's eyes glistened as a tear slipped free. "I don't think there's anything to tell Reagan Hart except that my brother-in-law wants his wife home and safe and they'll figure out all the other stuff later. Right now, Tracy coming home alive is our priority."

"Sounds good to me."

Missy placed her hand on the back of Malcom's neck. She bent down and gently pulled him closer until their foreheads were touching.

"Look at me," she said.

He did.

"Tell me one last time that you had nothing to do with what happened to my sister. Tell me the truth and I promise you won't hear me ask you ever again."

Malcolm could feel Missy's breath on his face. He could smell her perfume that mixed with perspiration and the cleaning spray she was using for the dishes. Her eyes were shining as they stared at him, her one hand still around the back of his neck, her other placed in the center of his chest. It somehow felt natural. It felt good. Like he finally had someone on his side.

"I didn't have anything to do with what happened to Tracy," he whispered. "I swear."

"Well, okay then."

Finn thumped down the stairs and ran through the hall toward the kitchen. Malcolm and Missy quickly let go of one another as Missy scurried back to her glasses that were on the counter.

"Here, Daddy," Finn said. He slid into the kitchen on his socks, the towel held out like a victory flag.

Malcolm snatched the towel from his son and winked at him. "Thanks, buddy."

He watched as Finn climbed back up and sat opposite him, his head buried right back into the picture he was drawing. The room grew quiet but for the music that kept playing from Missy's phone. Malcolm examined the scene. He watched Missy as she reached up to place the tallest glasses on the highest shelf, the bottom of her sweater pulling up as she reached. He turned his attention back to his son who stuck his tongue out one side of his mouth as he drew, a habit he'd inherited from his grandfather. Everything looked as it should have been except for the fact that his wife had been missing for the past eight days. The sensation of calm in that moment frightened him, and he got up from the table without another word, walked upstairs, and got in the shower. He didn't want to think that life without Tracy could ever seem normal again.

CHAPTER THIRTY-SIX

The bedroom door opened, slamming against the door, making Tracy jump.

"Who's there?"

"He came to see you," Sam said, his voice deep and angry. "I know he did. Finn came to see you while I was gone."

Tracy forced herself to smile. In that moment she decided to play along to see if she could disarm or manipulate Sam. It was the only thing she could think of that might eventually get her out of the chain. She had to find a way to escape from the house and call for help.

"I'm glad you're back," she said with a slight smile. "I missed you."

"Finn was in here while I was gone," Sam replied, ignoring her seductive tone.

Tracy shook her head. "No one came to see me."

"Don't lie to me. I put a playing card in the crease of the door. It only would've fallen on the floor if the door was opened. You can't get out of bed. I made sure of that. I wasn't here. That only leaves Finn. He came to see you."

"No one came to see me."

"Stop lying to me!"

Tracy recoiled against the headboard when she heard Sam scream. His breath came in heaves, his anger boiling to the surface.

"You keep lying to me and I won't tolerate it! I won't!"

"Then you stop lying to me!" Tracy shouted in return. She tried to stop herself, to keep up her flirty persona, but couldn't. "That boy is not my son!"

"What are you talking about? Of course he is. I brought Finn—"

"Don't you say his name!" Tracy surrendered to her fear and allowed the fury to take over, her voice choking on tears and anger and bile and terror. "You think a mother doesn't know her own child? You think just because I can't see him I wouldn't *know*? How dare you."

"That boy is your son," Sam said.

"That is not Finn. His name is Enzo."

"No!" Sam's voice shook the walls and froze Tracy in place. "That is your son! I brought him to you! I do everything for you! I saved your life, I gave you a place to stay, I shielded you from your husband who wants to kill you and now I'm giving you a new family! I'm giving you everything!"

"I don't want a new family! And I don't need you to shield me from Malcolm. I need Malcolm to shield me from you!"

"When will it be enough!"

Footsteps stomped toward her and before she could react, Sam grabbed her by her chin, yanking her to him.

"I give you everything and you spit in my face! Nothing's good enough!"

He pushed her away so hard that she hit the back of the headboard with a whack. White dots danced in her darkness while, in the background, footsteps stomped out of the bedroom and the door slammed behind them.

"You leave that boy alone! Don't you touch him!"

Tracy was left in the blackness that had become her new world. She bent down and frantically traced the chain that was fastened around her wrist down through the edge of the box spring. She sat back up and as she did, the door crashed open again.

"Get out!"

The footsteps—*his* footsteps—approached quickly. He was on her in seconds, his weight crashing down on top of her. She pushed at him, the heels of her hands making contact.

"Get away from me!"

"Shut up."

She felt Sam's hand grab the back of her hair and gently twist it until he had a fistful, taut and tense. He pulled and lifted her head off the pillow.

"You'll learn to appreciate me," he panted. "But don't push me. That would be a mistake. I care for you more than you can imagine, but everyone has a breaking point. I can be like Jake if I have to. Don't make me get there.

"Please," she muttered through tears. "It hurts."

Something sharp stabbed her in the bend of her arm. Sam let go of her hair and Tracy fell back into the pillow. Her head suddenly felt light while her body grew warm from her feet up to the top of her head. She began to relax and felt a sense of detachment from everything that was happening. The fear and anxiety she'd felt only seconds before was leaving her, and when she felt the weight of Sam's body disappear off her, there was no panic.

"You need to understand how I feel about you," Sam said. He was panting, talking through his teeth. That made her smile for some reason. "I love you. It'll take time before you can really appreciate me and what I did for us. I'll help you see things my way. You'll get it."

Tracy tried to speak, but it was getting so hard. "What... did you... give... me?"

"Go to sleep and we'll talk again later."

Tracy listened to Sam disappear and heard the door close gently, leaving her in the quiet bliss she found herself happily drowning in. This was her life now, but she didn't care. The blackness. The bedroom. Sam. This was her new existence, and for that singular moment, it was perfect, despite the message that echoed in the cavern of her mind.

He's going to kill you. It just a matter of time.

CHAPTER THIRTY-SEVEN

There was a knock and Tracy felt her body tense.

"Can I come in?" Sam asked. His voice was calm, small from outside the door. "I noticed the vomit before. I brought you a fresh comforter. Nice and clean."

Tracy didn't answer.

The door opened and Sam's footsteps carried into the room, stopping at what she figured was the foot of her bed.

"I'm sorry for getting mad again," he said. "I don't like when we fight. I just got upset when I saw the playing card on the floor. I like things to be in order. It's important for people to follow instructions. Sometimes I lose it a little when that doesn't happen."

Tracy tried to place the man she was hearing with the man she'd shared her most intimate details with over the past year. They were two completely different people. The Dr. Devi she knew was so intelligent and kind and patient. This man was anything but. It scared her to learn how two different people could inhabit the same body.

"Where's Enzo?" she finally asked.

"He fine," Sam replied. "I promise. He's in his room reading. I didn't do anything to him. I would never."

Tracy thought about the way he snatched her chin and slammed the back of her head against the headboard. Now he sounded normal again, unassuming, safe. She decided to try and play up to him again, to see if there was a way to get him to drop his guard.

"Look, I don't want to fight either," she said, trying so hard to keep her voice from trembling. "Let's be friends."

"I'd like that."

"Can you just tell me about Enzo? We don't have to argue about it. I'd like to know where he came from."

"That's Finn. He's your son."

"But he's not."

Tracy winced, hoping she wasn't pushing Sam toward another outburst. She just had to know. As a woman and a mother and a protector. She had to know.

A slow exhale. "I'll admit he's not your past version of your son, but he's the new version of him. His name is Finn, just like you remember. He's seven. All of that's the same."

"Except his name is Enzo, not Finn. He's not *my* Finn."

"He is now."

The footsteps came around the side of her bed and Tracy recoiled again, pushing herself back as she held her hands up in front of her. It was all she could do to protect herself.

"I'm not here to hurt you," Sam said. His voice was back to the way it was during their sessions. So calm. "I need you to understand that you don't have to be afraid of me. I saved you for a reason. I'm protecting you for that same reason."

"What's that?"

"I love you, Tracy. I'm all the things you wished Malcolm was. Remember all those things you told me in our sessions? That's who I can be for you. Someone you could depend on and be truly happy with. That's me. That can be us. I can love you like you deserve to be loved. I can give you everything you've ever wanted."

Sam gently grasped her hands. She wanted to push them away, but instead, leaned in.

"I want that too," she lied, trying to keep him steady.

"Really?"

"Yes. I want you to be everything Malcolm couldn't be. You know the real me. You know all of my secrets. We can start fresh and you can love me. I'll let you." She reached out and found his face. The tips of her fingers touched his cheek. "You shaved your beard?"

"For you."

"Just unlock me from this bed and we can be together. Like a normal couple."

Sam laughed quietly, then took her hand and placed it on her lap, pushing her down onto the bed. "You can't manipulate me, Tracy. That's not love. I'll make you see, though. I'm a patient man."

"I'm not manipulating you. I can love you. I can."

"And you will. Just not yet. You're not there yet."

Sam spread the blanket over her. "You'll learn to love me like I love you and we'll have Finn and you'll have the life you always wanted. I promise. We'll be equals. You don't need me to always be strong and overbearing and protective. You can take care of yourself and I respect you enough to understand that. We'll be an amazing couple. You'll see."

Tracy turned on her side, her back towards him, silent.

"I really am sorry about before," Sam said. "That's not like me to get so angry. I guess I was scared too. Scared you didn't like it here and that all the things I did for you were for nothing. Sometimes fear makes you angry. It's no excuse though. I know that."

Tracy felt the tip of a needle stab into her neck and jumped up. She clasped her hand over the wound and instantly felt woozy.

"What are you doing?"

"You'll be loved here," she heard Sam say, his voice immediately drawing distant. "I can promise you that. You, me, and Finn. We'll be so happy together. You'll see."

That same feeling came over her again. Her body growing warm. The instant relaxation. The bliss. The detachment. No fear or anxiety. No panic or despair. It was incredible.

"I want to go home," she slurred.

"You are home," Sam replied. "And you are loved here."

Then, nothing.

DAY TEN

CHAPTER THIRTY-EIGHT

Kelly sat in front of her computer monitor, staring at the feed, clicking the controls on the bottom of the screen to speed up, pause, or reverse the footage. The stationhouse around her was loud. A team of officers made a rather large bust of illegal firearms by the water in Mamaroneck and the seven suspected dealers were being marched in and processed. She tried to tune it all out and concentrate on the video she'd been sent. She'd have to celebrate with the guys later.

"You hear about our big day?"

Kelly looked up to find Sergeant Leeds leaning over her cubicle wall. A smile stretched across his face, his eyes alive like he was a rookie again.

"Oh, I heard. You guys are the talk to the town. Nice bust."

"Those were my guys. My team. I had two undercovers looking to purchase and these idiots handed us the entire case. Got into their self-storage spot. Must've been a thousand guns in there."

"Just remember me when they make you captain."

Leeds laughed. "I'll be well retired before that opportunity ever comes around." He pointed to the computer screen. "You got footage?"

Kelly nodded. "Yeah. One of the uniforms going door-to-door in the neighborhood around George's Island took down all the houses that had some kind of camera that faced the street. All of the owners gave us permission to download their recordings, but since most of the cameras are only motion-activated close to the house, we came up empty except for one camera this guy had. It's a trail cam. He had it set up to record raccoons that were raiding his garbage at night, and the motion field was large enough for the cars on the road to trigger it. We found Tracy's SUV going toward the park and a dark sedan follows behind after about five minutes. It's a late model Buick, but I can't tell which kind. The one headlight could be helpful. After about twenty minutes, we see the sedan come out. Can't tell how many people are inside though."

"Okay, so now we have the sedan with one working headlight on that camera and on the camera up by the entrance to the park. We know it's a Buick and it has a distinguishing feature. That's progress."

"I got more." Kelly took her mouse and minimized the screen, replacing it with a new screen and new footage. "I started going backward from the park based on what Malcolm Cowan told us Tracy said on the phone. I found a traffic cam by the train station and a security camera on the edge of the veterans' hospital grounds." She played the footage and Tracy's SUV was driving down Post Road, eventually slowing and making a left turn. Kelly fast-forwarded the footage and a few minutes later, the Buick appeared.

"That's him."

"Still no clear license plate though. I'm going to keep going backward to see if there are any other street cams or highway surveillance that I can use. Hopefully I can get a clear picture of the plate number or the person driving."

"Anything on the location tracker magnate we found?"

Kelly shook her head. "Tracks to a burner phone. Dead end."

"Damn."

The other officers called for Leeds to join them. He waved over and looked down at Kelly. "Keep digging. Something's gonna come up. Always does."

"It better come soon or the chief's going to take me off the case. I hear he's not happy about Malcolm Cowan's press conference and the fact that the media is really picking up the story. Pressure's mounting."

"You can handle it."

Kelly sighed and rewound the footage back to the beginning. "Let's hope so."

CHAPTER THIRTY-NINE

Detective Taft was at his desk in the corner of the department's second floor. All the pictures and computer printouts and stacks of files were gone, the only things remaining being a computer monitor and dust lines from items that he'd stared at for the good part of two decades. Retirement was a tricky thing. One moment you were part of the team, the next, just another face in the crowd. No longer being on the inside would be the biggest adjustment. He held his locket out in front of him, staring at his wife, thinking about the way they used to smile and laugh and carry on with their silliness. Now there was just sadness and grief and death snuffing out everything else. The life he'd known was gone forever. What lay ahead was a mystery he wasn't sure he wanted to solve.

Lena Blau snaked her way through the cubicles and desks until she reached Taft. She placed a folder on his desk, tearing him from his thoughts.

"Forensics wrapped on Kat," she said. "I never gave this to you, understand?"

"Got it."

"We didn't get anything else from the autopsy and her

apartment's been processed. We've got samples of fibers and skin and the semen. Even found some nail clippings in the garbage. But unless you have anyone to match it to, they're pretty useless."

Taft felt his body go limp. He nodded and pulled the file toward him. "Any hits on the prints?"

"A bunch were obviously the victim's so we eliminated those. We found two other sets, but neither were in our local database. We're running them through IAFIS to see if we get a hit on the national level."

"Okay, keep me posted."

"Anything on your end?"

"I've been going through her social media accounts, and it's all the same people. All the same pictures really. She'll post one picture to all three platforms."

"Anything you can go on?"

"Not really. From the way her friend describes Kat's lover, this Big Daddy guy, he would be older, most likely a client, and a guy who had a little money. Everything she posts is either just her or the same group of friends who all seem to be her age. I even went back to that Coldplay concert at Madison Square Garden hoping to catch the guy in the background of a photo or something, but she didn't post about the concert at all. The way I see it, she knew she wasn't supposed to be there with him and she kept it under wraps. Even the pictures we found on her phone that weren't posted have no older guys in them."

Lena sat on the edge of his desk. "Shows some pretty good restraint. Girl that age not posting about her boyfriend or the concert she went to? That's maturity right there."

"Unfortunately, her maturity leads us to another dead end. I'll go through the list of clients you gave me from the law firm. Hopefully I can match something there."

"Okay," Lena replied. "We also caught something on her phone records. Not sure if it's anything, but besides home, she had three numbers she called and received calls from on a regular basis. One is the law firm. The other is her friend, Jill Toomey. The third is where I think we may have something. Same number over and over, but she doesn't have it assigned in her contacts. The calls are both incoming and outgoing, and it's a burner."

Taft sat up. "Really."

"I called it myself and it rolls to a generic, automated voice-mail. I'm thinking this could be Big Daddy."

"You get a trace on it?"

"We're working with the cell carrier the burner phone goes through. Waiting to hear back. If Big Daddy used a credit or debit card, we'll have him, but I'm not getting my hopes up."

"Nice work."

Lena looked out over the floor, studying the detectives and officers who milled about. "If we do find the guy, and we can match his prints and semen from what we collected at the scene, this'll be open and shut for the DA. And for you. Would be good to have closure. Let's get a win."

Taft exhaled slowly as scenes from his life, both personal and professional, flashed through his mind. "My gut tells me we're close," he said. "And a win sounds pretty nice to me."

"I know it does."

He waited as Lena lingered for a few more seconds, then grabbed his cell phone from the desk as she walked away. He chose a number from his contacts list and waited.

"Yeah, George. It's Dennis Taft. Listen, I need you to do me a favor. Consider it the retirement gift you never got me. I need to be the first to know if any hits come up on the IAFIS search we're running for the Kat Masterson case. Lena put some prints in there for analysis. First to know. Got it?" He smiled. "Good."

CHAPTER FORTY

"Why did you do it?"

Jake stared at her from the corner of the living room, his eyes dark and swollen from crying. "I didn't do anything."

"So, all the evidence, the video, and the testimony from Angela is a lie?"

"Yes."

Tracy knelt up on the floor and leaned her arms on the couch cushions. "Just tell me why you did it. You and I both know these aren't lies, and maybe I can start to understand what you were thinking if you tell me why it happened in the first place."

Jake sighed, tapping the barrel of the gun against his chin, looking away and thinking.

"Tell me, Jake. Why'd you do it? Why couldn't you stay faithful to me? To us? What compelled you to rape an underage girl when you had me always and forever?"

"Because you wouldn't let me love you the way Angela let me love her."

"Finally, the truth."

"You're cold on the inside, Tracy. Lifeless. The way I see it, you're unlovable in the real sense of the word. I try and be *romantic and be the man you dream about or read about in your romance books, but that's not real life. I give you everything I can, but there's a void inside you. I can't explain it."*

Tracy fell onto the backs of her legs. "You think I'm unlovable?"

"I do."

She knew it in that moment. He was right. She was unlovable. And that gave her the clarity she needed to see things through. It was all crystal clear now. She knew what she had to do.

She had nothing more to lose.

———

Sleet fell hard against the side of the house. The beads of ice hit what sounded like metal, each one like mini explosions in the otherwise silence of the house. The wind roared and she could hear the waves crashing against the surf. The sea had turned violent again, which made the safety within feel all the more fragile. Tracy knew she wasn't safe where she was. Despite her memories betraying her and her mind always being caught in some kind of fog, she knew that what Sam said about trying to protect her and keeping her safe and hidden away from Malcolm were all lies. She was a prisoner. There was no two ways about. And her son needed her. She had to get out and get home and ensure what she had started would end the way they planned. The rest of her life was dependent on ending what Malcolm knew of his. It had to work.

The hinges on her bedroom door began to squeak, then abruptly stopped. Tracy tried to listen over the hail that pounded the house and the wind that howled outside. She touched the dressing on her face. Her eyes still hurt. The gauze seemed thicker than she remembered, the tape extra thick.

"Who's there?"

She could hear movement, but it was barely audible. Careful steps.

"Hello?"

"Shhhh," the voice replied. "He can hear you."

Relief washed over her. It was Enzo.

"Are you okay?" she whispered. "You never came back to see me."

Tiny footsteps crossed the room.

"He told me to stay in my room," Enzo whispered. "He told me if I came out, he would give me to bad people and I don't want that. I stayed like he said. But now he's sleeping and when he sleeps, I come out."

"You've been out of your room before when he sleeps?"

"Yes."

"And he doesn't hear you?"

"No."

Tracy nodded in her darkness. "Have you been able to see and hear things while you were in your room?"

"A little," Enzo replied.

"Do you know if anyone else has come here? A doctor or a policeman or anyone?"

"I didn't see anyone."

"I didn't think so."

Tracy thought for a moment, her mind racing. She bent over and tugged on the chain that was around her wrist. It gave just enough, but she couldn't get the fat part of her palm by her thumb through the loop.

"What's outside this room?" she asked. "When you leave here, what do you see?"

The boy moved closer, his voice even softer. "There's a hallway and a bathroom and then a space by the front door and in the back there's a kitchen and a living room and behind that there's a big room with a bunch of windows."

"Where does the man sleep?"

"Upstairs. Across from where my room is."

"Where are the stairs?"

"By the front door."

Tracy tried to picture it all in her mind. If she could get out of the room, all she'd have to do was make it to the end of the hall and the front door would be there. And if the boy could guide her, all the better. But she still had no idea where she was. Other than knowing she was by the ocean, there were no other details.

"What's outside?" she asked.

"Woods," Enzo replied. "Lots and lots of woods."

"And then the beach?"

"And the lighthouse."

"So, we're not in a lighthouse."

"No. The lighthouse is that way."

She couldn't see where he was pointing, but thought that maybe someone was working in it and she could run there and ask for help.

"You said the man was sleeping. Does that mean it's night?"

"Yes."

This was her best shot at escape. Even though her head still swam from whatever Sam kept giving her, she was alert enough to know she was in danger. She had to get out.

"Enzo," she began, reaching for the boy and finding his tiny shoulder. She gently pulled him closer so she could whisper under the noise of the storm outside. "I need you to sneak into the kitchen and find the dish soap. Do you know what that is?"

"Yes."

"Good. Find it and bring it back to me. But you have to be very quiet. We can't wake the man. Go."

She listened as the patter of tiny footsteps scurried out of the room and disappeared down the hall. The storm outside sounded rough. She was thankful that she could use the noise from the hail and wind to mask her movements, however, she was worried about maneuvering once she got outside. But she was already thinking too far ahead. If the dish soap didn't work, she'd be back to square one.

Enzo returned and placed the bottle in her hand. She smiled. It was exactly what she was hoping he'd find. She poured the soap all over her wrist and hand and the chain.

Please. This has to work. Please.

She turned her wrist around, twisting it and working the slick soap into all of the nooks and crannies of both her hand and the chain. Slowly, she felt a bit of give and she folded her thumb across her palm as far as she could and pulled.

It took a bit of manipulating, and she bit her bottom lip to keep from squealing when the pain came, but she slipped her hand through, catching the chain before it slammed to the floor.

She was free.

Tracy swung her legs over the side of the bed and placed her feet on the floor. She stood and immediately felt pain in her knees and shins. The bottom of her feet were pins and needles as she shuffled forward a few steps, testing herself before going any further. She hadn't stood in days and her legs felt uneasy, but they would hold.

"Give me your hand," she whispered.

Without a response, a small hand slipped into hers.

"Guide me to the door. We have to go slow and quiet."

The small hand pulled her and she followed. The storm outside continued, the wind and sleet thrashing the house, giving them cover. Tracy held her breath as she went, purposefully lifting each foot and placing it down so as not to make more noise than needed. Her free hand was out in front of her. She felt the bedroom door as she passed into the hallway. Almost there.

The floor was bare. There was no rug or runner. Just the hardwood. Enzo kept pulling her forward and she followed, lightly brushing her free hand against the wall as she went, balancing herself in the darkness. She felt a thin table as they passed and before she could course correct to go around the corner of it, her thigh knocked into it and a bell went off one time.

"Wait."

The boy stopped. Tracy stood still, holding her breath, listening for any movement above them. The only thing she heard was the storm outside. But the sound of the bell. She knew what that was. She bent down to be closer toward Enzo.

"Is that a phone on the table there?" she asked.

"I think so. It looks weird."

"Put my hand on it."

Enzo placed her hand atop of what felt like an old house phone. Her fingers traced the slightly curved shape of the receiver, then worked their way down to the buttons protruding from the plastic casing. She'd spent so many hours as a child on her parents' house phone calling friends and boys and anyone she could get a hold of. When she was a kid, cell phones didn't exist. Her parents had two landlines in the house, one hanging on the kitchen wall and one in the hallway on the second floor. The one on the second floor felt just like this one. Push button instead of rotary dial. At the time, almost state of the art.

Tracy slowly lifted the receiver off the base and felt a rush of relief when she heard a dial tone. She didn't know Malcolm's cell phone number off the top of her head. She just pressed his name from her phone's contacts list to connect. Same with Missy and pretty much everyone else she dealt with on a regular basis. But she knew her house number by heart. The same house number they'd gotten when they moved in and bought the triple product discount package from the cable company. The same house number that cost more to disconnect than keep on for the telemarketers. She knew Malcolm wasn't the person she needed to fear. Her gut told her he hadn't been the one who attacked her that night at George's Island. It had been Sam. She knew this. There was no doubt. She'd call home to tell Malcolm she was okay and then she'd call 911 to tell the police to come and get her.

"I need you to press the numbers when I tell you," she said to Enzo who was still holding her other hand. "Can you do that?"

"Yes."

"Okay, get ready. Here we go."

She began reciting, and Enzo started dialing.

CHAPTER FORTY-ONE

"They still there?"

Missy pushed the curtain back just an inch and craned her neck to see outside. It was snowing, the meteorologist calling for an inch an hour for the next six hours, and the front yard, driveway, and pavement below were already covered in white. But they were still there. Like fixtures on the corner of their street.

"Yeah. Still there."

"Figures."

She and Malcolm were hoping the cluster of news vans would be driven away by the storm that was heading up from the south but as she pulled away from the window in the formal living room she realized such hopes had been foolish. They were a big story. *He* was a big story. No way an investigative journalist would miss out on something breaking while they hid away in their motel room. A little snow would be easy to overcome. A lashing from their editor or news director would not.

Missy stumbled down the hall toward the family room. As she passed through the kitchen, she grabbed the half-empty bottle of wine—their third—and her glass next to it. It was a little past eleven o'clock and they'd started drinking right before dinner. Needless to say, she was seeing double and loving every minute of it. She was a happy drunk, and she realized, as she emptied yet another glass, that she needed a little happiness in her life. Tomorrow would be full of hangovers and headaches and inevitable irritability, but tonight was about taking the edge off and pretending—if only for a little while—that everything was normal and her sister wasn't missing and that everything would have a happy ending. For her and Tracy at least.

Malcolm was in the family room, on the sectional, half-watching the end of a Knicks' game that had gone into overtime. He'd turned to beer after they'd polished off the second bottle of Pinot and held the can of Coors loosely by the tips of his fingers. He was a pleasant drunk. Not as carefree as Missy, but nice enough for her to be able to joke with him and let her hair down without the fear of his mood changing on a dime. She'd dated enough assholes with beer muscles or a chemical imbalance when it came to the hard stuff. It was nice to spend some time with a guy who could keep his cool and keep knocking them back. She didn't think he was as drunk as she was, and if he was, he hid it well.

"Thought the snow might've caused them to scatter like the rats that they are," Malcolm said as she sat down next to him. "But, nah. They're cockroaches, and roaches don't scatter for nothing. Not even a nuclear bomb."

"They really don't leave, do they?" Missy placed the wine bottle on the table in front of them and took a sip from her glass. "I think they sleep in the vans. I get up, they're there. I come back late, they're there. It's crazy."

"They think they can smell a story, and there's no convincing them that there isn't one. Not here anyway."

"As long as we stay inside and they stay outside, we're good. No one's come knocking and no one's been trying to climb the back fence to get candids of us in here, so that's a plus. I guess it could be worse."

"How?" Malcom asked as he turned and looked at Missy. "How could it be worse?"

Missy thought for a moment. "You're right. I'm sorry. Forget it."

Malcolm got up from the couch and took a swig of his beer. "You don't have to be sorry. I didn't mean to call you out. I just wish everyone would leave us alone so we could concentrate on finding Tracy. They should be spending their time and energy helping us instead of trying to figure out how they can pin her disappearance on me."

Missy rose from the couch as well. Her happy buzz was starting to wane. "Those are just the reporters and internet trolls. The police don't think you're a suspect or you'd have been arrested by now. They're the ones looking for Tracy and they're the ones who have what it takes to find her. Don't worry about anyone else."

Malcolm nodded and finished his beer.

"Come on," Missy blurted, desperate to keep the happy mood going. "I'm going to take your mind off of the press and Tracy and everything else that's bothering you."

"Yeah? How you gonna do that?"

"We're going to dance."

Malcolm laughed. "I don't think so."

"I'm serious!" Missy replied, laughing herself. "We'll pretend we're in a bar and it's a shitty bar and we're the only two people there. We came in separately. Didn't know each other. But then we got to talking and realized that each of us thought the other was okay. A song comes on the jukebox and you ask me to dance. I accept."

She muted the Knicks' game, flipped through her phone, and played an old, slow, Jackson Brown song.

"Come on."

Malcolm smiled. "I can't dance."

"Anyone can slow dance," Missy replied. She placed her

glass of wine down on the coffee table, put Malcolm's beer next to it, and slid her arm around his waist, pulling him close while she put her other hand on his shoulder. "You got this."

The smile slid off Malcolm's face as he touched the small of her back with one hand and put the other on the top of her hip. They began moving slowly, drunk rocking more than dancing, their eyes fixed on one another, their breath short and shallow.

"You're doing fine," Missy whispered, moving just an inch closer.

"Can I buy you a drink after this song is over?" Malcolm asked.

"I don't know," Missy replied. "What if I like the next song that comes on? Might have to keep dancing."

"I can handle that."

"I know you can."

The family room melted away. With each passing second, there was no house or press outside or missing sister or prime suspect or the thousand what-ifs that played endlessly in her mind. There was only her and Malcolm, together, swaying back and forth, the music guiding them, their eyes focused only on each other.

The house phone began to ring.

Missy jumped at the sound and pulled away as reality forced its way back into her life. "I'll get it."

"Leave it," Malcolm said, his face turning red. "Only telemarketers call that line."

"No. It could have something to do with Tracy. I'll get it before it wakes Finn."

Missy stumbled out of the family room, back through the kitchen, and into the foyer by the front door. An old cordless phone sat on a decorative table near the stairs. She picked it up on the third ring as the room tilted sideways. In the background, the basketball game came back on.

"Hello?"

"On my God. Hello? Missy? Is that you? Missy!"

It was Tracy. There was no mistaking the voice, even though it was panicked and whispering. Missy knew that voice anywhere. It was her sister. She staggered back a step, her hand touching her heart.

"Tracy?"

"You have to help me! I don't know where I am! I'm by a beach and a lighthouse! He has me!"

"You're alive."

"Yes! I need you to help me. Please!"

Missy took the phone away from her ear, looked at it for a moment...

"Hello? Missy?"

...and she hit the button to end the call. She quietly placed the phone back in the cradle, bent down behind the table, and unplugged the jack. When she was done, she took a breath, tried on a smile, and staggered her way back into the family room.

"You were right," she said. "Telemarketer."

"Told you."

Malcolm had returned to the couch and she sat next to him, taking her glass from the coffee table and downing what was in it in one gulp. "No more dancing. Let's watch the end of the game. And then a fresh round for everyone."

CHAPTER FORTY-TWO

"Hello?" Tracy heard the call disconnect, but held on to the hope that her sister was still there. "Hello? Missy? Can you hear me?"

A second click.

Dial tone.

Tracy held the phone against her chest and whispered. "We need to dial the number again. Can you do that?"

"Yes," Enzo replied.

Tracy gave Enzo her home number for a second time and she held the receiver back up to her ear, listening as it rang once, then twice, then a third time, then a fourth.

"Hi, you've reached the Cowan residence. No one is available to take your call right now, but of you leave..."

No one was picking up. Missy knew it was her. She'd said her name and seemed surprised that she was alive. Then she hung up. Why? What was happening?

She was tempted to dial again, but didn't want to waste any more time standing in the hallway, exposed and vulnerable. Instead, she reached over and felt the two plastic bubbles protruding from the phone's base and pushed them down, resetting the call.

"Dial nine, one, one."

She heard the three numbers tone in the receiver and waited. Help was on the other line. This nightmare was almost over.

"East Hampton 911. What's your emergency?"

"Tracy?"

She heard his voice and froze for a moment. He was above her, probably at the top of the stairs. Her heart pound harder in her chest as she gripped the phone.

"What are you doing?"

"Hello?" the operator said. "Are you there? What's your emergency?"

"Help us!" Tracy cried, then hung up the phone and found Enzo's tiny hand. "Run! Go!"

"Tracy!"

The boy dragged her forward as footsteps galloped down the stairs. Somewhere in the depths of her darkness, she heard the door open, and before she even realized what exactly what happening, she felt the cold air and the sleet stabbing her in the face.

"Run!" Enzo screamed over the wind. "Come on!"

She tried to keep up, but slipped on the slick porch, landing on her right hip and rolling halfway down what she figured were the front steps. She lost her grip with the boy and instead of trying to find it again, got herself back up onto her feet and just started running.

"Enzo, run! Go hide and find help! Go!"

Tracy had no idea if the boy could hear her or where he was, but she shouted her instructions for a second time and got moving as fast as she could. She ran, stumbling along the way. Not being able to see knocked her balance off and it was hard to keep going in what she thought was a straight line. She was wearing a sweatshirt and sweatpants Sam had given her, and only had wool socks on her feet. Everything was soaked and half-frozen instantly, her hair sticking to her face, the bandage around her head becoming wet and unstable.

"Tracy! Finn!"

Sam's voice roared in the night, rising above the wind and rain like thunder in a hurricane. It sounded like he was far enough away that she'd gained some ground, but it was hard to be absolutely sure with the way the wind was changing direction.

The mud Tracy had started out on turned to underbrush and dead leaves. Enzo had mentioned they were surrounded by woods. She wondered if being lost and blind in a forest was a worse fate than being chained to a bed in a house where there was heat and food, but her instincts were to run, so she did the best she could.

"Tracy!"

It sounded like Sam was getting closer and there was no way to know if she was hidden in the woods enough or if he could see her from where he was. Branches slapped her in the face and scratched her cheeks and chin. Thorns got caught in her hair as she kept moving, listening to the sickening rip as she broke herself free. Rocks she couldn't see stubbed her toes and roots twisted her ankles. She kept running and staggering, arms outstretched in front of her, reacting to what she felt as quickly as she could without stopping.

"You have to wait!"

Sam sounded angry, panicked. He knew that if she got free and got someone to help her, his little game of keeping her safe wouldn't hold up and he'd be arrested. She wanted to be reunited with her family. She wanted to wrap her arms around Finn and never let go. She had to find help. Just one person to save her.

A thick branch protruding from a tree slipped above her

outstretched fingertips and slammed into her face, crashing her hard to the ground. Stars danced in her darkness and she immediately felt blood flowing freely from her nose. She touched the tip of it and pain shot through her.

"Tracy! Come back!"

Sam's voice shocked her into moving again. She climbed to her feet and staggered forward, her legs a little less stable than they were only moments before. She could hear the waves clearer as she stumbled ahead and when her foundation of muddy earth, fallen sticks, and dead leaves gave way to packed sand, she realized she was close to the water's edge. She hadn't gone further into a never-ending forest. She'd made it to the coast. Someone had to be there to help her. Even in a storm someone was always at the beach, right?

"Help me!" she screamed over the crashing waves and relentless wind. "If you can hear me, I need help! Please! Help me!"

Tracy ran forward as she cried out. The sand turned a bit rocky and she slipped on some lose gravel, catching her balance before falling for a third time.

"Tracy! Stop!"

Sam's voice sounded close, maybe twenty yards away, full of panic and fear.

"Leave me alone!"

"Don't take another step."

"Help me!" she screamed again.

"No one's out here!" Sam sounded like he was getting closer. "It's almost midnight and we're in the middle of an ice storm. Come back with me and we can forget about all this. I'm not mad. I just want to get you inside and safe."

"No! I want to go home!"

"Okay! We can call the police when we get back to the house. Just stay put and don't move. You're at the edge of a rock cliff. It's like a hundred feet down to the ocean. Stay there. I'm coming for you."

"You're lying!"

"I'm not. I swear. If you keep going, you'll fall."

Tracy heard a branch snap under Sam's feet and she instinctively stepped back. She didn't want to go to the house with him. She wanted to go home. She wanted to be saved.

Another step back.

"I'm serious. Don't move."

Anoth—

The ground disappeared and Tracy found herself falling.

CHAPTER FORTY-THREE

Before she had a chance to realize what was happening, someone grabbed her wrist as she dangled in midair.

"Climb up my arm!"

Sam had made it just in time. Tracy swung her other hand over and wrapped it around his neck. He grunted as he pulled back and she pulled up and for a moment it felt like they might both fall, but her flailing feet found the edge of a wet rock face and she steadied herself until she was back on solid ground.

"I told you," Sam panted as they both lay on the ground, the sleet pelting them. "These woods are surrounded by sand cliffs. I wasn't lying."

Tracy said nothing.

"But I was there. You see? I saved you again. That's what I do."

Tracy quickly flipped onto her stomach and climbed to her hands and knees, but before she could make another move, Sam was on her, one hand around her throat, a fistful of her sweatshirt in the other.

"No more tricks," he seethed, still panting. "Let's go. Back to the house."

He started walking, pulling and pushing her along the way. She could feel the anger emanating from him. They said nothing on the way back to the house. Even when she stumbled over roots and rocks and was slapped by branches and scratched by bushes, he kept pulling and pushing. She tried to fight him off, but he was stronger than she was. Push. Pull. Silence. It was only when she was back in her room, being chained to the bed again, that she heard Enzo sniffling in the corner.

"Enzo," she said. "Are you all right?"

"He's fine," Sam replied for the boy. "Just made a mistake listening to you. Finn's learned his lesson. It won't happen again."

He wrapped the chain much tighter around her wrist this time.

"That hurts."

"Too bad."

She didn't see the slap coming, but felt the impact across her cheek and chin. The pain from her already swollen nose and eyes exploded in her head and she yelped, recoiling as the sting spread across the rest of her face.

"I give you everything!" Sam screamed. "Safety. Love. Shelter. A family. You don't care. You don't appreciate any of it! You'd rather be miserable in a loveless, cheating, marriage so you can feel sorry for yourself instead of being thankful that I've given you a life you deserve. You don't think you're worthy. I'm starting to wonder if you're right."

Tracy started crying. "Get away from me!"

"You're not leaving this place. Ever. This is your new life now. I've tried to be kind and calm and allow you to find your way to me, but my patience has run out. If you want me to *make* you love me, I can do that. I'd rather not, but I can." He leaned in so close she could smell the ocean on his skin. "If you try and leave again, I'll kill you."

"Go away."

"No. I need to change your bandage. It's soaked."

"Leave me alone!"

Sam ignored her and pulled on the back of the bandage that was wrapped around her head. He was rough as he picked at the layers of tape with his fingernails, pulling and clawing until small clumps of fabric began breaking away. The band around her head started to move and he forced his fingers over the top edge and pulled.

"That hurts!"

He yanked the bandages up and off.

The blackness remained.

Tracy lifted both hands to her face and felt around her chin and cheeks and eyes and forehead. There were bumps and scratches and swelling, but there was no detail, no vision.

She still couldn't see.

No!

"This can't be," Tracy muttered to herself as she touched her eyes again, wincing as the pain shot through her. "This can't be."

"What's wrong?" Sam finally asked.

"I still can't see! What's happening?"

"The swelling in the brain hasn't gone down to the point of your vision returning. Your face still looks a bit battered, but better than when I first brought you here. Not as much bruising, and the cut on your chin is healing. It's going to be a matter of time before your vision returns. Can you see anything? Colors? Shapes? Anything at all?"

Tracy shook her head as panic set in. "No."

"Put your hand up close. Can you see that?"

"No!" She looked around the room again. Just blackness. "The only thing I see is the man who attacked me at the park that night. Malcolm was never there, was he? It was you. It's always been you."

Sam huffed a laugh. "You're delusional. I saved you."

"No. You captured me."

She could feel Sam's body freeze, then he suddenly leapt off the bed. His footsteps scurried to the far end of the room toward the window.

"Dammit," he said.

"What is it?" Tracy asked.

Sam ignored her. Instead, she listened as his footsteps hurried back toward her and he grabbed her chained wrist hard, pulling it toward him as he worked quickly to unlock the padlock. She could hear keys dangling from the belt loop on his pants.

"What's happening?"

"Get up."

He pulled her to her feet and before she had a chance to balance, he was pushing her into a corner.

"The police are coming," he explained, his voice almost hoarse with a combination of rage and fear. "You're going to stand in this corner and I'm going to open the bedroom door wide enough so the door hides you. I'll have Finn with me, and I'll have my shotgun too. If you make a sound or alert this cop in any way, I'll kill them both. And I'll make sure they suffer. Do you understand?"

"Yes."

"Not a sound."

Sam pulled the bedroom door all the way back on its hinges until it pinned Tracy in place. She held her breath and listened as she heard Enzo sniffling.

The doorbell rang.

"You ready?" she heard Sam ask Enzo.

"Yes," Enzo replied as he tried to catch his breath through sobs.

The front door opened.

CHAPTER FORTY-FOUR

"Hey, Chief."

"Sam."

"I think I know why you're here."

"Do you?"

"You got a 911 call?"

"We did. Someone yelled for help and then the phone hung up. I was on my way home and heard dispatch. Told them I'd handle it since I was so close."

Sam's voice sounded different. The accent seemed to drift way. Why? Tracy wanted so desperately to call out, but she knew doing so would set things in motion that she would not be able to undo. But she'd never been so close to salvation before. Only a few feet away.

"I'm really sorry about that," Sam said. "My godson here was trying to pull a prank and didn't realize that goofing on 911 was serious. We talked about it, hence the tears. He gets it now. Isn't that right?"

"Yes," Enzo muttered.

Tracy's heart broke when she heard the boy speak. He sounded so fragile and scared.

"You can't prank 911," the chief said. His voice was harsh and gravelly, but there was a gentleness in there somewhere. "We need to keep those lines open for folks who actually have an emergency. We clear?"

"Yes, sir. I'm sorry."

"Why're you all wet? Both of you."

"I started yelling when I caught him and he kinda freaked out and ran out of the house." Sam's voice was low. "I had to chase him down to make sure he didn't get into the woods or near the cliffs."

"His parents here?"

"Nope. Just us. Boys' weekend."

"What's your name?" the chief asked the boy.

Silence.

"Finn," Sam interjected.

"Okay, Finn. Where're you from?"

Nothing.

"Manhattan," Sam said. "Same as me. His mom lives in Soho."

There was a tight period of quiet and Tracy knew she could step out and call for help in that pocket of time, but she couldn't see and didn't know how ready the chief would be to react. She assumed his guard was down as he knew Sam and she also knew that Sam was ready to kill if he had to. His priority was keeping her. Not Enzo and not the chief. She had to remain quiet. Their lives depended on it.

"I gotta look around," the chief explained. "Protocol when you call 911."

"No problem. Come on in."

Tracy listened as the group of footsteps traveled from room to room. As they walked down the hall and approached the bedroom, she held her breath and pushed herself as far into the corner as she could.

Boots stopped at the threshold.

"Who's in here?"

"Finn and I had a campout in here last night. Pretended we were cavemen and the dinosaurs were outside in the woods."

"Sounds like fun."

"It was."

A raspy exhale filled the brief silence.

"Everything looks in order."

"Good."

"I just need a second with the kid."

"I'm sorry?"

"Protocol. Wait in the hall. Just take a sec."

Tracy heard the doorknob rattle as someone grabbed it. She grimaced as she realized what would happen next. The chief would close the door so he could talk privately with Enzo, and when he did, he'd find her hiding. After that, there would be the deafening roar of gunfire and the silence of the aftermath. People were going to die. Sam was going to kill them.

"I want to talk on the porch," Enzo suddenly said. His voice was louder, more in control.

"It's cold out there," the chief replied. "Let's talk here."

"No. Outside. I think I left my toy out there and I want to get it before it gets all wet."

The grip on the doorknob released.

"Okay, Finn. Lead the way."

The group of footsteps walked back down the hall, away from Tracy and her hiding spot. She let out a breath and leaned her head back against the wall. She listened as Enzo led the chief outside and again when they came back in. She actually felt her body give way when the chief reported that all was as it should be and heard him walk down the gravel path and get into the car that was idling in front. When it pulled away, Sam came back in, returned her to the bed, re-shackled her wrist, and began putting on a new set of bandages.

"Where's Enzo?" she asked. She hadn't heard him come into the bedroom with Sam.

"His name is Finn. Weren't you listening?"

"Where is he?"

"Don't worry about it."

"I do worry. Where is he?"

Sam sighed. "He's in his room eating a bowl of ice cream. He earned it. He saved two lives tonight. Maybe three."

Tracy was quiet while Sam wrapped the new bandages around her head. She thought about the call she'd made to the house. Why was Missy there? Why had her sister hung up on her? Had she been moving forward with what they'd planned or had things changed in her absence? The more questions she asked herself, the less she wanted to know.

CHAPTER FORTY-FIVE
SIX WEEKS EARLIER

"Kat!"

Kat spun around when she heard her name and stared at the woman standing across the street. At first her face didn't register, but then it clicked.

"Missy?"

She nodded.

"What're you doing here?"

Missy crossed the street. "I followed you from the office," she explained. "I'm sorry, I know that's a little weird, but I needed to talk to you and this wasn't about work. It's not the type of conversation you'd want to have at your office."

They were standing in front of Kat's building, a brick three-family home that looked a bit long in the tooth, but serviceable. Kat thought it had charm with the oversized windows and detail in the moldings and trim. A good power wash and some fresh paint would've done wonders, but the landlord didn't care too much about the upkeep. Still, she thought it was nicer than the soulless stainless-steel apartments of downtown. She liked the history in this neighborhood.

"What's up?" Kat asked. Her hand was on the small

wrought-iron gate that led to a slate path and eventually up the front steps, but she hadn't opened it yet. She didn't like that Missy had followed her from the office. There was something unnatural about seeing a client outside of her workspace. She gripped the tip of the gate in case she felt the need to push it open and run, but knew she was probably being paranoid. But when she glanced beyond Missy and saw how alone they were, it made her a little nervous.

Missy looked down at the ground, then back up. "It's about your Coldplay date," she began. "I knew he looked familiar when I saw you guys there. I do know him."

Kat fought a shiver that wanted to run through her body. She'd tried so hard to keep him a secret. "Impossible. What are the odds?"

"His name is Malcolm Cowan. Owns a construction company in Westchester. I've facilitated some subcontracting work for him."

Kat could feel the blood drain from her face. She knew.

"He's married," Missy continued. "And he has a kid. A little boy. That's all I wanted to say. I wasn't sure if you knew or if he was telling you a line or maybe all this is old news and you know more about him than I do, but just in case you didn't, I wanted you to be aware."

"We're just friends."

"Okay."

"It's not what you think."

Kat knew the words coming out of her mouth sounded ridiculous, but she couldn't think of anything else to say.

"That's not what I saw at the concert, but look, it's really none of my business. I just wanted you to know about his other life in case you didn't. No judgment from me."

Kat thought about making an excuse or trying to explain, but instead she simply turned around and walked through the iron gate without another word. Missy didn't call after her as

she reached the front door and Kat dared not turn back to see if
she was still standing there. A slight panic was beginning to rise
in her. If Missy knew the truth and Missy knew Malcolm, who
else did she know?

And who else might find out?

DAY ELEVEN

CHAPTER FORTY-SIX

Detective Taft shuffled down the hallway of his one-bedroom apartment and made his way into the small galley kitchen. With eyes still slits and a brain that hadn't fully woken yet, he flipped on the percolator and opened the cabinet next to the refrigerator where he snatched a mug and a bowl for his doctor-ordered intake of daily fiber. Outside, the storm had passed and the sound of gas-powered engines filled the morning air as snow blowers cleared paths and driveways so folks could get to work on time. He smiled at the thought of his car parked safely in the garage under the building. It was an extra hundred a month for a space, but on days like this, it was the perfect investment.

With the coffee brewing and the Fiber One waiting for milk, Taft retreated back down the hall and went into the bathroom. He brushed his teeth and took his shower and by the time he was out, the coffee was sitting in the pot, waiting, steam rising into the air, the aroma of what he considered to be the good stuff from Colombia wafting through the apartment. He poured the coffee into his mug, poured milk into his cereal, and took both over to a small bistro table that overlooked Van Rensselaer Avenue and the Long Island Sound.

He was aware that he'd become a living cliché. An overweight cop who was unhealthy, unloved, and addicted to the job. The only thing preventing the quadfecta was the fact that he didn't have a drinking problem. Just a few beers on the weekend or a drink after work with the guys every once in a while. That was it. He'd been blessed with the ability to know when to say when, and for that, he was eternally grateful.

The apartment seemed lonelier that morning. The nausea in the pit of his stomach had been a constant for the last few weeks. Retirement. Kat. His last chance to put a killer behind bars. It was all piling up on him. He had to find Kat's murderer if it was the last thing he did. For him and for her.

Taft's cell phone rang and he picked it up from the table.

"This is Taft."

"Hey, it's George. Listen, I didn't know anything when you called before or else I would've said something. I'm sorry. I didn't know."

"It's fine. Don't worry about it. What's up?"

"We got the prints back that Lena put through IAFIS. We got a hit."

"Talk to me."

"One set was from Kat's cleaning lady. She came up on the federal level because of her immigration status and work visa. I'll email you her address, but I think you can rule her out fairly quick since you found semen at the scene."

"Agreed. I'll talk to her though."

"The second hit is quite interesting. Came up on IAFIS because of a handgun license. All legal and clean, but this guy's got some backstory."

"Who is it?"

"Malcolm Cowan."

Taft leaned back in his chair and took a quick sip of coffee. "That name sounds familiar."

"Yeah, well, it should," George replied. "Malcolm Cowan's

been in the news lately. His wife went missing under myste-
rious circumstances a couple of weeks ago. Still no trace of her.
Online chat is pointing the finger at the husband, so I went back
and started matching dates."

"And?"

"Stamford PD found Kat's body the *same day* Malcolm
Cowan's wife went missing."

There was silence in the apartment for what seemed like an
eternity.

"Holy shit," Taft muttered.

"Mr. Cowan lives in Putnam Valley, New York," George
continued. "I know the town borders Connecticut, but why
would his fingerprints be in our victim's apartment?"

Taft put down his mug. "I don't know, but I can assure you,
I'm going to find out."

Papers rustled on the other end of the phone.

"Lead detective on the Cowan disappearance is Kelly
Evans. Westchester PD."

"You got a contact number?"

"Everything's coming your way via email."

Taft stood from his chair and hurried to the bedroom.
Perhaps he was wrong when he said he wasn't addicted to
anything. That wasn't completely true. He was addicted to
moments like these. The times when the puzzle pieces
suddenly fit together and the adrenaline of a case forming a
conclusion was enough to make him feel like he did in his
younger days. That's what he was addicted to. That's what kept
him wanting to come back for more. That's what kept him
relevant.

"I'll call over to Westchester to speak with Detective Evans.
Hopefully we can have this guy in custody by dinner."

"I would have to agree with that plan."

"Do me a favor and delay the report to Lena. I'd like to be

down the road on this a bit before she starts calling in the cavalry."

"I can't hold it off forever."

"I know. Just give me some time."

"I get it," George replied. "Go. Do your thing. Just don't take too long."

CHAPTER FORTY-SEVEN

The cold air stung Kelly's face as she ran through the neighborhood, hopping through the snow that had fallen overnight and dodging plows and pedestrians shoveling out their driveways and sidewalks. Normally, she'd wait until the streets were clear before bothering to go for a run, but she'd been up all night, tossing and turning, thinking about Tracy Cowan and the Buick they'd found on the security cameras. She'd spent as much time as she could in front of her monitor, tracing Tracy's SUV and the Buick backward, but lost Tracy's car somewhere between the Taconic Parkway and Route 9. By then her eyes had started blurring and a headache had come on. She had to pull herself away from the screen, but in doing so, left an itch that she couldn't scratch, a task on her to-do list that seemed impossible to complete. So, she woke up as soon as the sun crested the horizon, layered up, and started jogging. It was slow going and frustratingly sloppy, but at least her heart was pumping and her head was starting to clear.

Her phone rang, interrupting the Billie Eilish song that was streaming through her earbuds. She checked her smartwatch and saw it was the stationhouse. She let the call go to voicemail, figuring she'd be back home in a few minutes and could call back when she was in the house and not panting through a conversation. The song picked back up and she kept moving.

It had been over a week since Tracy had gone missing. Her early theory of the woman abandoning her car and disappearing from her life had long been cut loose. The damage to her SUV, which had clearly been pushed into the river, spoke of something violent and unplanned. The only question that remained was whether Tracy was still alive or not, and with each passing day, those odds dwindled. The Buick with one headlight was their most solid lead in a case that didn't have many. She had to get back to her computer and start back-tracing surveillance footage and street cams again in the hopes of getting an image that would clearly show the Buick's license plate number. If she had the plate number, she'd have the driver. And if she had the driver, she'd have her first real suspect.

Kelly turned the corner and started running the final block before reaching her house. In the distance, she could see a lone news van sitting across the street from her home. The press had been growing relentless as each day passed without discovering Tracy's whereabouts. The case was gaining national attention, which meant pressure was mounting on the mayor and her chief. There was a growing push to assign a more experienced detective to the case, and she heard that Leeds had been advocating for her to stay on, but she knew it was only a matter of time before someone more senior got the go-ahead. If any more time passed, the governor would get involved, and then the FBI would be called in to assist, and she'd be the rookie who lost her department a national case.

Her phone rang again, cutting off the music. Kelly checked her watch and it was the stationhouse for a second time. She stopped running and engaged the call. Something was up.

"Yeah, this is Kelly."

"Hey, Kelly," a young voice replied. "This is Cooper on the

desk. I got a call I need to patch through. A Detective Taft from Stamford PD. He says it's urgent."

"Stamford, Connecticut?"

"Yup."

"Okay. Put him through."

Kelly walked back toward her house. She tried to steady her breathing as the call clicked into her earbuds.

"Detective Evans?" a gruff voice asked.

"Yes, this is Kelly Evans."

"Dennis Taft. Stamford Police. Listen, I'm working a homicide that I think you need a heads up on?"

Kelly braced herself, waiting for the detective to tell her he'd found Tracy's body. "Okay, what's up?"

"Victim's name is Kat Masterson."

Kelly exhaled. "Don't know her."

"She's a real estate attorney here in town. Found in her apartment. Strangled. Been working the case for almost two weeks and just got a match on some prints. They belong to Malcolm Cowan."

Kelly stopped in her tracks as the name was like a punch to the gut. "Are you serious?"

"It gets better," Detective Taft replied. "We found the body the same day Malcolm's wife disappeared. We also have traces of semen left behind. It appears the victim had sex with her assailant before she was killed. No sign of forced entry, so the fact that she knew her killer fits."

Kelly picked up her pace. She ignored the reporter who hopped out of his news van and started shouting questions.

"I took swabs of everyone in Tracy's family," she said. "Including Malcolm."

"Excellent. Then we'll have prints and DNA to test a match. I'd like to take Mr. Cowan in for questioning. We can do it at your place instead of having to bring him all the way to

Stamford. And I'd like you to assist me when we go by his house later to get him. That sound okay?"

"I'd be happy to."

"I'm not trying to step on toes or screw up your investigation. Kinda just worked out this way."

"No, I get it. It's not a problem."

Kelly walked up the front steps to her house as she worked out the logistics of when and where she'd meet Detective Taft in anticipation of bringing Malcolm Cowan in for questioning. Things began to click into place in her mind and suddenly the brash reporter behind her and the stress of an unsolved case building national attention didn't matter. This was as solid a lead as she could've hoped for, and if it took someone else's murder to close her case, so be it. Sometimes you just had to take what you could get.

CHAPTER FORTY-EIGHT

Malcom sat in the family room watching some sports program on ESPN, but his mind was a million miles away. Finn was next to him playing quietly on Tracy's iPad. Missy was in the kitchen making sandwiches for their locked-down picnic in the backyard. He could hear her rummaging through the cabinets and opening the refrigerator and replayed the scene of them drunk-dancing the night before. He could picture them floating through the room, could still feel her body in his arms, and searched for a trace of guilt or anger or remorse, but found nothing but emptiness. He knew he should've felt regret or shame, but he was a shell of himself, a stranger in his own skin. He simply didn't care.

It was starting to feel like Tracy was never coming home, but what was more frightening was the fact that it was hard to remember what it had felt like when she'd been there. He felt ashamed for having trouble remembering her laugh or how she called Finn down each night for dinner, but with all the stress and the avalanche of crap coming down on him, it was difficult to see past that moment or look back to two weeks earlier. He needed his wife home. He needed to feel her presence again.

"Hey, Malcolm," Missy called from the kitchen. "Something's going on outside. The press is getting all stirred up."

Malcolm turned away from his thoughts just as he heard a ruckus coming from outside the house. He looked toward the windows in the living room that faced the street, but the shades were drawn and he couldn't see anything. He could hear, however, and the increased volume of movement and van doors slamming shut and voices turning from murmur to talking to shouting told him something was up.

"Stay here," he told Finn as he rose from the couch. The boy ignored him, too entrenched in his game to notice.

Missy poked her head into the family room. "What's going on?"

"I don't know. I'm going to have a look."

He walked down the hall, and into the foyer. The voices and commotion outside grew louder as he approached the front door. He carefully slid a curtain to the side and peeked out the side window next to the door. There were two patrol cars and an unmarked sedan sitting in front of his house. He watched as four officers, Detective Evans, and an older man he'd never seen before climbed from the cars and made their way toward the house.

They've found her.

Malcolm choked back tears that suddenly wanted to burst forth. The emotions he'd been trying to turn off came back and he clutched his stomach as all the pent-up anguish and shame and guilt and worry that had been building over the last ten days was now threatening to break loose. He did his best to hold it together as the team of police personnel climbed the front steps and knocked on his door.

"What's going on?" he heard Missy ask from behind him.

Malcolm didn't answer. Instead, he opened the door and stepped back, waving two of the officers and the detective and the older man inside. The remaining two officers stood guard outside on the porch.

"Hello, Mr. Cowan," Detective Evans said as they gathered in the foyer. "We need to speak with you for a moment."

"Did you find her?"

"Can we talk in private?"

Malcolm turned and saw that Missy was in the hallway, her arms wrapped around Finn who was standing in front of her.

"We can talk in the living room," he said. "This way."

Malcom led Detective Evans and the older man into the living room while the two officers stayed in the foyer. Malcolm sat down on one couch while the older man sat opposite him on the loveseat. Detective Evans remained standing.

"Malcolm, this is Detective Taft from the Stamford Police Department."

Malcolm looked at the older man who stared back at him with an intensity that was unnerving. "Stamford? You found Tracy in Stamford?"

"This isn't about Tracy."

A wave of relief washed over him for a moment, but was quickly replaced with confusion. "What's going on?" he asked.

"You own a construction company, is that right?" Detective Taft began, his voice more of a growl than anything else. "Cowan Construction?"

"Yeah, that's right."

"And you do business with Triaglia and Brown?"

A quick nod. "Triaglia and Brown is my law firm. They handle my business with licenses and bonding and workers comp and all that stuff. Has something happened?"

"Are you familiar with a Kat Masterson there at the firm? She's been your contact there for the most part?"

"I know Kat, sure."

"She was found dead in her apartment. Strangled."

Malcolm heard the words, but it took a moment for the

actual sentence to sink in. He felt his throat go dry and his heart thump in his chest. Kat was dead. Did that mean Tracy was too? What was happening? "Dead?"

"That's right. Have you heard from her?"

"No."

"When was the last time you spoke to her?"

Malcolm tried to think. He needed to get his story straight. He rubbed his face as his world crumbled in on itself. Everything around him seemed to dim. "I don't know. A few weeks?"

"What did you talk about the last time you spoke?"

The detective's questions came one after the other, like he knew the answers Malcolm was going to give before he gave them.

"I don't know. Probably the new project I was working on in Hastings."

"And where did you meet?"

"Her office."

"Ever meet in her apartment?"

"No."

The old man shook his head. "Try again."

"What?"

"You're lying and I'm giving you the opportunity to try again. Did you ever meet her in her apartment? Have you ever been to her apartment?"

Malcolm fell back on the couch and looked up at Detective Evans who was staring at him with hate in her eyes.

They know.

"Yes, I've been to her apartment."

The detective nodded. "Which would explain the fingerprints we found there."

"I guess."

"When were you there?"

Malcolm shrugged. "A couple of weeks ago."

"How about the night before your wife went missing?"

Malcolm could feel his entire body seize.

Detective Evans took a step forward. "Detective Taft shared a few details of his case with me this morning," she said, her voice sharp and impatient. "Showed me Kat's phone records and there was this number that kept coming up. Untraceable because it was a burner phone." She took her phone out of her pocket and hit the screen.

The house went quiet.

Somewhere in the background, faint and distant, a digital tone was sounding off.

"I think we found the owner of that burner," she said.

Detective Taft stood from the loveseat. "We're going to need you to come down to the station so we can talk in more detail. Can you do that?"

Malcolm nodded as words escaped him. He let the older man guide him out of the family room and allowed one of the officers to take him gently by the arm as they left the house and walked down the path toward the street, a chorus of questions and excitement from the rabid reporters coming one after the other as they surrounded the police car he was put in the back of. He looked down for fear of making eye contact with anyone, especially afraid of seeing his son watching all of it unfold, the same two words churning through his mind, over and over.

They know.

There would be no recovering from this.

CHAPTER FORTY-NINE

The interview room at the Westchester Police headquarters was purposely small. There was a plastic chair on one side of a tiny table, a second chair facing it, and a third chair in the corner of the room. Unlike some of the larger departments or what one might see on a TV show or in a movie, there was no oversized one-way mirror with an observation room on the other side. In lieu of an observation room, there was a single camera on a tripod that recorded both audio and video. The room was designed to make a suspect feel claustrophobic. The chairs were supposed to be uncomfortable. The atmosphere was going to be either too hot or too cold, depending on the time of year. The object was to make the suspect want to get out of the room as quickly as possible. In order to do that, he or she had to give up information the police wanted. The more intense the situation became, the smaller the room seemed. Three humans in such a tight space could make the heat unbearable sometimes. It was an effective technique. One both Kelly and Taft hoped would work on Malcolm Cowan. Only time would tell.

The prints alone weren't enough to bring any kind of charges against Malcolm. Both she and Taft knew that even before speaking with the Fairfield County District Attorney, thus the formal interview versus an official interrogation. Taft would have to tread gently to keep Malcolm from leaving or calling for an attorney. It was important to maintain the illusion that Malcolm was there to help in Kat Masterson's homicide investigation and not there as a primary suspect.

Malcolm and Taft were at the table sitting face-to-face. Kelly was in the corner, in the third chair, observing. The reason Malcolm had been brought in for questioning had nothing to do with her case, so she was an observer for the time being. If something came up involving Tracy and her where-abouts, she would be there. Until then, she was quiet, ready to take notes, listening for anything that might connect the death of Kat Masterson and the location of Tracy Cowan.

Taft put the locket he'd been holding back in his pocket and smiled. "We appreciate you talking with us today, Mr. Cowan," he began. "You're not under arrest. We just need you to answer a few questions for us to help us understand better what happened to Kat Masterson. You can do that for us, right?"

Malcolm looked shaken. He was pale and the edges of his eyes were red. He kept brushing his hair away from his face like it was a tick. He looked up at Taft and nodded, but said nothing. The officers had told Kelly that he'd been quiet for the entire ride. Not a word. The room was already hot and a thin line of perspiration was forming on his brow.

"Let's start with your relationship to the victim," Taft said. "Who is she to you?"

"She's my attorney," Malcolm replied. "She helped me with my business dealings. I was introduced to the firm by a friend and they helped me file the paperwork to form my corporation. Kat was assigned to me, I guess you'd say, and over the years she's helped me file for bonding, deal with a worker's comp issue, help with permits in certain counties I'm doing a job in. Stuff like that."

"And were you seeing her romantically?"

"No. We were just friends."

Taft paused. "Just friends? You sure about that?"

Malcolm nodded.

"If she was your attorney from a business standpoint and you guys were just friends, why did you need a disposable phone to talk to her and text?"

"Because sometimes my wife uses my phone and I knew that if she saw a bunch of texts and calls, she'd think something else was going on just like you guys do. It was easier to have the separate phone."

"You don't think just explaining to your wife that she was your attorney would be enough? You could show her the texts if they were all professional."

"It wouldn't have been enough. You don't know Tracy."

Taft looked at his suspect. "Mr. Cowan, now that we have it, we're going to be able to pull texts from that burner phone in a matter of days. Are you sure you don't want to come clean and save yourself the need to explain what we might find a few days from now?"

Malcolm shifted in his seat. "I'll admit some of the texts could get a little flirty," he said. "But she wasn't my lover. I wasn't cheating on my wife."

"Yet the two of you called each other obsessively. Ten calls a day on average according to her phone records. And she never put that number in her contacts list. You'd think if you were talking that much, she'd just add that number to her contacts."

"I don't know what to tell you."

Taft nodded as he skimmed through the file. "Kat had a sugar daddy kind of guy she was seeing. Took her to fancy shows and out to dinners and concerts and all kinds of fun things. Did you know that?"

"No."

"She and her friends called him Big Daddy. You ever hear

Kat reference Big Daddy in the conversations or texts you had with her?"

"No."

Taft wrote a few notes in the pad that was next to the file. He looked up when he was done. "Are you Big Daddy?"

"No."

"Okay." More notes. "When was the last time you were at Kat Masterson's apartment?"

Malcolm shook his head. "I told you at the house, I was there a couple of weeks ago."

Taft smiled. "Yes, sorry. I forgot. What were you doing there?"

"I had documents that had to be reviewed on a job I have lined up after my Hastings job that I'm working on now. I got the documents from my client's lawyer at the last minute and I drove them to Kat's place because the office was already closed and I needed her to review them ASAP. That's why I was there."

"And what day was that?"

"I honestly don't remember. I can look at the paperwork when I get home and let you know."

"How long did you stay?"

"Half hour maybe? I had a drink and she skimmed the docs and told me everything looked like it was in order and she'd do a formal pass that night." He looked up at Taft, his eyes wide. "And I got the docs back the next day, which proves I wasn't at her place the night she was killed. If that was the case, I never would've gotten the documents back."

Taft made a few more notes and paused. Kelly watched intently, waiting for the elder detective to make a move she knew he had up his sleeve. All the good ones did.

"I want you to close your eyes," Taft began.

"What?"

"Close your eyes. Humor me."

Malcolm closed his eyes.

"I want you to think back to the night you were at Kat's apartment. The night you were dropping off those documents. Can you see it?"

"Yes."

"Good. Put yourself in the hallway at the exact moment she opens the door to greet you. Are you there?"

"Yes."

"Excellent. From that moment, talk me through where you go in the apartment until you leave."

Malcolm swallowed once, his eyes closed, his left leg bouncing up and down relentlessly.

"I followed her down the hall into the living room. I gave her the file with the paperwork in it and she placed it on the coffee table. She offered me a drink and I said yes. I followed her into the kitchen and she made me a vodka tonic. We went back into the living room and she skimmed through the file. Then I left."

"So, you only went into the living room and kitchen."

"Yes."

"Did you use the bathroom?"

"I don't think so. Maybe, but I honestly can't remember."

"Okay, open your eyes."

Malcolm did as he was told and looked back and forth between Kelly and Taft. It appeared as though he wanted an assessment of how he'd done. Kelly met his gaze for a moment, then glanced back down at her own notepad, afraid she might give something away with an unintended expression or movement.

Taft cleared his throat and made more notes. "You said earlier that the texts we'll find when we upload the information from your disposable phone might be flirtatious."

"That's right."

"Flirtatious on both ends or was one of you more aggressive than the other?"

Malcolm thought about the question. "I'd say they were pretty even. I'm not going to lie, if I wasn't married, I definitely would've pursued Kat, but I couldn't cross that line."

Taft shuffled through his pad. "Let's go back to this Big Daddy person Kat and her friends talked about. You say that's not you."

"Correct."

"Any idea who it might be?"

"None."

"Did Kat ever mention him to you?"

"No."

"You ever buy Kat anything that she could misconstrue as a gift a boyfriend would buy his girlfriend?"

Malcolm shook his head. "No. I've gotten her flowers a couple of times after her help closing a large job, but I sent those to her office and they weren't, like, roses or anything."

"Any jewelry or perfume or something more intimate?"

"No."

"Any idea who might've wanted to hurt Kat?"

"None. I really, truly, have no idea who could've done something like that."

Taft closed both his notepad and the notebook. He stood up from his seat. "I appreciate your time, Mr. Cowan. I think that's all I have for you at this point. I may need to circle back on a few things as they come across my desk, but I got what I needed. We'll have an officer drive you home."

Malcolm exhaled again and fell back in his seat. "So, what now?"

"What do you mean?"

"It's bad enough the entire world thinks I had something to do with Tracy disappearing. You guys just perp-walked me from my house in front of national news reporters. Can you give a statement or something saying that you only brought me in to help with a separate investigation and that I'm not a suspect? I don't need people thinking I'm a goddamned serial killer."

Taft motioned toward Kelly. "I'm sure Detective Evans and I can draft a statement to get out to the media. Shouldn't be a problem."

Malcolm stopped when he got to the door. He turned toward Kelly. "Any progress on your end?" he asked.

"We're still working a few leads," Kelly replied.

"It's been too long. And now Kat. Do you think this has something to do with me?"

"I don't know. Does it?"

"I can't see how."

"If there's a connection, we'll find it."

Kelly watched as Malcolm disappeared out the door without saying anything further. She stood from her seat and turned off the video recorder. "I think he's lying," she said. "Something doesn't sit right."

Taft pushed his chair in. "He was lying for sure. And we got more than we could've hoped."

"Explain."

They walked out of the interview room together.

"We needed to build a baseline of his lies," Taft explained. "And he keeps feeding us what we need. We didn't have enough for charges, so, we brought him in and listened to one bullshit answer after the other, which will tangle him up when we do file charges and bring him in for a real interrogation. He said he only went into her living room and kitchen, and maybe the bathroom. We have his prints in her bedroom. He said they weren't romantic, but if that semen sample comes back as a DNA match, we'll have him there too. Unless, of course, the sex wasn't consensual. Either way he's cooked because if that DNA sample is a match, we'll have caught him in his lie about going to her apartment to drop off the paperwork on his new deal several nights before her murder. If the semen is his, that means he was there that night. Then we bring charges and really turn it up."

Everything Taft said made sense. Kelly thought about how deft he'd been setting up the questions and allowing Malcolm to walk into each lie. It was all to construct a net to catch him in down the road, and the veteran detective had played it flawlessly.

"When do we get the DNA test back?" she asked.

"A few days," Taft replied. "Maybe sooner if we're lucky. Lena put a high-priority rush on them, so they should be able to get us at the top of the list and execute pretty quickly. Won't be long."

Both Kelly and Taft turned the corner into the main area of the stationhouse just in time to see Malcolm signing out with a uniformed officer standing next to him. The man looked disheveled and lost, his movements slow and muddled. He didn't look like a guy who'd committed one murder and possibly a second. He didn't look like a guy who'd hurt anyone, but she reminded herself they rarely did. Every news feed showing neighbors interviewed after one of their own was taken into custody for a horrendous crime always had them quoted saying they couldn't imagine that person being so evil. He was so quiet. She was so nice. He was such a good neighbor. She took care of everyone on the block. It was their kindness that was their camouflage, their thoughtfulness that took the spotlight of guilt off them. Malcolm Cowan was probably no exception. Still, doubt scratched at the back of her mind. If he'd done what Taft had shown her and made his wife disappear, she would've thought she'd be able to see even a slight glimpse of madness behind Malcolm's eyes, but there was none. None that she could see anyway. And that was what kept her up at night. What was she missing?

CHAPTER FIFTY

Tracy heard the bedroom door open and cowered back as far against the headboard as she could. Her skin crawled and her headache was getting worse. She felt on edge, like her body was on the verge of exploding. The pins in her eyes were throbbing. "Who's there?"

"It's me. I wanted to show you something."

Sam's voice sounded a little lighter than it had the previous night when he'd caught her and Enzo trying to escape. Even that morning he'd been cold and unwilling to talk when he brought her breakfast and changed her bedpan. Now he seemed a bit more relaxed and in control.

"What have you been giving me?" Tracy asked as she scratched her arms. "I don't feel good."

"Just something to calm you down and help you sleep," Sam replied.

"But what is it?"

"Nothing you need to worry about."

More scratching. The headache pulsated with her heartbeat.

"Where's Enzo?"

The footsteps that had been approaching her bed stopped.

"*Finn* is fine. He's in his room."

"I want to see him. I want to make sure he's okay."

"You can see him later. He's taking a nap."

"I don't believe you."

"I don't care what you believe. I'm telling you the truth. I get that you're worried because he helped you out of that chain and helped you run from the house. I'm not mad about that. Not anymore. He's just a kid and he was listening to an adult tell him what to do. Makes perfect sense. We talked about it and he's now aware of how unstable you are and how you being fastened to the bed is for your safety. At least until you get your eyesight back. It's amazing how deep a conversation you can have with a child over a peanut butter and jelly sandwich and a glass of milk."

Tracy fought the urge to rip her skin off. She spoke through gritted teeth. "I want to make sure you didn't do something to him."

"I didn't. You can see him as soon as he wakes up and you can apologize for making him your accomplice."

Sam chuckled and that unnerved Tracy. She couldn't understand why he was in such an upbeat mood. He should've been furious. She should have been punished for what she did. Her escaping and the close encounter with the police chief the night before should have had his nerves frayed. Instead, he seemed carefree, which made things so much scarier. What did he have planned for her next?

The footsteps continued toward her and Tracy felt the mattress give under Sam's weight as he sat on the edge of the bed.

"I need you to listen to this," he said. "It's a video clip from Channel 2 news."

In the blackness, Tracy fought through the pain in her head and the needles in her eyes and the itching of her skin and concentrated on the anchor's words. It was a woman. Professional. Her diction almost perfect.

"Local businessman, Malcolm Cowan, was escorted by Westchester County police and Stamford, Connecticut detectives to the County Police Headquarters in Hawthorne today as a person of interest in the homicide investigation of Kat Masterson in Stamford. Mr. Cowan is currently the main suspect in his wife Tracy's disappearance almost two weeks ago. The police would not confirm whether the two cases are linked, but sources tell Channel 2 that Ms. Masterson was Mr. Cowan's attorney for his construction business and that the two knew each other."

Suddenly everything went away. No more itching or pain or needles. Just the news anchor's words. It was happening.

"Oh my God," Tracy whispered.

"There's more," Sam said. "Listen."

"Ms. Masterson was found inside her Stamford apartment after failing to show up for work. She was strangled, but there was no sign of forced entry and nothing appeared to have been stolen. Police believe the victim knew her assailant and that they were able to recover key evidence that could shed light on the case in the coming days. It is unknown if Ms. Masterson knew Tracy Cowan, but police from both jurisdictions are working together to connect any dots that may arise from the two cases. Channel 2 will keep you updated as the story unfolds."

Tracy could hear Sam slipping his phone back in his pocket.

"You obviously can't see the video, but they show Malcolm being walked out of the house surrounded by police officers and the two detectives. He looks guilty if you ask me. You can see it in his eyes."

"And you'd be an expert in madness, right?" she said, her voice full of sarcasm.

Sam didn't rebut. "It's what I do and what I know. Your husband killed that woman. No doubt about it."

Tracy nodded and fell back onto her pillows. It was all finally coming to a head.

Finally.

CHAPTER FIFTY-ONE

Reagan Hart sat behind her anchor chair looking both glamorous and serious all at the same time. Her lighting was perfect. The color swatches on the set matched with her outfit that, in turn, matched with her makeup. She stared into the camera, her eyes adept at not reading each word the teleprompter scripted her to say. She was the consummate professional. America loved her. And that was only Malcolm's second most serious problem. The first were the words so delicately, yet somberly, coming from her exquisitely shaped lips. Words that spelled nothing but doom.

"In an incredible plot twist to the story we've been following about Tracy Cowan, the missing mother whose car was found half-submerged in the Hudson River over a week ago, her husband, Malcolm Cowan, was brought into Westchester County police headquarters today for questioning around the murder of attorney, Kat Masterson, in Stamford, Connecticut. Sources tell us that Ms. Masterson was Mr. Cowan's attorney and that her murder took place the day Tracy Cowan went missing. When asked about the details of Mr. Cowan's detainment, police said—"

Malcolm muted the television and threw the remote down next to him on the couch.

"That's not what happened!" he yelled. "I wasn't brought in for questioning as a suspect. They're interviewing all of her clients. Jesus!"

Missy said nothing. She stared at the beautiful reporter as she mimed her story in the silence of the family room. Malcolm had been brought in. The police had made the connection.

It was happening.

"This is insane," Malcolm continued. "The police marched me past all those reporters and then tell me I'm not a suspect after I'm alone at the station. They have to tell *them* that! They said they'd make a statement. What's taking so long? The entire world already thinks I made Tracy disappear. I don't need this too. Not when I'm innocent."

Missy was only half-listening. Tracy was alive. She'd heard her voice. Her exchange with her sister replayed in her mind. She had no idea what had happened to her, but she'd never thought it was possible that she'd still be alive after all this time. And now the plan was coming to fruition. Like it was all meant to be.

She could hear Finn playing upstairs. After the police had dropped Malcolm off at the house, the press had swarmed and it took all three uniformed officers to hold the reporters back off the front yard. Malcolm had come in disheveled and angry. She sent the boy up to his room so he didn't have to see the scene unfolding out on the street or see his father looking so fraught and abused. Missy could still hear the reporters outside even though it had been an hour since he'd returned.

"I don't understand why the police haven't put something out saying I'm not a suspect to get these people off our backs. They said they would. I should sue the department when this is over."

Missy put down the glass of wine she was holding, leaned her elbows on her knees, and stared at Malcolm so he knew she was serious.

"The police aren't going to say you're not a suspect because you *are* a suspect."

"I'm not!"

"You are, hon. Don't be blind. The police had you pegged for this the second your name came up and got cross-referenced with Tracy's disappearance. You're their number one man and they ain't taking their eyes off you until your alibi is verified by a hundred different people or you're behind bars."

"But I didn't do anything," Malcolm whined. "To Tracy or to Kat."

"Well," Missy replied as she clapped her hands together once. "You were screwing them both and now they're both gone. It ain't looking good for you."

Malcolm climbed off the couch and began pacing the room, his hands flailing as he spoke. "What happened to innocent until proven guilty?"

"Still applies, but they're gathering the proof. And as far as the public is concerned, you're guilty. Case closed."

"This is spinning out of control."

"Why didn't you just admit to the affair with Kat?"

"Because I know it would've made things even worse."

Missy laughed and shook her head. "Things are already worse, Malcolm. You think they're not going to find out about the affair? And when they do, you'll be officially lying to the police during a murder investigation while having taken part in a love triangle between you, Kat, and Tracy. One's dead and one's missing. You think they're not going to pin that on you? Come on, you're a smart guy. Use your head. If I were you, I'd start looking into a lawyer. Choose a man this time."

"Neil's getting me a lawyer."

"Tell him to hurry up about it, and when you get him, call the detective and tell him you were having an affair with Kat and come clean. That would be the smartest move you could make right now. At least it would show you're not trying to hide anything. You can say you were scared at first knowing what it would look like, but then you then realized it would look worse if you didn't say anything. They'd have to appreciate that."

Malcolm shook his head. "No. I can't paint a bullseye on my back like that. Not when I'm innocent. The second I admit I lied in the interview, I'm a goner."

"The bullseye's already there," Missy said. "I can see it from here. Not sure why you can't. You're a goner the second they find out about the affair. Think about it."

Malcolm leaned against the wall and started to cry. He cupped his face in his hands and sobbed. Missy climbed off the couch and walked up to him. She placed her hands on his trembling shoulders.

"I believe you when you say you didn't have anything to do with Tracy's disappearance. And I believe you when you say you had nothing to do with this Kat Masterson woman's murder. But this is way beyond what I'm willing to believe. At this point, I have to be here for Finn because it looks like he's going to lose both of his parents soon, and I need to step up and protect him. This isn't about you anymore. This is about your child."

"I know," Malcolm stuttered. "I appreciate you looking out for him."

"You need to start thinking about protecting your family."

"I am."

Missy paused. "I think you should put me on as an owner or signer on your business."

Malcolm looked up and Missy kept speaking, slow and even. No emotion.

"If you get arrested and Tracy stays missing, the government is going to come in and seize the assets of your company and Finn will be left with nothing. If I'm part of the company, I can keep the existing jobs moving and I can make sure Finn is taken care of when Uncle Sam does come in and starts grabbing what ain't his. It's not safe that you're the sole owner right now. And I'd be saying the same thing if Tracy was still part of your company but missing. It doesn't even have to be me who's on there with you. Make it your CPA or another lawyer at the firm you use. Just make sure it's someone more than just you. Someone you can trust. For Finn's sake. This is about legacy."

Malcolm nodded and wiped tears from his eyes. "You really think they're going to pin Kat's murder on me?"

"I think that ball's already rolling."

"My God."

She gently touched the bottom of his chin and kept him from lowering his head again. "I'm here," she said quietly. "Always have been. I believe you when you tell me you're innocent and I'll stay by your side as long as you need me to. I'm here for you, but I need to be here for Finn even more. Remember that. For your son."

Malcolm leaned in and as he got closer, she let go of his chin and closed her eyes. She felt his lips touch hers and then felt him step into her as his tongue slipped into her mouth. She let it happen, pulling him closer, her hands moving up and down his back, her nails gently scratching the bottom of his hairline, all the while thinking of her sister's voice on the other end of the phone, telling her that she was alive, and the plastic sound the phone made as Missy placed it back in its cradle, cutting her off.

Malcolm pulled away and looked at her. "I'm sorry."

"It's okay."

"I shouldn't have done that."

She stepped toward him again. "It's okay."

Malcolm turned away from her and began to walk out of the

room. "I'll sign the paperwork to put you on as an owner. I'll call Neil now."

Missy nodded. "Good. Tell him it has to happen today. We're not sure when the police will be back. Could be any second."

CHAPTER FIFTY-TWO

Lena was waiting for him when Taft pulled into his apartment parking garage. From the expression on her face, he knew she'd found out about his interview with Malcom Cowan, and she was not pleased. He shut off the engine and climbed out of his car. She was on him before he could engage the alarm.

"Did you think with all the media surrounding Malcolm Cowan that I wouldn't find out?" she spat. "You perp-walked him out of his house, for Christ's sake. Did you think you could keep this a secret when fifty cameras are on this guy every time he blows his nose? You can't possibly be that stupid. Or reckless."

Taft put his hands up. "I know. I'm sorry. I screwed up."

"Screwed up? No, Dennis, you jeopardized the entire case. We finally got some evidence that can stick and you went behind my back and conducted an unapproved interview in another police department while trying to keep me out? What's the matter with you?"

"I don't know. I jumped the gun. I felt like we were on to something and I wanted to nail this guy."

"We *are* on to something. But I was waiting to see if the

DNA also came back as a match. This way we'd have him on both prints and DNA and we could actually get a conviction."

Taft looked to the ground. He wasn't used to getting called to the carpet like that, and her words stung because he knew she was right. If another cop ever went over his head on an active case, he would've gone ballistic.

"I know what I'm doing," Lena continued. "I don't need you leading the way. And I sure as hell don't need you handing the other side an out with an interview we can't use in court. You're better than this, regardless of the situation."

"I'm sorry."

Lena stepped so close he could smell the mint from her gum on her breath.

"This is my case," she said. "You understand? You're here because I'm allowing it, and the second I tell the department you're out, you're in Florida living the rest of your life fishing off a dock and having two o'clock Mai Tais. You're here because I'm giving you a chance at closure. Don't spit in my face like that ever again."

Before he could respond, Lena turned on her heels and stomped back up the ramp and out of the garage. He didn't start moving again until he heard her car pull back out into the street.

DAY TWELVE

CHAPTER FIFTY-THREE

The snow had picked up again in the Hudson Valley and although the accumulation forecast for Manhattan was light, Dr. Devi had to stamp his feet on the rubber mat when he stepped into his building to knock the slush off. He unbuttoned his jacket and untied his scarf as he hurried down the hall toward his office. The young man was already sitting in the wingback by the window when he walked in, his hood pulled up all the way, almost covering his face.

"I'm sorry I'm late," Dr. Devi said as he hung up his coat and scarf and rushed to the unoccupied chair opposite his patient. "Traffic had me tied up with the weather."

"Where you coming in from?" the young man asked.

"I was up north. Had to see someone last minute."

The young man studied the doctor, looking him up and down. He crossed his arms in front of his chest. "I haven't seen you around in a while."

"I could say the same."

"Where've you been?"

"Here and there. Seeing patients. Mostly here at the office. Sometimes at their homes like the appointment I just came from. What about you? Every time I come here, I don't see you with the other two."

A small shrug. "You must not be looking hard enough. I'm with those guys all the time."

"I see. I guess I'm mistaken." Dr. Devi pulled his eyeglasses from the breast pocket of his shirt and slipped them on. "You don't have to take on the persona you use out there with your friends. You're with me now."

"I wish I wasn't."

"I know, but don't think of it as such a clinical visit. Think of it as a check-in and an opportunity for us to talk. It doesn't have to be a doctor–patient thing. It's just us, Samesh. You and me."

"I told you not to call me that."

"I'm sorry. Quiet Boy. You're right. You did tell me that."

"Many, many times."

Dr. Devi opened his notebook and took a breath. Thoughts clamored in his mind and he tried his best to clear it all so he could be present with his patient. All he could think about for the past few weeks had been Tracy. He could hear her voice and see her face and listen as she told her stories in his office, sitting so innocently across from him, wanting so desperately to know how to fix what was ailing her. She'd been good at the process. Now she was a face on the news and others who never really knew her were trying to give her a new persona. They were already assuming she was dead or that she abandoned her family. They didn't know her like he did. They'd never take the time to. But he had to focus on the people sitting in sessions with him regardless of what else was happening with the investigation. He had a job to do and it wasn't fair to the others.

"Can you take the hood off so we can get started?" Dr. Devi asked Quiet Boy. "It's a bit distracting."

Quiet Boy tugged at his hood until it fell on his shoulders. A tuft of thick black hair emerged, his brown eyes hidden behind bangs that fell past his nose. He was skinny under the layers of baggy clothes, but he was tough. Trouble when he wanted to be. Dr. Devi had been trying to get to the root of his anger, but so far he'd been unsuccessful in even scratching the surface. All those years of picking away and it felt like they hadn't gotten very far.

"Why do you like to be called Quiet Boy?" Dr. Devi asked, his pen at the ready. "After all this time, why not use your birth name or a different nickname? You're too old and too smart for a street name like that."

"I already told you, I don't like my birth name. And I like that people think I'm quiet. When I don't want to talk or interact, they get it because it fits the name. But also, I like it because they underestimate me. Just because I'm quiet doesn't mean I can't scrap. I think the name has some mystery to it."

"You're such a smart young man. Don't you think it's time to start looking ahead toward your future instead of playing games with your life? Your mother told me your teachers have called her on several occasions. You're not going to school on a regular basis?"

"I am. Maybe I'm so quiet they don't know I'm there."

Quiet Boy smirked and Dr. Devi made more notes.

"You have to go to school."

"I am."

"I'm serious."

"I am too."

Horns began honking outside and Dr. Devi glanced out the window to see a taxi trying to get around a double-parked garbage truck. He glanced down at the parking spot Tracy always used to park in. A red Jeep Cherokee was in it instead.

"You hear about that lady, Tracy, who used to come here?" Quiet Boy asked, breaking through the horns and somehow reading his mind. "The one who used to come in before me? I saw on the news she's missing and everyone thinks the husband did it."

Dr. Devi tore himself away from the window and nodded. "Yes, I know the story."

"She disappeared after she was here with you."

"I know."

"The police question you about that? You a suspect?"

Dr. Devi looked at the young man who chuckled in the quiet.

"I can't discuss other patients with you. You know that. And I'm certainly not discussing open police investigations. Let's talk about you instead."

Quiet Boy fell back in his seat. "I'm tired of talking about me. I'm good. I keep to myself and mind my own business. I get good enough grades to keep Mom off my back and I'll be ready for college next year. I don't need to see you."

Dr. Devi pulled a file out from under his notebook. He opened it and began reading.

"Actually, you're not good. Your grades have plummeted and you haven't even visited a campus let alone done any of the required paperwork for college admissions. You missed the SATs and you're here because there's a restraining order against you that was filed by a girl you wouldn't stop harassing. This is serious."

"That restraining order is ancient history and it was a misunderstanding in the first place. You know this."

"Misunderstanding or not, these are the things I'm talking about that you need to get a handle on. The next phase of your life is waiting. You can't waste it on the stoop with your friends who are going nowhere fast."

Quiet Boy pulled his hood back over his head and leaned forward in his chair. "Look, I heard all this before and I don't have time for another lecture. All my shit's under control. I promise."

"I need to see progress for me to believe you."

"I gotta go."

"We're not even halfway done. You can at least give me half an hour."

"I'm not in the right frame of mind and if I stay, we'll just fight. We can go longer in the next session. I got to clear my head right now and all this talk about college and bad grades and the restraining order is adding too much stress."

"It's not stress, it's life."

"Yeah, well, I'm not talking about it right now."

"You have to get yourself back on track."

"I am!"

Quiet Boy got up to leave, and as he looked down at the floor, he stopped. Dr. Devi stared down to see what he was staring at, then they both looked up at each other, locking eyes.

"I gotta go," the young man said.

"Wait."

Quiet Boy shot out of his chair and hurried from the office before Dr. Devi could object further. He shut the door behind him and Dr. Devi sat in the wingback, stunned at the sudden end to the session. He looked back down to the section of rug that was between the two chairs and saw it among the melting slush.

Sand.

He stood up and checked the bottom of his shoes, then walked back the same way he'd come in and saw more grains of sand sprinkled onto the dark carpet. Without hesitation, he walked into the closet and grabbed the vacuum. He turned it on and began vacuuming the office, sucking up the slush and sand, getting under the chairs and in the nooks and crannies of the office. He bent down to push the vacuum further under his desk and something caught his eye.

What was that?

He turned the vacuum off and stood it up, then crawled

toward his desk on his hands and knees, studying the object that was stuck underneath. It was small, like a wart growing out of the flat wood. He picked it off with his fingers and studied it as it lay in the palm of his hand. Things connected, and suddenly he knew. All the pieces suddenly fell into place. Murder was such a dirty game.

CHAPTER FIFTY-FOUR

Detective Taft was at his favorite Portuguese takeout joint eating the best empanadas in the county while he watched traffic crawl down Summer Street. The snow that had begun earlier as flurries was now coming down at a clip of about a half an inch per hour. The cars sat bumper-to-bumper, slipping and sliding their way toward I-95. Conditions were getting worse by the minute.

A copy of Kat's file was laid out on the small table in front of him. Next to the crime scene photos was a picture of Kat, taken during her last birthday party, and a picture of Malcolm, his main suspect. He thought about the interview and the lies Malcolm let roll off his tongue. If it had been that easy for the man to lie in such a setting, how easy would it have been for him to lie about his missing wife? The two cases were connected. He had no doubt in his mind about that. It was just a matter of finding the thread that joined the two together, and the most plausible angle he could come up with was the classic love triangle. He needed impenetrable proof so he knew he had the right man. Once he knew that, he could take the next step. It was just a matter of beating the others to the arrest.

He began playing out the most logical scenario. Malcom started seeing Kat. They got involved. First it was sex, but then it became something more, something deeper. Maybe things got too serious and Malcolm decided the young lawyer wasn't worth losing his family over, so he decided to break off the affair. Kat flips out because she was really falling for the guy and threatens to tell Tracy. Malcolm kills Kat before she can say anything, but doesn't realize she'd already told his wife, and when he gets home after killing Kat, Tracy is there asking for a divorce. That's why she was going to leave him. It had nothing to do with growing apart or wanting a change as Detective Evans had told him. It was Kat. Tracy knew, asked for the divorce, and was about to get one hell of an alimony payout. Malcolm couldn't have that. He'd worked too hard to let a divorce take half his wealth, but she won't forgive him. His wife can't be talked out of leaving him. So, he waits until she leaves the therapist's office in the city, follows her to the park in Buchanan, and kills her. Dumps the car. Makes it look like something crazy happened. And then he plays the worried and grieving husband. Malcolm had no idea the two cases would be connected because the murders took place in two different states and two different jurisdictions. He didn't count on anyone in Connecticut finding his prints. It all went downhill from there.

Taft took a sip of his soda and nodded to himself. That was the only way he could figure things as he saw them. That was the scenario he was going with until more evidence changed his mind.

His cell phone rang and he grabbed it from his jacket pocket.

"This is Taft."

"It's Lena. Against my better judgment, I'm giving you an update. You don't deserve to still be on the inside of this, but things are what they are. I get that."

"I appreciate it. And I really am sorry."

"We got the DNA back from the semen we found on Kat."

Taft sat up in his seat. "Tell me it's Malcolm Cowan's."

"It's Malcolm Cowan's. Almost a one hundred percent probability."

"And that gives us proof that he was there the night Kat was killed. No old fingerprint bullshit about working on some paperwork for his business weeks earlier. This puts him there *that night*."

"We got something else that puts him there that night," Lena replied.

"Talk to me."

"There's a house across the street and a block away from Kat Masterson's. He has a camera over his garage."

"I thought we did a sweep of the neighborhood. The uniforms did the knocks."

"This guy was in Seattle on business. Just got back. He was on our follow-up list, so an officer went by this morning and got the footage from the cloud storage. At 9:06 p.m. we see Malcom Cowan's car park just south of this guy's camera and we see Malcolm and Kat get out and walk toward Kat Masterson's house. It's him. Clear as day. Only Malcolm comes back to the car at 10:30 p.m."

Taft hopped off his seat and gathered his file folder while closing the lid on his empanada container. "I'll be at the station in ten minutes. I want to see everything you got and then I want to drag Mr. Cowan's ass to Connecticut this time."

"Correction. You want to see *me* drag Mr. Cowan's ass to Connecticut this time."

"Right. Sorry."

"Boundaries, Dennis."

"Copy that."

Taft disconnected the call and made his way out of the

restaurant. Information was starting to snowball and it looked like he'd miss the opportunity he needed, but it appeared they'd found their guy; the proof was irrefutable.

Kat's killer would be brought to justice, but Taft wouldn't be the one delivering it.

CHAPTER FIFTY-FIVE

The interrogation room at the Norwalk Police Department was a little larger than the one Kelly was used to in New York and was close to what one would expect from TV shows and movies. The room was painted gray and the table that sat in the center was longer. There were two chairs on either side and an oversized one-way mirror that connected to an observation room no one could see. Kelly and Taft watched through the mirror as Lena Blau sat with her back to them and Malcolm Cowan and his attorney, Logan Sickle, faced them. Logan looked a bit on the younger side, but well put together. His suit appeared high-end and his overall appearance gave her the impression that he came from a prestigious firm. His black hair was short and kept in place. His cheeks and chin were smooth. His brown eyes were dark and alive. And his teeth were absolutely perfect when he smiled his soulless smile. He was sitting with arms on the table, calm and in control, while his client was slumped in the seat next to him, left knee bouncing endlessly, chewing on his thumbnail, looking down at the floor.

Lena cleared her throat to begin. "Mr. Cowan, I'm just going to come right out and ask. Did you kill Kat Masterson?"

Malcolm looked up from the floor. "No."

"You're sure?"

"Yes."

"Then explain to me why, when you had the opportunity to tell the truth the first time you were interviewed, you chose to lie? I can't understand it. If you didn't have anything to do with Kat Masterson's murder, why would you lie and make yourself look even more suspicious? You knew we were looking at you as a person of interest, so why not cooperate?"

Silence fell upon the room. Kelly felt herself lean forward.

"Okay." Lena opened the folder that was sitting in front of her. "Mr. Cowan, you said you went to Kat Masterson's apartment a few days before she was killed to drop off documents for her to look over. Is that correct?"

Malcolm looked back down to the floor. "Yes."

"You stated you only went to her living room and kitchen. Maybe the bathroom. Is that correct?"

Malcolm didn't answer.

"You stated you weren't having an affair with the victim and that you were not this person she was secretly seeing that she and her friends called Big Daddy. Is that accurate?"

"Yes."

Lena closed the file and sat back in her chair. She looked back and forth between Malcolm and his attorney. Kelly could feel the tension building.

"This is your last chance to come clean," she said. "Because I know everything you said last time was a lie. Even the half-truths you offered had lies intermingled with them. I want the absolute truth from this point forward because every lie you tell from now on will only add to the list of very bad things that are happening to you."

"The veiled threats are a bit much," Logan Sickle snapped. "Just ask your questions and we'll decide what we want to answer."

Lena slid a second file over and opened it.

"Why did we find your fingerprints in Kat Masterson's bedroom when you said you'd never been in there?"

Malcolm looked at his attorney and the young man gave a slight nod of approval.

"Because I was having an affair with her."

"For how long?"

"A few months."

"Are you Big Daddy?"

"Yes."

"And the transcripts of the texts between the two of you that I'm about to get delivered from your carrier?"

Malcolm sighed. "They'll show conversations about how much we like each other and where we're going to meet up. There's some sexting on there and dirty talk. That kinda thing."

"That's a far cry from you saying they were just a little flirtatious. Why lie when you knew we were going to get the texts?"

"I was scared. I've never been in a situation like this before. I didn't know what to do."

Lena nodded and as she made some notes. "Were things starting to get a little more serious between you and Kat?"

"Not really. It was just fun for the both of us."

"She wanted to take the relationship to the next level, but you didn't want to leave your family?"

"No. Nothing like that."

"She wanted you to leave Tracy or she was going to tell her what was going on between you two?"

"No."

"And you knew if Tracy found out, she'd leave you. And if she left, she'd take half of everything you worked for with her. You couldn't have that. You had to take matters into your own hands and stop Kat from saying anything. You had to save your marriage and your fortune."

Malcolm looked up, his eyes wide and glassy. "I don't have a fortune to save. Nothing like what you're saying happened."

"But after you killed Kat, your wife asked for a divorce. Out of the blue. And you knew right then and there that you were too late. Kat told her and Tracy was leaving and your world was falling apart."

"This is why I didn't say anything the first time. I knew you'd jump to conclusions like this."

"I'm not jumping to anything. I'm just telling you what things look like from my side of the table."

"Well, you're wrong."

"And after you realized you were too late with Kat, you had to take care of Tracy too."

"No!"

Malcolm pushed forward against the table, leaning toward Lena as his eyes got wider and more crazed. Kelly could feel Taft's body tense up next to her. Logan Sickle eased Malcolm back in his chair and tried to interject.

"That's enough with the false accusations. My client isn't here to feed into your fictional theories. He admitted to the affair and that's the end of it. There's nothing more to tell."

Lena looked at the attorney, then back at her suspect.

"Okay, answer this. Were you at Kat's apartment the night she was killed?"

"We don't have to answer that," Logan said.

"You're right, you don't," Lena replied. "We already have the answer. We found your client's semen on the victim's leg the night she was killed. One hundred percent match on the DNA."

Malcolm's face turned white.

"Stand up, Mr. Cowan. I am placing you under arrest for the murder of Kat Masterson. You have the right to remain silent. If you give up that right, anything you say..."

Kelly felt herself relax and watched as Lena recited the

Miranda Rights to Malcolm Cowan while two uniformed officers came into the interrogation room and placed Malcolm in handcuffs. His attorney was whispering something into his ear, but Kelly doubted he heard any of it. Complete shock was written on his face. His wide and angry eyes were now full of fear and bewilderment. His mouth was hanging open as if the hinges on his jaw were no longer operational. He said nothing as the officers escorted him out of the room with Logan Sickle in tow. They had Malcolm for Kat Masterson's murder. Now it was a matter of getting him for whatever happened to his wife.

"That was good," Kelly said, turning toward Taft. "I learned a lot."

"Comes with experience," Taft replied. He dug into his pocket and came away with the locket she'd seen before. He started rubbing it with his thumb. "And Lena's been doing this for a while. It's nothing to be good or bad at. It just comes. One day you'll be writing things down that you want to cover in an interview, the next day you'll be freestyling off the top of your head. You'll get there." He smiled. "Don't let them tell you otherwise."

"Hey, what's that?" Kelly asked, pointing to the locket. "I've seen you playing with it a couple of times. A good luck charm?"

Taft held it up and tried to smile. "It was my daughter's locket. Has a picture of her mother in it. My wife. She left us about six months ago."

"I'm sorry."

"I guess I have it for luck. I don't know. Makes me feel better. Makes her feel closer."

Kelly nodded as she followed Taft out of the observation room. Before she could respond, Detective Blau was there and they began talking about Malcolm and the interview that had just taken place. Taft's sorrow got lost in the shuffle. Such was the life of a detective when the case was reaching its climax. They had their man. Now Kelly had to get hers.

DAY THIRTEEN

CHAPTER FIFTY-SIX

The doorbell rang and Missy was certain she was going to be sick. She held her head over the kitchen sink and waited. Her stomach turned and gurgled, but nothing came up. Ever since Malcolm had called her from the police station the night before and told her about being arrested, her nerves had been on edge. She wasn't expecting to feel this way once things were set in motion, but then again, she'd thought her sister would be there with her, guiding her. And now the detective was at the door, an opportunity that forced her to act quickly. Malcolm was scheduled to be arraigned later that afternoon at the Stamford Courthouse and they'd learn at that time if bail would be offered and for how much. She was planning to be there when all that was determined, but before she wasted any more time, she knew she had to speak with Detective Evans.

Missy walked from the kitchen and down the hallway holding her stomach. She opened the door and Detective Evans was standing in front of her, the backdrop a pristine white from the snow that had fallen over the region, the cold air nipping at her bare feet. The woman in front of her was stiff and professional. She glared at Missy, saying nothing.

"Thank you for coming." Missy stepped back and allowed the detective to come inside. "Can I get you a coffee or tea? Something to warm you up?"

"No, thanks," Detective Evans replied. "If we could just get right down to it, that would be great. Things have been a little hectic since Malcolm's arrest. I have to get back to Connecticut as soon as possible. And if you called me over here to yell about how many days it's been since Tracy's been missing, let me just leave now. We're making progress. I can't waste time at this point."

"No, it's nothing like that."

Missy led them into the family room. Her hands were shaking as she rolled them into fists and she sat on the edge of the couch.

"I need to tell you something, and I know you're going to be mad and I know it's going to make me look like a very bad person, but you gotta understand that I did what I did for a reason. I'm not bad. You need to know that."

Detective Evans remained standing, silent.

Missy paused, trying to get her stomach to settle so she could talk.

"When I came here to stay with Malcolm and Finn, I did that because I was pretty sure Malcolm had something to do with my sister's disappearance. I came here to protect Finn just like I used to protect Tracy. That was always my number one goal. I knew that whatever happened to Tracy, she'd want me to look after her boy, and I didn't trust Malcolm. He's a good provider and all that, but I knew she was asking for a divorce and I was afraid he'd done something to her, and I knew Tracy found out about his affair, so I got here to protect Finn."

"Okay."

"When I first came, I was angry and scared and I let that son of a bitch know that I was on to him and that I thought he made Tracy disappear, but I ain't dumb and I could see that my aggressive approach was making him shut down. So, I took a new angle. I decided to play the role of replacement wife. I started being kinder to him and doing the housework and trying to reassure him that I believed he was innocent and trying to get him to trust me so I could find out what happened to my sister. Or at the very least, stay in the house so I could keep an eye on Finn. It worked."

"Did he tell you something?" Detective Evans asked. She took out a pen and notepad.

"No," Missy replied. "He never said anything except he didn't have nothing to do with what happened to Tracy. I thought she was dead. But I was wrong."

"How do you know you were wrong?"

"Three nights ago, me and Malcolm were watching TV and the house phone rang. The landline. Malcolm thought it was a telemarketer because no one ever calls that phone. I figured he was right, but something made me pick it up anyway. Tracy was on the other end."

Detective Evans stopped writing and looked up from her notepad. "What?"

"Tracy's alive. She called the house and I heard her voice myself."

"And you're just telling me this now?"

"I had to wait. I couldn't risk telling you when Malcolm was still roaming around. If he found out I knew Tracy was alive and told you, I was afraid he'd go kill her or kill me. I didn't say anything in order to protect my sister. I figured if she'd been alive that long, she'd stay alive a little bit longer. She didn't sound hurt or anything. Scared, maybe. And now that you've arrested Malcolm and he can't get to her, I wanted to tell you about it."

Detective Evans looked at Tracy. "But why would your sister call the house if Malcolm was the one who abducted her?"

A shrug. "I don't know. Maybe she was calling him to plead for her life or to convince him to let her go."

The detective took out her phone. "What did Tracy say?" she asked. Her voice was excited, amped up.

"There was no time for a conversation. She said she was by a beach and a lighthouse, but I hung up on her before she could say anything else. Then I disconnected the line so she couldn't call back."

"Jesus, Missy!"

"I know! It sounds horrible, but I did it to protect her. I called you here to tell you everything and I was thinking that if you could get some kind of phone records from the cable company, maybe they can show the number she was calling from and you can trace that number to where she is."

"And if the phone number's unlisted or there's no ID associated with the phone, where does that put us?"

Missy lowered her head. "I was just trying to help."

"All you had to do was ask her a few more questions about the beach and the lighthouse," Detective Evans snapped. "Hang up after that."

"I'm sorry. It was all happening so fast. I panicked."

Detective Evans turned and rushed toward the front door.

"Where are you going?" Missy asked.

"I'm going to try and trace that incoming number like you said. And then I'm going to scour the northeast for a beach and a lighthouse. Nothing like a needle in a haystack."

CHAPTER FIFTY-SEVEN

"This ends now," Jake panted. "Me and you. We're going to be together like we were always meant to. You can't change fate, Tracy. We were meant to be together until the end of time. This is the end."

The world around her was quiet except for the army of police personnel outside of the house. Tracy could hear the radio chatter and calls for backup as officers ran from position to position, some trying to see inside while others covered any and all exits should Jake try and escape. She knew escape wasn't part of his plan. She could see it as plainly as she could see the shotgun that was in his hand. He had no intention of ever leaving her house again.

Boots thumped above them and they both looked up at the pellet-pocked ceiling as the haze of his last shotgun blast still lingered in the living room. The SWAT team was moving in. It wouldn't be long now.

"Okay, listen," Tracy said, her hands out in front of her as she slowly climbed to her feet. "These guys are going to come busting in here soon, and I don't want to see you get hurt."

Jake's eyes were wide. He pushed himself further into the corner by the window as he watched her approach.

"I don't want to live in a world without you," she continued. Her voice was shaking and hoarse from crying. "I was angry before, but the truth is, I love you more than life itself. I can't watch you go to jail and suffer like that, and I won't sit here and let you take your own life alone."

She crossed the living room and was only a few feet from Jake.

"I think you're right. We need to die. Right now. Together." She reached out and gently touched his cheeks, wiping away his tears. "I love you so much, Jake. More than you can ever know, and more than I could ever say. I loved you the second I met you back when we were kids and I'm so happy you chose me. I forgive you for what you did, and I agree with you one hundred percent. We need to leave this life so we can be together in the next. Let's do it. Now."

Jake slowly shook his head, his eyes still wide, watching her, melting when she touched him.

"You forgive me?"

"I do."

"I love you so much."

Tracy smiled. "I love you more."

She leaned in and kissed him. He kissed her back hard, knowing this would be the last time. She traced her right hand down his shoulder, down his arm, and caressed his hand as she poked her thumb through the trigger guard and laid it on his finger. Her left hand rubbed the outside of his pants, eliciting a small moan from her fiancé as she moved up to his stomach, then his chest, then over to his arm where she carefully reached for the barrel of the shotgun.

"I love you," she whispered.

"I love you, too," Jake moaned in response.

In a flash of movement, Tracy pushed the barrel of the

shotgun under Jake's chin and pressed her thumb down, firing a round up into his head and ending her nightmare. The sound of the shot stole her hearing and replaced it with a ringing as she fell backward onto the floor. Jake's lifeless and half-decapitated body fell on top of her and she could taste his blood in her mouth along with the gunpowder that coated her tongue. She didn't hear the SWAT team advance after the round was fired. She didn't start to hear anything until she was already in the back of the police car, heading to the hospital, covered in her vengeance.

Tracy could remember it all as if it happened the day before. She could see every detail in her mind and could still smell every stench that afternoon offered. But that horrific event had given her what she needed to survive, a strength she never knew she had. She knew what she had to do to escape. It had been there all along, but she hadn't concentrated enough to grasp it. She could see it now. As plain as if she had her eyesight back. She could tap into her resolve and end the nightmare like she ended her nightmare with Jake. It was time to take matters into her own hands. She was strong enough.

And she had a plan.

CHAPTER FIFTY-EIGHT

Sergeant Leeds poked his head over Kelly's cubicle. "You get that number back from the cable company yet?"

Kelly didn't look up from her computer. "Should be any minute. They put a priority on it and said it won't take more than an hour."

"What're you doing?"

"Scrolling through the Cowans' Ring camera to see if I can match the time Malcolm leaves his house with Kat Masterson's time of death."

"Any luck?"

"No. Malcolm left for work that morning and never came back. He must've gone to Kat's apartment from the job site."

Leeds came around the corner and looked over her shoulder as she scrolled through. The camera captured Malcolm walking down the front steps of his porch with a thermos of coffee in his hand. It's morning. He gets in his car and drives away.

"That's the last time you see him?" Leeds asked.

Kelly nodded. "That's it."

As soon as Malcolm's car pulls out of frame, Leeds leaned in. "Wait a second. There it is."

"What?"

"Rewind to when Malcolm pulls off camera."

Kelly rewound the footage.

"Stop. Look."

Now it was Kelly who leaned in. "Holy shit."

"Exactly."

Kelly minimized the video feed from the Ring cam and opened a file on her desktop. She clicked through a few subfolders and pulled up the footage from the entrance to George's Island. She pulled the Ring footage back up and placed each video side by side.

"Bingo," she whispered.

Kelly looked at the frozen pictures on the screen. The second car that came into frame after Malcolm pulled away was a black Buick. She could see someone sitting behind the wheel, but there was a sun glare on the glass making a pure identification impossible. She pointed.

"I can see a plate."

"Blow it up."

She enlarged the picture on the screen.

"Charlie, Echo, Tango, Six, Three, Nine," Leeds read. "New York."

"We got him."

Leeds smiled. "Great work. You're going to be one of the good ones. I can tell."

Kelly blushed. "Yeah, yeah. Just get the registration for an address."

"Ten-four."

She watched as Leeds jotted down the plate number and marched back to his desk. Adrenaline began churning through her body. They were close. She could feel it.

"Detective Evans?"

Kelly spun around to find an officer standing on the opposite side of her cubicle. He held a piece of paper in his hand.

"We got the number from the cable company," he said. "Seventeen Bluffs Way, Montauk."

"The Hamptons?" Kelly took the paper from the officer. "Montauk has a lighthouse, right?"

"Montauk Point Lighthouse. The most famous one out here."

"Good. Now let's see who lives at Seventeen Bluffs Way."

"Yes, ma'am."

She got him. She finally got him.

CHAPTER FIFTY-NINE

She'd been trapped before. She'd looked into the face of death and was forced to take control in order to survive. She'd done it then. She could do it now.

There was no real way to tell time, but Tracy sensed it had been a while since Sam had come in to see her. Her stomach growled from hunger and her bedpan was filling up. Her head ached and the nausea remained. From what she could tell, the house was quiet. No creaking floorboards or squeaking hinges from doors opening and closing. She hadn't heard from Enzo since they'd tried to escape, and she wondered if the boy was okay. A little voice in the back of her mind told her he was probably dead, but she did her best to ignore it. If she was going to do this, she had to stay focused and in the moment. The fact that she couldn't see made things so much more dangerous, but the time for hope had come and gone.

She could hear the gravel crunching outside. He was home. A car door opened, then closed. Footsteps on the porch. The front door opened.

It was now time for action.

"Hello!" she cried. "Is anyone there? Sam? I need help."

She strained to listen for a response, but none came.

"Hello!"

Tracy caressed the chain that was wrapped around her wrist and felt the tiny padlock keeping it in place. She traced the chain down the left side of the mattress and followed it as it went around the metal edge of the bedframe and was fastened in place by a second tiny padlock. She tugged on the chain, listening to the metal clatter against the steel.

Footsteps approaching. Heavy. Thumping.

The door opened.

"Sam?"

"Yes."

"Something's wrong. I can't breathe."

"What do you mean?"

"I don't know! Help me. I can't breathe right! Come here."

The footsteps hurried closer and Tracy held her breath. The mattress sunk as Sam leaned his weight on it. She could feel his body poised over hers as he moved in closer, the aroma of sweat and a faint aftershave filling the space around her.

"I... I can't," Tracy wheezed.

"What's wrong?"

Sam's voice was panicked. She fell back onto the mattress and waited for him to lean forward. When he did, she swung the chain up and around from the side of the bed and wrapped it around his neck. Before Sam could register what was happening, she slipped out from underneath him and pushed him facedown on the bed while she climbed on his back, pulling on the chain as hard as she could. Light danced in her darkness like fireworks exploding in the night sky. She pulled, her hands hurting as the chain dug into her skin and scraped her wrists. Her arms trembled.

Sam thrashed about, his hands flailing, trying to reach behind him to grab Tracy. He flung his right hand up and managed to get a quick grip on the bandages she had around her head. Frantic fingers found their way into the seam of the bandage and yanked downward. Her head followed and she almost toppled off him, but she twisted her head from side to side until the bandage loosened and the wrapping fell off in his grip. Her darkness remained.

Sam tried throwing elbows but she was on top of him, straddling him, and he didn't have the leverage. He tried bucking her off, but he was losing too much oxygen too quickly and the strength it took to knock her off disappeared within moments, leaving him helpless and choking.

Tracy kept pulling on the chain as she thought about Finn and Enzo and going home and returning to her life. She wanted to escape. Killing Sam was her only option. It had worked with Jake. It had to work here.

The sound of gargled choking and labored breathing filled the house. Tracy pulled until she felt Sam's body finally go limp, and then she pulled some more. She only relented when her arms couldn't stand to pull any longer, and she let go, feeling Sam's head fall the rest of the way onto the bed, then silence.

Go! Quickly!

Tracy climbed off Sam and knelt on the floor next to him. Her hands fumbled through the pockets of his jeans until she wrapped her fingers around a set of keys. She pulled them out and felt each one, trying to determine what key might fit the tiny padlock that had her fastened to the bedframe. She felt a key that was small and thin and tried to insert it into the lock, but it wouldn't go. She kept feeling each key and came upon another one, a little smaller than the first. She concentrated on inserting it into the lock as her hands shook violently. The key slipped in and she turned it, the sound of the lock popping open like a cork shooting from a celebratory bottle of champagne.

She fed the lock through the chain and felt the entire thing fall away. Still focused, with no time to let up, she dropped the keys, stood on weak legs, and began feeling her way back around the room, her mind too full of fear to remember the layout. Her arms were outstretched in front of her as she bumped into the bed, a dresser, the wall, tripping along the edge of the room, desperate to find the door. She paused for a moment to try and steady herself when she heard movement and a low growl.

"No."

Tracy spun around toward the noise and hands grabbed her by the shoulders, pushing her backward as she lost her balance. She crashed onto the floor and slammed the side of her face onto the hardwood, knocking her out for a split second. When she came to, she flipped herself onto her back and pushed herself against the wall. She looked around and could see the room she'd been trapped in. White walls. Unfinished wood dresser and matching nightstand. Iron headboard on a farm bed. A red and white quilt. Her bedpan. Her pillows. An empty food tray on the floor next to a black rocking chair. She could see it all, even though it was distorted. But...

She could see.

Tracy looked down at the floor where she fell and noticed a small black piece of plastic. It took her eye a minute to focus on it, and when she did, she recognized it instantly. It was a contact lens, blacked out. They'd been in her eyes the entire time. In fact, one of the contacts still was, which was why her vision was off. She was never blind. The lenses kept her from seeing, which in turn kept her from knowing the truth about where she was. That's why her eyes were hurting as much as they were. The contacts were irritating them. She looked up and saw the man standing over her. But it wasn't a man. It was a boy. Not Dr. Devi after all.

"Quiet Boy," Tracy whispered more to herself than her captor. "It's you."

CHAPTER SIXTY

"How can this be?"

Tracy pushed herself away from the boy standing over her. She remained on the floor, vulnerable. She could see, which was a welcome change, but he still had the upper hand. They stared at each other for what seemed like forever, then, without warning, she flipped onto her hands and knees and scrambled to her feet.

"Wait!" Quiet Boy cried. "I'm not going to hurt you! We have to hurry. He's coming."

Tracy stopped when she got to the bedroom door. "What are you talking about?"

"Dr. Devi. He knows I know. He's coming up here for both of us."

"What are you talking about?"

Quiet Boy took a single step closer as he rubbed his neck and coughed, wheezing as he spoke through a raspy whisper. "I was in his office. I was asking about you because you haven't been around. He was acting all strange, and then I saw sand on the floor. He saw me staring at it. I knew he'd been up here. As soon as I saw the sand, I figured you were here too. He's done this kind of thing before."

Tracy gripped the molding around the bedroom door. She was confused and frightened. Questions ran through her mind, one after the other. She fumbled with the other contact that was in her eye, pulling it out and tossing it on the floor.

"How did you know to come up here?"

"This is his summer home."

"How do you know that?"

Quiet Boy took a breath. "Dr. Devi is my father."

The revelation almost knocked Tracy back down to the ground. She was speechless, staring at the young man who took another step forward.

"He knew I was coming here and he knows I'll find you when I do. He's on his way. We have to get out of here."

Tracy nodded and turned to run down the hall. When she got to the front door, she stopped. "Wait!"

Quiet Boy ran past her and opened the door. "There's no time. We have to go."

"But—"

The young man pointed. "That's him! I can see the head-lights coming up from the road. Come on!"

He took her by the hand and pulled her out of the house, down the front steps, and around the back. She stopped when she saw the car parked next to the house. It was a black Buick Lacrosse, new but for the smashed up front end.

"Is that your car?" she asked.

Quiet Boy shook his head and pulled her forward. "No. It's my dad's. He said he hit a deer with it one night coming home from an appointment. I didn't put two and two together until I saw the sand. This was the car he used to smash into yours. I saw it on the news."

Tracy could still hear the crunching of metal and feel the impact from the car with one headlight—the Buick—as she ran past it, cowering, as if it might reach out and grab her. That was the car that followed her. That almost killed her. The car that Dr. Devi had been driving.

They passed the car just as a larger SUV was pulling into the driveway. They got caught in the SUV's headlights as they broke into the tree line leading toward the sand cliffs.

"Samesh!" Dr. Devi's voice thundered over the waves that crashed upon the beach below them. "Tracy!"

Quiet Boy stopped halfway through the woods and put his finger up to his lips, telling Tracy to stay quiet. Tracy nodded and they fell to their knees to stay hidden in the brush.

"Samesh, bring Tracy out now." Dr. Devi was standing at the edge of the woods, peering into the darkness. "This is not a game. There are serious ramifications to what you've done. I can't hide this kind of behavior. You've gone too far this time. Please, Samesh. This has to end."

Tracy watched the young man staring at the silhouette of his father, shaking his head as Dr. Devi spoke.

"Tracy, I'm so sorry for this," Dr. Devi shouted. "My son tends to become highly focused on things, and I'm afraid his interests have fallen on you. I've seen you talking with him before our sessions, but I never would've imagined he'd do something like this."

"He's lying," Quiet Boy whispered, his eyes never wavering from his father's silhouette. "He wants you to think I'm crazy or unsafe so you'll go to him. Once you do, he'll kill us both."

"Samesh is my son. I've seen this kind of behavior before. He was convinced that he was in love with you and that you would love him back. He had a fantasy of you two getting married and living together. He saw this as an absolute reality with no alternatives. His love for you was absolute, and he saw it as his mission to get you to love him back."

"No. No, that's not true." Quiet Boy finally turned to face

Tracy. His eyes were wide and glassy with tears. "That's not true."

Tracy nodded. She didn't know what to believe.

"Samesh has been following you for some time. He had a tracking device on your car. He'd follow you whenever he could, but you never noticed. I believe he was trying to fight his compulsion, but when he heard you were leaving, he panicked and attacked you and kidnapped you. He got you up here, kept you sedated with his valium, and when he ran out of that, bought heroin and injected you with that to keep you calm and controllable. Then he got on with the task of making you fall in love with him."

"Lies!"

"I know all this because I found his journal this afternoon. We had a session together today and after he left and I saw the sand in my office, I found a small recording device he hid under my desk. He's been listening to my sessions. All of them. He knows everything we talked about. I went to the house to confront him and found the journal. That's how I knew he was here. That's why I'm here now. I'm so sorry. I never meant to put you in such danger."

Tracy made a move to stand and Quiet Boy grabbed her by the arm.

"I promise you he's lying," he whispered. "He's the one who's obsessive about things. He's the one who wants you to fall in love with him. But now he knows he can't have you, so he's going to kill you. The second we come out of these woods, he'll kill you and me and then he'll kill Enzo too. We have to get out of here. If we can slip through the back of these woods and come around, we can hop in my car and get to the police. That's the only way."

Tracy's eyes immediately widened as she pulled her arm from Quiet Boy's grip. She stood up and stumbled back.

"What're you doing?" Quiet Boy asked.

"It's you," Tracy said. "You're the person who's been keeping me in that house. Samesh. Sam."

"I'm not!"

"Then how do you know Enzo's in there? You came straight into my room when you got here. I called for you and you came in. If you've never been here, how do you know about Enzo?"

CHAPTER SIXTY-ONE

Kelly swerved through traffic with her dashboard lights on and siren blaring. She grabbed her cell phone and dialed the number for the East Hampton Police Department.

"East Hampton Police," a male voice answered.

"This is Detective Kelly Evans of the Westchester County Police. I'm working the Tracy Cowan missing person case. You hear about it?"

"I did. Missing mom, right? Car was found in the Hudson?"

"That's right. We have reason to believe Tracy is in your neck of the woods. She called her house from a landline that traces to Viraj Devi's house on Seventeen Bluffs Way. We also have video evidence that shows a car registered to Viraj sitting across from Tracy's house on the day she went missing."

"Seventeen Bluffs Way is right off of Old Montauk Highway by the cliffs and Camp Hero," the officer said.

"You need to get an officer out there right now. I don't know what the situation is, so approach with extreme caution. She may be there voluntarily. She may be hiding out. She may be there against her will. I can confirm that she was seeing a Dr. Viraj Devi for psychological reasons. He was her therapist, so there may be no malice involved, but I would approach as if there is. Do you understand?"

"Yes, we copy. I'll send a unit to check it out right away."

Kelly maneuvered through the traffic and sped onto the ramp that brought her over the Whitestone Bridge and onto the Long Island Expressway.

"I'm on my way. I want you to hold whoever's at the house in custody until I get there and we can figure things out. She may be alone or Dr. Devi might be with her."

"Ten-four."

"I can't stress this enough. Extreme caution. I don't know what you guys are stepping into."

"We'll be careful," the officer replied.

"Google Maps says it'll take a little under two hours to get there. I'll make it in one. Just hold them."

"Copy."

Kelly disconnected the phone and pushed down on the accelerator. The cars in front of her pulled to the side as she passed them in a blur.

CHAPTER SIXTY-TWO

Quiet Boy's face contorted into a cold and heartless scowl. He stared at Tracy as he slowly climbed to his feet, his eyes locked on hers.

"It was you all along," Tracy said again, backing away. "Pretending to be your father. Talking like him. Using words he'd used. Matching his accent. You knew how he spoke to me. You knew all my secrets because you recorded them in his office. You were in the car with one headlight. You tried to push me into the river. You never saved me. You kidnapped me after you knocked me out. It was all you."

Quiet Boy stood all the way up, his eyes cold, his breath heaving from his lips in white puffs, instantly evaporating in the cold wind. "It was for love," he said. "I love you. From the second I saw you, I knew I loved you."

Tracy shook her head. "No." She turned and ran as fast as she could through the dark woods, the same branches slapping at her, the same thorns tugging at her skin. The underbrush and pine needles stabbed at the bottom of her socked feet as she made her way through the icy slush and snow that was blanketing the ground. She could hear Quiet Boy behind her, but this time she could see. The house just beyond the trees. She was almost there.

"Tracy, wait!"

Quiet Boy's voice boomed in the night. Tracy broke from the tree line and fell into Dr. Devi's arms, who was waiting.

"Get to the house!" Dr. Devi cried, pushing her off him. "Call the police. I'll hold Samesh out here. Go!"

Tracy nodded and sprinted toward the house, hopping up the front steps and throwing herself through the front door. She ran down the hall toward her room and stopped at the small table she'd bumped into during her attempt to escape.

The phone was gone.

"No!"

She fumbled around the table, looking under it and noticing the line that had been cut. Quiet Boy must've cut the line and removed the phone to ensure she couldn't make any more calls out. She ran around the bottom floor of the home, searching for a second phone that she hoped was on another end table or hanging on a wall. In the back of her mind, she knew that if he removed one, he would've removed them all, but still she searched, praying for a miracle.

Tracy flew around the corner that led from the kitchen to the hallway. As soon as she did, she felt something knock her in the face and she crumpled to the floor. She was dazed and shocked as she felt herself being pulled down the narrow corridor and tossed into the room she'd been locked in for what seemed like forever. She looked up just in time to see Quiet Boy closing the door behind him. A lock engaged from the outside. She'd never heard that before.

She was trapped.

"I fell in love with you the second I saw you," Quiet Boy said through the door. He was calm, his voice even. "You walked up the front stairs to my dad's office and you took my breath away. I couldn't believe someone so pretty and so nice could be an actual person." His voice grew louder as he moved through the bottom floor. "At first I just wanted to find out why you were there. I mean, how could such a beautiful, wonderful, kind person need a psychologist? What could possibly be going wrong in your life that you'd need to talk to someone like my dad? So, I planted a wireless microphone under his desk. It connected to an app in my phone and I'd listen to every session you had with him. I saved them and would play them back and would listen to the heartache in your voice and the stories you told him about you and your husband growing apart and your struggle through your cancer."

"Samesh, let me out."

"It was all so sad. I knew I had to take you away from the pain. You deserved a chance to start a new life. The more we got to know one another, I was positive that you deserved a chance to be happy. And I could tell I made you happy. Every time I gave you new music, I saw that smile on your face and I knew it was real. I could make you that happy all the time. Not just with trading music and talking about what we liked and didn't like. I wanted to make you happy for the rest of your life."

"Open the door."

"I was listening live that day on my earbuds when you told my dad that you'd finally gotten the courage to tell Malcolm you were leaving. I was so excited, but the next thing you said was that you were leaving us too. I couldn't believe it. How could you leave without giving us a chance? There was no way I could get through a day knowing I was never going to see you again. I couldn't let that happen. I couldn't let you leave."

Tracy scurried around the room trying to find something she could break the knob with or cut through the thin door with. She picked up the chain and wrapped it around her hand.

"I followed you home that night," Quiet Boy continued. His voice was faint. "I'd been following you for weeks before. I knew where you lived and where Finn's school was and what time you got him on and off the bus. I knew what stores you liked to shop in and who you met for coffee. My plan the day you were leaving was to follow you to your house, kill Malcolm for you, and then you and me and Finn could run away together. But then you took that exit and ended up at that park, and I had to come up with a last-minute alternative plan. We were going to end up here either way, so I knew what my end game was. I decided to just force you out of the car by pushing it into the river and chase you down once you got out. I never wanted to hurt you. I just needed you to get out of the car. Anyway, I brought you here, put the contacts in your eyes that I painted black so you couldn't see, and waited for you to fall in love with me. I thought maybe I could go back to your house and kill Malcolm and take Finn, but the police were always around and the news vans kept coming. I brought you a new son instead. I brought you a new life."

Tracy listened as the front door opened and Quiet Boy's footsteps walked outside. The crunching of gravel filled the air as she ran to the windows to try and see what he was doing. She pushed the curtains away and saw the metal hurricane shutters covering the glass. There was no way out.

"But you don't care. Never did. You're a liar and a tease. You're just like all the other people who pretend to care about me. You ruined everything. We could've been so happy together."

"I don't even know you," Tracy cried through the window. "You were pretending to be someone else."

"I was trying to build trust."

"By lying?"

"By making you think you were with someone you were already comfortable with. But whatever. That doesn't matter now."

The smell of gasoline began as a faint aroma, but grew

stronger as Quiet Boy's footsteps carried back inside the house. She could hear it splashing onto the floor.

He's going to burn the place down.

"I'm sorry, but I can't let you leave. You'll tell everyone what happened and my life will be over. I can't let that happen."

"Samesh, please. You don't have to do this."

"I do."

"Where's your father?"

The footsteps stopped outside her door. Everything quiet.

"Where's your father?"

"I love you," Quiet Boy whispered from the other side of the door. "You need to know that. I didn't want any of this, but here we are. I hope you find peace."

CHAPTER SIXTY-THREE

The roar of fire exploded in the quiet and the bedroom door was suddenly awash in flame. Tracy grabbed a blanket from the bed, covering herself as the room filled with black smoke. With the windows blocked, she knew she had to wait until the locked door burned down enough to get through, then hope there was still time to get out. She fell onto her stomach and watched as the fire burned through the bedroom door, chewing its way toward her as flames licked the inside walls and ceiling.

The room became nothing but black smoke, twisting and churning in a breeze she couldn't feel, hunting her down and choking her. She struggled to breathe and knew she had to make a run for it at that moment or risk suffocating. She climbed to her feet, pulled the blanket tight around her, and ran through the door, crashing through the splintered wood and flames. She got through and managed to scurry down the hall that was almost completely engulfed. She was by the front door when she heard a tiny voice one floor above.

"Help!"

It was Enzo.

Tracy ran up the stairs, which were quickly burning and

losing their stability. She high-stepped as best she could but could feel the fire on the bottom of her feet. There was no time to register the pain. She had to get Enzo and get out of the house. She made it to the top of the stairs where the smoke was thick but there were no flames. Not yet, anyway.

"Help!"

"Enzo!" she screamed, choking on the smoke that was moving in like a thick fog. "Enzo, where are you? We have to get out of here. Where are you? Talk to me!"

"In here!"

The voice was weak and sounded far away, but Tracy followed the call and made it to a closed door at the end of the hall. She opened it, letting in the smoke which quickly filled the small room, and flipped on the light. She saw the boy sitting on the floor in the corner, his tiny hands and ankles bound with duct tape. She knelt beside him and tore at the tape, ripping it downward as if she was shredding a piece of paper, biting at it and yanking and pulling until it finally came off. She did the same with his ankles once she was done with his wrists.

"I want to go," the boy cried. He began coughing and Tracy held him against her.

"I'll find a way. Take my hand."

They stood up and ran back toward the hall. Tracy peeked out of the bedroom and could see the flames climbing the stairs toward the second floor. There's no way they would make it. The fire was growing out of control.

She pulled them back inside and shut the door.

"Roll up the blankets from the bed and stuff them under the door," she said. "I'll help you in a minute."

The boy started pulling the blanket and sheet off the bed and pushed them under the space at the bottom of the door. Tracy moved toward the window and opened the shade. Another hurricane shutter was blocking their way, but this one was different. It wasn't the rolled down metal shutters like the ones on the first floor. This looked more decorative, made from a heavy plastic, and instead of rolling into place, it was on top hinges and swung out from the bottom so the shutters could stay on year-round, but could also open to offer a view and ventilation.

"The smoke keeps coming in!" Enzo shouted.

Tracy opened the window, unlatched the shutter, and pushed it out as far as it would go. It looked like it would be enough.

"Come here!"

Enzo ran over and she took him by the shoulders.

"The only way out is through this window. I'll hang you out and drop you and you land the best you can in the bushes below. You think you can do that?"

The boy nodded.

"Good. Let's go."

She lifted Enzo up and poured him out of the window, feet first, shimmying him down until she was gripping his bony wrists.

"You ready?"

"I'm scared."

"You'll be fine. I'm right behind you."

She let go and listened to the boy drop to the ground. She heard whimpering and crying.

"Are you okay?"

"That hurt."

"Can you move? Can you walk?"

"Yes."

"Good. I'm coming now."

Tracy propped her feet up on the windowsill and turned herself around as if she was doing a pushup. She walked herself backward on her hands until her legs were hanging off the side of the house. The flames were approaching, devouring the wood and carpet and plastic and anything else that got in its way. The smoke was too thick to even see the bedroom door. The bulb in the overheard light burst. She pushed herself the rest of the way through and fell.

Tracy hit the ground on her side, which knocked the wind out of her. Despite that, she was okay. Enzo was immediately by her side, trying to help her to her feet. The house was mostly engulfed now and she scrambled away from it.

"Come on," she said as she pulled the boy to the edge of the property. "We need to stay back."

They walked up the driveway and she saw Dr. Devi's body, facedown and unmoving. Blood pooled around his head. Out of the corner of her eye she could see the flashing lights of an emergency vehicle making its way toward them. She watched as it approached, knowing it was finally over. She hugged Enzo against her and waited to be rescued.

"You can't leave!"

Quiet Boy's voice roared over the flames as he staggered out from the side of the house, an axe in his hand, his eyes wide with anger.

"You can't leave! They're not sending me away again! I'm not going back. You have to die! They can't know I did this!"

"Run," she cried to Enzo and pushed him toward the road where the emergency lights were approaching, hoping the boy could get to safety while she distracted Quiet Boy by running in the opposite direction. The boy hung on for a moment, then disappeared into the darkness that encircled the burning house. As soon as he broke to her left, Tracy ran right and hopped back into the woods.

CHAPTER SIXTY-FOUR

"No!"

Quiet Boy's voice exploded in the night as she ran through the trees again, knowing the cliffs were somewhere up ahead. She followed the glow of the lighthouse figuring if she could make it to the cliffs, she could circle back to the house and get the police.

The woods were not as deep as she'd originally thought. Within only about one hundred yards, she was out in a clearing and could see the edge of the cliffs and the lighthouse to her left. The black ocean was below, somewhere in front of her, but it was too dark to see. She could hear the familiar surf, pounding the coast, over and over.

Tracy ran along the edge to try and find a place to hide so she could circle back. Before she could tuck herself away, Quiet Boy broke through the tree line and she stopped. He held the axe in front of him, his knuckles white from gripping it so tight.

"You can't leave!" he shouted over the wind and the surf. "You need to die tonight. I'm not going back to that hospital! They can't make me! If you die you can't tell on me and I won't have to go back. And if you won't love me, then you have to die! It's one or the other."

Tracy stared at him, trapped between the cliffs' edge and the woods. She was panting from running, the smoke still burning in her lungs, her legs weak from being in the bed for so long. She wanted to lie down and rest, but instead waited for Quiet Boy to make his next move.

"Samesh!" a voice cried from behind them. "I want you to stop this right now!"

Tracy watched as Quiet Boy turned toward the voice. Dr. Devi stepped out from the shadows of the woods holding a piece of cloth to his head, his face bloodied and swollen. Both men were silent as the waves crashed against the sand somewhere out in the darkness. The wind carried the madness out toward the sea.

"Put the axe down and leave her alone. The police are here. It's over."

Quiet Boy began to cry and shook his head, looking back and forth between Dr. Devi and Tracy.

"You shouldn't be here," he whimpered. "I killed you."

"You didn't," Dr. Devi replied. "I'm exactly where I should be."

"You can't help me." Quiet Boy cried harder. "You help everybody else so why can't you help me? You promised you would, but you can't. I heard you on my microphone telling one of your doctor friends that you thought my obsessions were too far gone. I heard you! Those were your exact words!"

Dr. Devi walked closer, his voice growing louder over the surf below. "That doesn't mean we stop trying. You were getting there. I saw signs of progress. I think we can still keep moving forward."

"You said it yourself. I become manic and overwhelming. Look at me right now. Look at her! All of this is because I love her, and I can't help how I feel. Why can't I let her go?"

"The police are in the woods," Dr. Devi explained. He stopped about twenty feet from his son. "They said if you drop the axe and come back with me, no one will get hurt. But this is over, Samesh."

"I can't be helped."

"We can keep trying."

"I'm broken."

"I know."

"I'm not going back to the hospital."

"We can talk about that."

Quiet Boy turned back to Tracy. He let one hand go from the axe and when he wiped his tears with the back of his hand, his face changed. His brow furrowed and his eyes glazed over. The tip of his tongue licked his bottom lip.

"She doesn't love me," he cried over his shoulder, his eyes never leaving hers. "After everything I've done for her, she still doesn't love me."

His knees bent and his torso leaned forward as if he was about to run. Tracy could see his left foot digging into the muddy ground.

"She needs to die."

"Samesh," Dr. Devi growled. "Enough."

Tracy moved closer toward the edge of the cliff and braced herself.

Seagulls squawked overhead.

"Tonight. She dies tonight."

CHAPTER SIXTY-FIVE

"Samesh!"

Dr. Devi's voice echoed in the night, but Quiet Boy ignored it as he sprinted, full speed, toward Tracy, his axe up and ready to strike. She could see the monstrous look on his face, the hate so plain in his eyes. He'd been betrayed and he was scared and she had been the cause of it all. Someone had to pay. She had to pay.

She knew exactly how he felt.

Tracy waited as long as she could, and just as Quiet Boy was about to lunge and bring the axe down, she fell to the ground and kicked herself sideways. Quiet Boy tried to stop, but his momentum carried him past her and she kept spinning, kicking her leg out, and tripping him. He dropped the axe and fell, sliding as his body was carried over the edge of the cliff, the mud and ice unable to stop him. Tracy watched half of his body disappear over the edge, but then felt a hand clasp around the ankle she'd tripped him with. Before she could react, it pulled her with him and she watched in horror as the edge of the cliff quickly approached.

She twisted around and tried to dig her fingers into the

earth, but Quiet Boy's weight and momentum were too much for her to stop. His entire body went over the edge, pulling her with him. As she was about to fall to the rocks and ocean below, she grasped the thin trunk of a dead tree that had grown out of the side of the dirt. The two of them hung over the ocean, Tracy hanging on to the tree trunk, Quiet Boy hanging on to her, the wind whipping them around, trying to pull them to their deaths.

"Let go and come with me," Quiet Boy cried over the crashing waves. "We can die together."

Tracy heard those familiar words and could feel her grip loosening. The spray from the sea below made the tree bark slick and difficult to grasp. She looked down and saw Quiet Boy staring up at her, waiting for the inevitable, somehow at peace with where he was.

"Let go," he said again.

Her fingers were slipping. Somewhere above her she could hear Dr. Devi and a woman calling to them, but she ignored what they were saying, instead concentrating on the hand Quiet Boy was holding on to her ankle with. She lifted her free leg and kicked at it, trying to get him off.

"What are you doing?" Quiet Boy asked, a sense of panic suddenly rising in his voice. "Don't do that."

She kicked again.

"Stop it! Just let go! We can die together!"

Tracy grunted as she kicked for a third time.

"Stop!"

She was hanging on to the tree trunk by her fingertips now. She didn't have much time left. A fourth kick to his hand loosened his grip.

"Stop it!"

With a final scream of determination, Tracy used what remained of her energy and brought her heel down as hard as she could on his fingers. She heard the sound of knuckles crunching and finally felt his weight disappear off of her. She watched as her captor vanished into the night, waiting until she thought she heard a splash below, then shimmied herself up a bit to regrip the tree she hung from.

"Help! I'm slipping!"

Tracy closed her eyes and waited to be rescued, listening as the waves crashed below and the wind howled in her ears. The woman, who she'd never seen before, began yelling instructions to her, but she couldn't hear what she was saying over the scream of a terrified and anguished father who'd just watched his son fall to his death.

DAY SIXTEEN

CHAPTER SIXTY-SIX

Kelly stood over Tracy Cowan's hospital bed, watching her sleep, the stress of the case finally behind her. She'd received commendations from both the Chief and the Mayor as they were eager to get in front of the cameras and express their confidence in her and the department. Her colleagues teased her about being the flavor of the month and then invited her out for beers to celebrate closing her first assignment as a detective. She accepted, knowing she was one of the gang now, and that made her happy.

Tracy looked peaceful despite the tubes running in and out of her body, hydrating her with IV fluids and helping her heal with antibiotics. The press had descended upon Montauk the moment they got word that she'd been found and was being treated at a local hospital. The mob waiting in the lobby was an obnoxious by-product of today's media age. Their hunger for information was insatiable, and they would not go away no matter how many statements the doctors or superiors made about her current state.

Kelly thought about all the days Tracy had had to endure and wondered how many more months or years of nightmares and post-traumatic stress might come from them. This hadn't been the first time she'd had to endure something so extreme and Kelly wondered if Tracy's past would help or hurt in that regard. She made a mental note to keep tabs on her in the months to come. It wouldn't hurt to stop by and check in every once in a while. She might even make a friend along the way.

Tracy stirred and slowly opened her eyes. It took a second for her to fully regain consciousness and look up at Kelly.

"Where am I?"

"You're at Weill Cornell Burn Center in Manhattan. You were brought here by medivac. Do you remember?"

Kelly could see the moment the memories returned. Tracy's face went white and her eyes looked away, widening a bit, then closing into slits as she bit her bottom lip.

"Where's Dr. Devi?"

"He's okay. He's back home."

"And his son?"

Kelly paused for a moment. "Samesh is dead. He fell from the cliff near Camp Hero on Montauk. Do you remember that?"

Tracy nodded.

"My name is Kelly Evans. I'm a detective with the Westchester County Police. I was the person put in charge of your case when you went missing."

"You were the one who saved me," Tracy whispered. Her voice was hoarse from the smoke she'd inhaled. "You pulled me back up from the cliffs. You and Dr. Devi."

"That's right."

"How did you find me?"

"Your sister let us know you called your house and we were able to trace that call to Dr. Devi's summer home. She was instrumental in us being able to find you."

Tracy tried to sit up, but winced and remained in place.

Her breath came in short bursts. "Missy hung up on me. I couldn't figure out why."

"She was afraid your husband had something to do with your disappearance and didn't want him to know she took your call. She came to us after…" Her voice trailed off.

"After what?"

There was no use in delaying things any longer. She was there for a reason and it was time to get her questions answered. Kelly took her notepad from her bag. "I know this might seem like a bad time, but I have a few loose ends I need to tie up. Do you mind?"

"No."

"How did you know Samesh Devi?"

"I didn't," Tracy replied. "I knew him in passing. His friends called him Quiet Boy. To me, he was just a kid in a hoodie who hung out in front of Dr. Devi's office. We got to know each other a bit and we had this thing where we traded music every time I came for an appointment. That was about the extent of it. I thought he was a patient because I saw him going into Dr. Devi's office a few times after I'd come out. I had no idea he was his son."

"Did Samesh ever give you any indication that you were on his radar? Anything that might've tipped you off that he liked you?"

"Nothing. We always talked about each other's music and it was always a good few minutes before I had to go in. His friends would joke around. We'd all laugh. I had no idea he was attracted to me or obsessed or anything. And to go as far as he did? I never would've imagined."

"Ever notice him following you? Showing up in places you didn't expect him? Ever see his car where it shouldn't have been?"

"No. I didn't know what kind of car he drove. The only

reason I noticed the Buick that night was because one of his headlights wasn't working."

Tracy nodded as she wrote. "Dr. Devi confirmed that Samesh has done something like this before. He was getting help after an incident with a girl in his school. The police and the courts were involved."

Tears welled in Tracy's eyes. "Can you tell Dr. Devi I'm okay? I want him to know that."

"I'll tell him," Kelly replied. "He keeps asking about you. He feels awful."

There was a moment of silence between the two women, each of them looking at the other, waiting. It was finally Tracy who spoke.

"Why was my sister scared to tell my husband I was alive?"

"She thought he might've had something to do with your disappearance."

"There's something else," Tracy said. Again, she tried sit up and couldn't. "Tell me. Please."

Kelly paused, trying to figure out what she wanted to say. She looked down at her notepad. "It's about Kat Masterson?"

"She was my husband's attorney. She was also the person my husband was having an affair with. That's why I asked him for a divorce."

"I'm not sure how to put this gently," Kelly said. She could hear her voice trembling just a bit. "Kat Masterson was found murdered the same day you were abducted. We obtained proof that your husband was at Kat's apartment the night she died and he's been arrested for her murder."

Tracy looked up at Kelly. "Are you serious?"

"I'm afraid so."

"Is that why he's not here?"

"It is."

"He *killed* someone?"

"Evidence looks that way."

Tracy let her head fall back on the stack of pillows that were propped under her shoulders. She closed her eyes and tears ran down the sides of her face.

"You have proof?"

"We do."

"My God."

"There she is!"

The voice from the hallway caused both women to turn. Missy was holding the door open while Finn ran under her arm and jumped up onto his mother's bed. Tracy quickly wiped her tears away and held him tight, planting kisses all over his face, the two of them laughing and crying and rocking back and forth. There was no more wincing or pain. It was apparent that Tracy felt nothing but the love between a mother and child. Everything else simply melted away.

"I couldn't keep him in the waiting room any longer," Missy said. "He hasn't seen his mom in two weeks."

"It's fine," Kelly replied. "We were done anyway."

Finn sat up and pointed to the boy who was hanging on to Missy's coat. "Mommy, that's Enzo. He's my friend."

Tracy smiled. "He's my friend too."

"The doctor brought him out to us when me and Aunt Missy were waiting to see you. He doesn't have any boo-boos."

"Well, that's the best news I heard all day," Tracy replied. She looked at the boy cowering behind her sister. "Enzo is a very brave boy. He helped me even when he knew he could get in trouble. I owe him my life." She turned back to her son. "And you know what? Enzo has no place to live. Do you think you'd like it if he came and lived with us?"

Finn's face lit up. "Yes!"

She found the young boy half-hiding behind Missy. "And what about you?" she asked him. "If it's okay with you I'd like to start the process to become your foster mom. Maybe just Mom one day. Does that sound okay?"

Enzo smiled and nodded.

"Then get over here and give me a hug. I need both my boys right now."

Missy walked him over to the bed and helped him climb up. As Kelly was shutting the door, she saw Tracy grab her sister's hand and pull her close.

"Thanks for watching over him," she said.

Missy shrugged. "You know I've always got your back. Always have, always will. Thick or thin. I got you."

DAY TWENTY

CHAPTER SIXTY-SEVEN

Tracy sat at her kitchen table across from Reagan Hart who looked at her with the most exquisite expression of empathy and anger. She was a pro for sure, knowing what to say and how to say it, how to react to an answer, and how to change her mannerisms and expressions at the drop of a hat. She took one look at the bottom floor when they arrived and immediately instructed her crew to move the table by the bay window so the sun rising behind the house could give a natural glow without shining too bright. The lights were on the side of them to ensure neither would get a glowing forehead, and the boom mic hovering in between, just out of frame so one voice wouldn't overpower the other. She even told the makeup artist to accentuate some of the bruising that had begun to heal instead of hiding it. She wanted her viewers to see what Samesh had done to Tracy. She didn't want anything covered up.

The interview was almost over. They'd been talking for a half hour as part of a one-hour special Reagan planned to run in the coming weeks. There had been countless requests for interviews when she arrived home, but Missy had convinced her to

choose Reagan and let it end there. Tracy stretched her back a
bit. The hard chair was getting uncomfortable.

"So sum it all up for us," Reagan said in her soft and caring
voice. "You were a victim of domestic abuse when you were
younger, you were held against your will by a man who was
obsessed with you, and you come home to find your husband
was arrested for killing his mistress. How can you deal with all
of this tragedy?"

Tracy took a moment to think of everything she'd been
through since her time with Jake Bollard. So much pain. So
many failed relationships. People died. Lives were changed
forever.

"I guess I'm a fighter," she said with a shrug. "Sure, I've
gone through the things you mentioned, but in the end, I keep
getting up and getting back to my life. I have a great support
system in my sister and my son, and I keep moving forward for
them. If I stopped to think about the totality of it all, I might
never recover. So, I keep moving."

"Do you think you could ever fall in love again after what
you've been through."

A small smile. "I don't know. Probably not. But never say
never, right?"

"And what about your husband, Malcolm? Will you be at
his side at the trial? Will you support Finn's father?"

The smile disappeared. "I can't really answer that right
now. I haven't come to terms with what he's done to that poor
girl. That could've been me. What if he'd decided to kill me to
be with her? And her family. I pray for them. I don't know if I
can support Malcolm right now. Maybe in time, but the wound
is too fresh. I guess we'll have to wait and see."

Reagan nodded, smiled, and turned to the camera.

"This is Reagan Hart signing off with the strongest woman I
know. You can't keep Tracy Cowan down. She said it herself.
She just keeps moving."

A pause.

"And we're out!" a voice cried behind them.

Reagan clapped her hands and jumped out of her seat. She began raving about how well the interview had gone and how confident she was that her audience was going to love it. She started predicting viewing numbers and streaming downloads they could expect. Tracy pretended to listen as she smiled and laughed and nodded and did whatever else she needed to while the crew packed up and moved out of the house. She just wanted everyone to leave. She wanted to be alone. She never thought she'd have that desire again after all she'd been through, but she couldn't wait to have the quiet house all to herself.

And she couldn't wait for Reagan Hart to shut the fuck up.

CHAPTER SIXTY-EIGHT

Malcom was already seated when Missy arrived at the visitation room of Bridgeport Correctional Center. He sat alone at a table for four, his hands on the concrete slab of a tabletop, his left leg forever bouncing up and down. The stubble on his face had grown into a fairly thick beard since the last time she saw him at the house. His hair looked dirty and his skin was oily. The orange jumpsuit didn't quite fit him, making him appear smaller than he actually was, meeker among the carnivores he walked among. When he saw Missy, he straightened up and tried to smile, but the endless nights of restless sleep and the constant worry had already taken all of the joy out of him. The smile was superficial.

"Hey, Missy," he said when she approached. His voice was swallowed among the other conversations that surrounded them. "Thanks for coming."

Missy sat across from him. It had been eight days since he'd been charged with the murder of Kat Masterson and he was still waiting on a court date for his arraignment. He was part of the system now and that system didn't care about the outside world or timetables or families that might be waiting. It got to you when it got to you and not a second earlier. All Malcolm could do was wait, and in only eight days he already looked like a shell of himself.

"Tracy's home," Missy said. "Doc said the burns on her feet will heal fine and there's no lasting damage to her face from when Samesh attacked her at George's Island."

"I wish I could have five minutes with that freak."

"Let's not forget she was there because of you."

"Don't say that."

"I'm saying it." Missy fell back in her seat and folded her arms. "If you weren't so selfish and had kept your dick in your pants, none of this would've happened. Tracy wouldn't have had to go through what she went through and you wouldn't be sitting here now. This is on you."

Malcolm was silent, staring at her.

"You were even willing to take our relationship somewhere it had no business going. How could you try and get with me when your wife was missing? That's so gross."

"I was alone and scared. You were there at home with Finn and helping me. It felt like you were Tracy. I don't know, it just happened."

"Like Kat just happened."

"Yeah, maybe. Something like that." Malcolm looked down at the table. "But I swear I didn't kill her."

Missy leaned forward and lowered her voice. "I know you didn't, but it doesn't matter. We left enough evidence around the apartment to make sure you go down for it anyway."

It took a few seconds for the words to seep in. When they did, Malcolm looked up. His eyes glassed over as he thought through everything.

"It's a shame that young woman had to die, but we couldn't kill you. We wanted to, but too many questions would've come up if you were dead. The police would start pulling up pieces of Tracy's past and they'd learn about Jake and Frank and I mean, how many people could be part of your life and end up dead, you know? So, we killed Kat and we put it all on you. It's still revenge. Just a different version of it."

Malcolm tried to speak, but only a low choking sound came out.

"The medical examiner finding semen on Kat was just pure luck. That's what sealed your fate and made this case open and shut. We made sure to put some hairs from your brush around her place and some nail clippings in her bathroom garbage, but I don't think the forensics team even processed that stuff after they found the semen. And we knew you left your fingerprints in her place. We watched you walk in that night and then back out. But that semen. That was a blessing."

"You set me up?"

Missy nodded. "Your price to pay for cheating on Tracy. That was like the apple in the Garden of Eden, Malcolm. The only thing Adam and Eve were forbidden to eat, and they ate it. Cheating was Tracy's apple. After what she went through with Jake, that was the only thing she could never get past. You knew that. So did Frank. Why can't you guys just be happy with the woman you have? Why do you always need more?"

Malcolm scanned the room as the entirety of his predicament started sinking in. "Frank died in a car accident."

"Yes, he did." Missy got up from her seat. "This is the last time you'll see me. And trust me when I say that Tracy has no desire to ever come here. You'll be convicted and Finn will grow up without a father, but we'll take care of him."

Malcolm jumped up as she turned to walk away.

"Wait! Don't go!"

"I have to. Tracy just finished her interview with Reagan Hart to make sure the court of public opinion is against you too. I'm dying to hear how it went. Can you believe it? Reagan Hart?"

"Come back!"

"After that, we'll have to sit down and figure out how to properly run a successful construction company now that I'm the owner. I'm thinking I sell it. I'd like to get a good price for it, but I'm willing to bet Tracy could convince me to sell it at a discount just to be rid of it. I don't know. We'll see."

"Get back here!"

"Good luck, Malcolm. You'll need it since there's no chance you'll be able to afford bail. All that's ours now."

"Come back!"

Missy ignored him as she strolled through the tables. The last thing she heard was the sound of guards moving in as Malcolm screamed after her and tried to leave his seat. His struggles against their strength was music to her ears.

CHAPTER SIXTY-NINE

Tracy made her way into her bedroom, moving slowly and deliberately so as not to make the pain in the bottom of her feet worse. The swelling had gone down and, thankfully, there hadn't been any major damage to the skin or tissue, so recovery was a certainty. The socks she had on protected her to a certain extent. It was just a matter of staying off her feet as much as possible for the first week out of the hospital.

She and Finn and Enzo were moving. Not to Vermont or Maine like she'd first told Dr. Devi and Malcolm. She wanted a fresh start, a real chance to hit the reset button. Her mind was on Colorado or Montana, but she wouldn't rule out heading all the way to the coast and settling in Washington or Oregon. She didn't want to stick around with the press hounding her and the notoriety being in everyone's face. Her plan was to get in the car and drive. No map or timetable or specific destination. Just a chance to see what was out there, and if a particular place touched her in a certain way, that would be the place she'd call home.

Flattened boxes, waiting to be put together, lined the perimeter of her bedroom as they did the hallway, Finn's room, and the entire main floor. She'd put almost all of it in storage until she found a place to settle in, then she'd arrange for a moving truck to bring what she wanted out to her. Missy could sell the rest.

There was a small black ring box sitting in the center of her bed. It was wrapped in red ribbon with a red bow stuck to the center. Tracy sat on the edge of the mattress and took the box in her hand, examining it, the laughter of Finn and Enzo faint as they played in the snow in the backyard. There was no card or any indication of who'd sent the gift. She popped the bow off, slid the ribbon away, and opened the top. She smiled when she saw it.

It was a single brass bullet.

"Thought you might want that."

Tracy looked up to find her sister walking down the hall toward her.

"I didn't hear you come in."

"Came in through the back. Played with the kids for a sec. I had to drop some stuff off in the garage."

She held up the box. "Thank you."

"I know it's not really *your* memory, but that was the next bullet in the chamber of Malcolm's gun the night I thought he killed you and I was going to shoot him for you. Turns out it was just a bunch of misunderstood texts, but it makes a good memory nonetheless."

"You can say that again."

"How was Reagan Hart?"

"Fine. I think I said everything that needed to be said. And the press knows that's the only interview I'm giving, so hopefully the bulk of them will leave me alone. I'll ditch the rest when I leave."

Tracy closed the ring box and walked across the room. She pulled up the edge of the carpet and lifted a loose piece of plywood she'd installed when they'd first moved in. She reached

into the hole in the floor and came away with an antique
jewelry box. She opened it and placed the ring box inside next
to the shell casing from the shotgun Jake was killed with and an
empty bottle of ketamine she'd slipped into Frank's drink to
ensure he'd pass out while he was driving. Those were the
memories—the reminders—that despite her willingness to give
men chance after chance, they continued to disappoint her. She
wished she never had to keep such mementos, but there they
were. Why was it so hard for a man to be faithful? Why
couldn't monogamy ever seem to work? Still, these items repre-
sented more than just her lovers' shortcomings. They reminded
her of her own inner strength and her uncompromising nature
when it came to love. She would always be the one to control
her destiny and no one could take that away. She closed the
jewelry box, and with it, this chapter of her life. It was time to
begin anew.

"How're you feeling today?" Missy asked. "You had a hectic
morning."

"I'm good."

"You still got the shakes from the heroin he was giving
you?"

"No. That mostly stopped in the hospital, but they have me
on low dose methadone to help." Tracy put the jewelry box
back into the floor and put the rug back into place. "Reagan
showed me some of the news reports she did about me. You did
good feeding her that information you were getting from the
police."

"I didn't know what to do. I mean, you were missing for real,
but Kat was dead, so I had to keep things moving. I'd never been
so scared and confused. I was looking for you, and at the same
time feeding Reagan just enough info to get her to sway the
public toward Malcolm for when the time came and he got
arrested. Everyone needed to believe he killed Kat. I think we
accomplished that part of it."

Tracy leaned against the wall and put her hands in her pockets. "How is he?" she asked.

"He's a mess," Missy replied. "He keeps crying about being innocent, but no one believes him at this point."

"And he knows what we did?"

"He does."

"Good." She turned around and grabbed a moving box that was leaning against the wall. "How are we doing with the sale of the business?"

"Word just got out, but our broker said we have three people interested already. If we can get an offer or two, maybe we can get some kind of bidding war started. Then we'd be sitting pretty."

"And you promise you'll come out to wherever I land?"

Missy held up her hand as if she was a witness about to testify. "I promise. Let me tie up the sale of the business and make sure Malcolm's found guilty. After that, I'll sell Mom and Dad's place and we can start fresh wherever you end up. You, me, and the kids."

Tracy finished putting the box together and placed it on the bed. She walked over to her sister and hugged her close. "Thank you. I owe you for this."

"I told you," Missy replied, her voice a hushed whisper. "I always have your back. Had it with Jake. Had it with Frank. And I have it now."

"I love you."

"I love you too, sis. Forever."

CHAPTER SEVENTY
TWENTY DAYS EARLIER

Kat Masterson stumbled through the hallway and into the dark living room, tripping over the corner of an end table she'd walked past too many times before, catching herself before falling onto her knees. She was still half-asleep when she made her way to the door and stopped, one hand on the knob, the other clasping the deadbolt she was about to unlock without thinking. She froze as the fogginess suddenly lifted and things became clearer. She turned around and looked at the clock on her cable box. It was almost midnight.

Who was on the other side of the door?

"Who's there?" she said, trying to sound assertive. Her voice was still croaky from sleeping.

"It's me."

Kat recognized the voice, but didn't feel any better about it.

"What are you doing here?"

"I had to see you. It's about Malcolm."

"Seriously? This can't wait until morning?"

"Kat, she knows. Tracy knows."

Kat quickly unlocked the deadbolt and turned the knob.

She pulled the door open, catching the door chain. She was awake now, alert. And she was scared.

"She knows?"

"Yes."

Without saying anything further, she closed the door, slid the chain from the track and opened it back up.

Kat stepped aside and let Missy walk past her, quickly shutting the door behind them. Missy stopped just inside the front hallway and spun around.

"She can't know," Kat said. Her stomach churned at the thought of Malcolm's wife knowing about the affair and all the implications that might come with it. "It's not possible."

"It is."

"Did you tell her?"

"Don't be ridiculous."

It was never supposed to be like this. Malcolm was an accident, something that just happened. She knew he was married, but never wanted to know anything more than that. He wasn't anything serious, but it felt good to be with him. He was like a warm blanket in her otherwise cold life. Experts might say she had daddy issues and longed to be in the arms of an older man, but the truth was, he was good company. He made her laugh and always allowed her to be the center of his attention. She never had to work at whatever it was they had. It all came naturally, so she let it continue. It wasn't until just then when Missy was standing in front of her with this news did she really ever consider the implications of her actions and the effect it might have on everyone else in Malcom's life.

"What do we do?" Kat asked, breaking the silence. She paced back and forth, thinking, playing with the edge of her white satin nightgown, then took off for the living room where she stopped and spun back around to face Missy. "This is not good. We have to fix this."

"We will."

"How?"

"I can help."

"Oh my God. We were so careful."

The sound of the dog chain unfurling in the silence of the apartment made a strange metallic jingle. Kat watched as the chrome danced in the glow of the streetlight outside the window. The bottom of the chain swung like a pendulum.

"What're you doing?" she asked.

Missy stepped forward. "Tracy knows. And now we have to fix that."

Kat backed up a step. "What are you talking about? What are you doing?"

Missy matched her steps. "All that time you were seeing Malcolm. Fucking him behind his wife's back. All that time, you knew. You knew he was married. And then I told you he was married just in case, for some reason, you were under the delusion that he wasn't. I told you the truth, and you still didn't care."

"Missy, stop."

"You didn't care because you're young and selfish and think you deserve to get whatever you want. You just take it. You never paused for a single second to realize that his cheating was ruining a marriage and breaking up a family and leaving a son without his father."

Kat began to cry. The look in Missy's eyes was dark. "Please. I need you to stop."

Missy scowled. "And the thing that really burns me is that you're so selfish and caught up in your own world that you never even bothered to look up Malcolm online. If you had, you would've seen he was married. You would've seen his posts with his wife and son. But you didn't want to know. You wanted to live in your own selfish fantasy and pretend he was single. You wanted to keep your head in the sand because looking him up online would've confirmed you were the house-wrecker that you are."

"No. It's not like that."

"You would've known all this was a lie if you just bothered to look."

Missy stepped closer and wrapped her gloved hand around a paperweight that sat atop a stack of legal papers on the coffee table.

"You would've seen that the woman you've been talking to all these months wasn't Missy. I'm not Missy. I'm Tracy. I'm Malcolm's wife."

Kat's eyes widened further and she brought her hands to her mouth. The reality of what she'd done and the situation she found herself in finally dawned on her. She was facing Malcom's wife. It had been Tracy all along.

Kat turned to run as the rumbles of a scream emanated from the depths of her throat. Tracy was on her in seconds. Kat heard her footsteps cross the room and then something slammed into the back of her head. The blackness crept in as she crumpled to the ground, semi-conscious.

Tracy pulled Kat's limp body to the couch and sat her up so she was sitting on the floor and leaning against the couch.

"Please... stop," Kat mumbled. She was fading fast.

Tracy looped the dog chain around her neck and stood on the cushions behind her. She began to pull and Kat could hear the sound of herself choking as the blackness crept in. She reached up to try and pull Tracy away from the chain, scratching at her hands and fingers, but her strength dwindled and the blackness consumed her. The last thought she had was of the bell ringing above the law firm's door and how it reminded her of Cape Cod and all the good things that came with Aunt Bimy.

CHAPTER SEVENTY-ONE

Kelly took a breath and looked toward Detective Taft who was standing next to her.

"You ready?"

"Yup."

She rang the doorbell.

She could hear Finn and Enzo playing in the side yard and wished there could've been another outcome to the case, but there was simply no other explanation. It made her sick to think she'd almost gotten away with it, and Taft assured her that, over time, that feeling of betrayal would be replaced with resignation. It didn't matter who did what and when. As long as she caught the person guilty of the crime, she was doing her job. Everything else was just noise.

Tracy Cowan answered the door and Kelly could see the corner of the woman's mouth turn down just a bit when recognition set in.

"Detective Evans," she said, pulling the door open wider. "I didn't know you were coming by. Do you have more news?"

"I do," Kelly replied. She took a step forward and Tracy

backed into the foyer. When they were inside, Taft shut the door behind him.

"This is Detective Taft from the Stamford Police. He was one of the detectives handling Kat Masterson's case."

"Okay."

"We've been comparing notes ever since we learned your husband was involved in his homicide. We came across a few things we need to discuss with you."

Tracy nodded, but didn't say anything. She folded her arms across her chest and took another step back.

"Detective Taft and I shared our DNA reports when we found the link between Malcolm and Kat. His team had taken the semen found on Kat leg as well as skin fibers, hair, and nail clippings from her apartment. I had swabs and prints from you guys. Neither of us had anything to match them to, but once Malcolm was arrested, Detective Taft's team was able to match his DNA to most of the items found at the apartment."

Tracy nodded.

"Most everything was either Kat's or Malcolm's. We found some old prints from one of Kat's friends, but she was never a suspect. Another from her cleaning lady. We also found a couple of things didn't match."

Tracy shifted her weight from side to side. Kelly could see her eyes looking around, not wanting to meet hers.

"We found a hair. Belongs to you. Why would one of your hairs be in Kat Masterson's apartment?"

Tracy finally looked at her. It took a moment for her to respond. She could see the woman struggling to come up with an answer. Her face suddenly relaxed and she smiled a tight smile.

"Must've been transference. I've seen those true-crime shows. One of my hairs got caught on Malcolm's clothes and when he went to Kat's house, it fell off."

Now it was Kelly's turn to smile. "Yeah, that could be it. But how do you explain the skin found under one of Kat's nails? It's your skin, Tracy. One hundred percent match. How'd that get there?"

Kelly watched as Tracy absently rubbed a small cut on her hand.

"We thought Kat was unconscious when she was strangled because there were no scratches on her neck to pull the chain away. But she was awake. She wasn't scratching at the chain. She was scratching at the person using the chain."

Tracy was quiet now, thinking, her mind churning.

"I also had a chance to go over inventory items with Detective Taft," Kelly continued. "It's funny how something could be meaningless in one case but be everything in another." She turned toward Taft. "You want to show her?"

Taft pulled a plastic evidence bag out of his pocket and held it up.

"When I was in Kat's bedroom, I noticed she had a frame with a missing picture," he said. "I figured it was a picture of the killer, but I was wrong. Her friend told me it was a guitar pick she caught at a Coldplay concert. She framed it because they were her favorite band. Wasn't in the frame."

Tracy was transfixed on the bag.

"That's because it was in your purse," Kelly said. "We found it when the dive team pulled your belongings from your car in the Hudson. I didn't think anything of it, but when Detective Taft saw my inventory report, he called me right away."

"What's going on?"

Everyone spun around to see Missy Rollins standing at the top of the stairs. Tracy looked at her, her eyes glassed over with tears.

"Hello, Ms. Rollins," Kelly said. "I think you and I are going to hang out here and watch the boys for a bit. Detective Taft needs to take Tracy to Stamford so he can figure all this out, and I may have a few questions for you."

"Like what?"

"Like who's innocent? Who's guilty? Who might've been framed? Could take a while." She turned toward Tracy and Taft. "You guys all set?"

"I want my lawyer," Tracy said. Her face had turned pale, almost completely white. Tears slipped down her cheeks.

"Not a problem," Taft replied. "You can call him when we get to the station. I hope he's good too, because you're really going to need someone with skills on this one. Murder can be a tricky thing to get out of. You know. You've seen the true-crime shows. They all end the same way. The person who thought they got away with it didn't, and justice is served."

Taft led Tracy out of the house while Missy ran down the stairs and out onto the porch, shouting instructions as they went. Kelly looked toward Taft who gave her a little wink, silently telling her that she'd done good. She winked back and watched as a handful of neighbors came out of their homes to watch Tracy be led away just like her husband had been several days earlier. They watched and gawked and tried to pretend they were out there for reasons other than snooping. Kelly concentrated on Taft securing his suspect in the backseat of his car and stayed fixed on the sedan as it backed out of the driveway and disappeared down the street.

Case closed.

CHAPTER SEVENTY-TWO

It had been six hours since Taft had taken Tracy into custody and left Kelly at the Cowan house to look after Missy and the kids. Kelly was standing in the foyer, peering out one of the windows that flanked the front door. The sky was turning dark, the streetlamps outside popping on one after the other. The news vans were gone as were the neighbors who'd come out earlier to rubberneck their latest arrest. The block looked like any other suburban block in any other suburban neighborhood; calm, peaceful, dull. The excitement of the past twenty days had finally died away. Life could go back to normal now. This was the end of it.

Kelly looked down at the phone in her hand. She'd called Taft twice since he'd left and both had rolled to voicemail. She left a message the first time, but not the second. She didn't want to keep bothering him if he was in the middle of booking Tracy or was conducting a final interview with Tracy's lawyer present, but she did want to know how things were going. There hadn't been anything on the local news or online, and no one had followed up from her department after she called Leeds and the chief to let them know what happened. The anticipation was killing her.

Missy played dumb when Kelly tried to interview her. She acted like she had no idea what was going on, and, for the most part, she was convincing. Kelly couldn't tell if something was there or not, but her gut told her to keep digging, so she would. For now, Missy was in the family room watching a movie with the boys. She'd been quiet since they last spoke; the smart-mouthed, rambunctious woman Kelly had come to know had been replaced with a silent, almost weakened, version. She'd spent the rest of the day with the kids, ignoring Kelly as best she could.

She dialed Taft's number for a third time.

"You've reached Dennis. I can't take your call. Leave a message."

"Come on."

She hung up and dialed Stamford headquarters as she watched a car drive slowly down the block and turn into an empty garage two houses away.

"Stamford Police, Officer Hogan speaking."

"Yeah, this is Detective Evans, Westchester County PD. I was wondering if Detective Taft was available to talk."

"I'm sorry, who were you looking for?"

"Detective Taft. Dennis Taft."

She turned away from the door and began walking toward the kitchen.

"Um, Detective Taft's not here."

"Are you sure? He and I just picked up Tracy Cowan as part of the Kat Masterson homicide. He brought her in to you guys this afternoon. Maybe he's in booking?"

"I don't think so."

"Okay, how about Detective Blau then?"

"Please hold."

She walked through the kitchen and craned her neck to see

Missy sitting between Finn and Enzo in the family room. They were watching a *Star Wars* movie, but she didn't know which one. The three of them looked peaceful enough, but there was no denying the undercurrent of stress and anger in the house. Things could boil over at any moment.

The phone clicked.

"Detective Evans?"

Kelly spun away back toward the hallway. "Yes."

"This is Lena Blau."

"Hey, Lena. Is Dennis done booking Tracy Cowan yet? I don't want to be a pest, but I need to know where we are with things so I can report back to my superiors."

There was a slight pause on the other end.

"What are you talking about?" Lena finally asked. "Why are you looking for Dennis?"

Kelly stopped walking and stood still at the edge of the kitchen, facing the hall that led back to the foyer. There was something in Lena's voice that didn't sound right.

"Dennis came in to book Tracy Cowan. He said he called you. Tracy was the one who killed Kat Masterson."

"I'm sorry, what?"

Kelly started talking faster now. Something was wrong. "Dennis and I were going over our case files a couple of days ago as a final pass-through. When he read the inventory list from when my department processed Tracy's car that was in the river, he recognized a guitar pick that was an item missing from Kat Masterson's apartment. I also had Tracy's DNA from when we took samples from the family, and he matched her DNA to skin and blood found under Kat's nails. We picked her up a little before noon today. Dennis was bringing her in to book. She's Kat's killer. I was calling for an update."

There was no response from Lena. Kelly could hear the activity of the stationhouse in the background and held her breath, waiting for the detective to start talking again.

"Kelly," Lena finally said. "Dennis Taft is no longer a detective with the Stamford PD. He retired three months ago. He was only in on Kat's case as an observer. I was lead detective on the case."

Kelly's stomach knotted as she stopped herself from keeling over. "What do you mean he retired? I thought he was assisting you. Why would he be observing if he retired? It was a homicide investigation. Insiders only, right?"

"He was an insider. I let him in as a courtesy. Kat Masterson was his stepdaughter."

Kelly opened her mouth to speak, but no words came out. She thought about all the times Taft had met her in New York instead of inviting her to Stamford and how quiet he was when Lena was interviewing Malcolm, the complete opposite of how outgoing and in control he was when he conducted his interview at her department. He didn't give her his personal cell number because she was earning his respect, he gave it to her because there was no other official number to provide. Everything clicked into place the moment Lena told her the truth. But how could she know? Why wouldn't she trust another cop?

"Where is Dennis now?" Lena asked. Her voice was sharp, but trembling. "When did you last speak to him?"

"When he took Tracy into custody. Six hours ago. He said he was bringing her to Stamford to book her. I called his cell three times and they all rolled to his voicemail."

"He tried the same thing when we thought Malcolm Cowan was good for Kat's murder. He tried to get to Malcolm before we could, but I intervened and he backed down. I knew he was looking for vengeance, so I kept a close eye on him. I had no idea you found new evidence that pointed to someone else. He did it. He got her. Shit. He found the real killer and now he can have his revenge. Tracy Cowan killed the girl he'd raised since she was six years old. He told me he promised his ex-wife he'd get whoever was responsible."

"Wait. I thought his wife was dead. I asked him about that locket he was always holding."

"The locket was Kat's. His wife isn't dead. They're divorced. She left him six months ago. Said he worked too much and he refused to retire, and I guess she finally had enough and moved to Arizona with family. He retired a few months later to show her he could change and try and win her back. Didn't work. Then Kat's murder happened and I let a lonely father who had spent his entire life on the inside in one more time. I never thought it would backfire like this."

There was rustling on the other end.

"What do you want me to do?" Kelly asked. She could feel her breath growing short, her heart pounding in her chest.

"Keep calling his cell and put a BOLO out for him through your department. I'll do the same here. I don't know where he's going, but I'm pretty sure if we don't find him soon, Tracy Cowan won't be alive much longer."

The phone disconnected and Kelly stood in between the kitchen and the hallway, her phone shaking in her hand, tears welling in her eyes. She'd found one killer and given her to another. It couldn't end like that. It just couldn't.

She called her chief and explained what had happened. Both departments scrambled to spread the word up and down the east coast, then went west from there. In the days and weeks that followed, the news outlets picked up the story as did bloggers, true-crime podcasters, and web sleuths. Everyone was looking for Dennis Taft and Tracy Cowan.

No one ever found them.

A LETTER FROM MATTHEW

Dear reader,

I'm so excited to have shared this book with you and want you to know how thankful I am to you for choosing to read *The Woman at Number 6*. If you enjoyed it, and want to keep up to date with all my latest releases, I encourage you to sign up at the following link. Your email address will never be shared and you can unsubscribe at any time.

www.bookouture.com/matthew-farrell

I hope you loved *The Woman at Number 6*, and if you did, I would be very grateful if you could write a review. I'd love to hear what you think, and it makes such a difference helping new readers to discover one of my books for the first time.

I also enjoy hearing from my readers—you can get in touch on my Facebook page, through Twitter, Goodreads or my website.

Thanks, and happy reading!

Matthew

KEEP IN TOUCH WITH MATTHEW

www.mfarrellwriter.com

 facebook.com/mfarrellwriter2

twitter.com/mfarrellwriter

instagram.com/mfarrellwriterbooks

ACKNOWLEDGMENTS

I would like to take a moment to thank those people who helped with this book:

To my agent, Curtis Russell, of PS Literary Agency. Thank you for always being my champion. We make a good team and I enjoy working with you.

To my editor at Bookouture, Kelsie Marsden. Thank you for all you've done to make this story better at every turn.

To the support staff at PS Literary who are always pushing my work out through social media. I appreciate you helping to get the word out, each and every day.

To Kim Nash and the Bookouture marketing team. Thank you for helping to spread the word about this book and *We Have Your Daughter* and getting me and my books in front of readers, reviewers, and influencers.

To my friend and police professional, Investigator Brian Martin of the New York State Police. Thank you for sharing your insights on the inner workings of the police departments you work for and for always being there with answers to my random questions. If I got anything wrong, that's on me.

To my wife, Cathy, and my daughters, Mackenzie and Jillian. Thank you for always being patient while I'm writing and supportive in this crazy world as an author. Your enthusiasm is inspiring and I couldn't do this without you guys. I love you.

To my family and friends, to whom this book is dedicated. Thank you for the support and love and encouragement and for always being willing to spread the word about my books. I love you all.

To my readers, your support and willingness to get the word out about my books continues to inspire me and fills me with such gratefulness. I'm so happy you've chosen my books to read and post about when there are so many options out there. Thank you, from the bottom of my heart. I truly mean that.

Happy reading!

MF

Made in United States
Orlando, FL
07 May 2023

32876059R00232